THE GAME
OF HEARTS

THE GAME
OF HEARTS

A Novel

Suzanne D. Lonn

To order additional copies of this book, contact:
Xlibris Corporation
1-888-795-4274
www.Xlibris.com
Orders@Xlibris.com
22067

The Game of Hearts is dedicated with love and gratitude to:

My editor, Bev Stumpf, whose encouragement, expertise,
and endurance were key in finishing the book.
My husband, Bob, for Marine Corps
and historical knowledge and for computer skills
that helped my manuscript become a book.
My grown children, Kristin and Dallas,
for their inspiration and suggestions.
My mother for endowing me with
a love of reading and writing.
My other family members and
friends for your unending encouragement.
My Lord and Savior for words and books and
the wonderful joy that writers experience as
the story develops and is completed.

"An emotionally gripping novel with exquisite character development. This novel provides a deep examination of the human heart—love, betrayal, hypocrisy, jealousy and greed—with which the reader will identify. You won't be able to put this one down!"

—Mandy Moore, former student of author

"Move over, women's fiction writers! This powerful novel takes the reader through a gamut of emotions as it explores family relationships in small-town America and tells an amazing adoption story with a strange twist!"

—Lucille Erickson, professional book reviewer

"A good book is a friend to savor with each visit. The characters are so believable that they are like new-found friends. I'm looking for a sequel."

—M. Karen Carlson, Montana artist

"After reading this book I felt personally acquainted with the characters and was drawn into their lives. The author captured a variety of human emotions that most readers experience in life."

—Adrienne Teterud, former colleague and fellow teacher

Fate has written a tragedy;
Its name is 'The Human Heart."
The theater is the house of life,
Woman the mummer's part;
The Devil enters the prompter's box
And the play is ready to start.
—Robert W. Service, "The Harpy"

Chapter I

When Amanda gently pulled back the bedroom curtains and peeked out, she gazed down on a glistening, pure-white morning. A light snowfall during the night had kissed the ground just enough to cleanse and sparkle the earth. The whole town of Wheatland shone like the diamonds on Amanda's left hand.

December 25, 1944, was Robert and Amanda's first Christmas as man and wife, and as Marine First Lieutenant Robert Shaw slept under the down comforter in their bed by the window, Amanda pulled on a pink chenille bathrobe and tip-toed to the living room. The setting was all beautiful—the wonderful snow, her man in bed, and decorations—but, nevertheless, she had a bittersweet taste in her mouth.

The scent of pine from the table-top Christmas tree filled the room of the small apartment. She plugged in the string of tree lights and lit a bayberry candle on the maple coffee table.

She was glad to be up before Robert. Her quiet moments in the mornings gave her time to think and plan and prepare herself for another day. A lot was on her mind, even on Christmas.

Today she and Robert would drop by her family's old home just up the hill before traveling out to the country estate for Christmas dinner with Robert's parents, Ed and Belle Shaw. She could picture her family now—her older sister Margie and their mother Zoe, sitting at the yellow wooden kitchen table, sipping tea from their flowered china cups and lamenting the fact that Amanda would not be joining them for Christmas dinner.

Margie had wept over it earlier in the week when Amanda had announced that she and Robert would be spending the day with Ed and Belle. At her age Margie was too old to cry over such matters, Amanda had bluntly told her, which only made Margie blubber all the more.

"You just don't understand what family means to me; you NEVER understand."

"Mother Wentworth," as Zoe preferred to be called, had straightened herself up and accepted the news as graciously as was possible for a seventy-six year old widow, whose forty-year-old Amanda obviously preferred the Shaw's company over theirs. Her nose was up in the air, and the deeply lined furrows between her gray eyebrows were more deeply lined than ever before. The wire-framed glasses couldn't hide her worries and disappointments indelibly etched on her countenance forever, and her iron-gray hair drawn tightly back into a bun made her look all the more severe.

Amanda had little sympathy for either of them. Although the spinster Margie was five years older than Amanda, she acted like the baby of the family. She had been a sickly child, then returned home from college twenty-five years ago due to debilitating migraines, and even now everyone catered to her. She had the idea that she had gallstones, but even the Mayo Clinic couldn't pinpoint a specific problem. Mother only made it worse by giving in to her cries of pain and serving her a special non-fat diet.

"It's all in her head. I'm so glad to be away from it all," sighed Amanda out loud to herself, just as Robert entered the room.

"Talking to yourself again, dear?" Robert asked, as he stepped up behind Amanda's rocking chair and scared her out of her reverie.

As she jumped up to greet him and throw her arms around his tall lean body, she felt slightly dizzy and nauseous, but it passed as quickly as it had come. She thought little of it, and they admired their little tree, the snowfall outside, and each other before they wandered into the kitchen for the morning coffee routine.

"C'mon, let's drink it by the tree as we open our gifts," Robert suggested, and Amanda agreed.

"Here's some coffee cake that Mother sent down yesterday," Amanda volunteered, as she pulled two small plates from the cupboard. "It seems fairly moist, so Mother must have made it. Margie's are always so dry."

"Oh, well, the coffee will wash it down, whoever made it. Come here and relax. It will be fine."

Amanda set the breakfast tray on the coffee table and snuggled up against Robert on the love seat. He could almost always turn her negative feelings into positives—Robert, her big, brave Marine, home from Camp Pendleton. His leave was almost over. Soon she'd be seeing him off again on the train, due to report back to Camp Pendleton on January 2.

It was wartime. Every other morning they'd turned on the radio for news around the world, but not today.

No, I'll not give in to lonely feelings today. It's Christmas, Amanda thought, as she swallowed her last bite of coffee cake.

Robert, sensing her feelings as he looked into her sad brown eyes, cupped her face in his hands. "Hey, dear, are you ready to open your gifts? I brought you some special little treasures. Do you want the big package first or the little box? They go together."

Amanda knew that often the best presents come in small packages, so she carefully removed the ribbon from the bigger box. It was beautifully wrapped with a big green bow, which Amanda playfully looped around Robert's closely cropped hair and tied under his chin. In turn, Robert yanked it off and, grabbing her hands, cinched the ribbon tightly around her wrists.

He laughed at her as she struggled to tear the Christmas paper off. "I never knew you were so clumsy," he said, as he tickled her waist and made the opening even more difficult.

They ended up on the floor where he finally untied her hands. He quickly squirmed away as she tried to tickle his bare toes.

Hopping to his feet, he grabbed the half-opened package. "Why don't you open this?" he teased.

Amanda loved this funny side of him. Her life had been so serious, and she'd grown up so fast. It seemed like she'd been an adult forever.

Finally, like an eager little kid, she tossed the box lid on the floor, threw back the white tissue paper, and pulled out a bright red wool dress. "Oh, Robert, it's gorgeous," she exclaimed, as she held it up to her body. At age forty, Amanda still had a curvy, graceful figure, and she hoped it would fit. "I'll try it on after we open the rest and wear it today," she said eagerly. "Now you open one, Robert."

Robert liked to shake his presents before he unwrapped them, but since he'd been doing that for the last week, he ripped into one quickly. It was a photo album of their wedding pictures, and Robert had never seen any of them.

Amanda had been dodging questions since he'd returned from California.

"Where are the wedding pictures? How much longer do we have to wait? Will they be here before I leave?"

"Ah, you are a tricky one," Robert said, as he slowly savored them, looking at every picture for a long time.

Amanda sat beside him, and they kissed and talked about the little wedding that now seemed so long ago. In late August Robert and Amanda exchanged vows in front of family and friends in the little Presbyterian Church in their hometown. Mother Wentworth was a charter member of the church and, although Margie and she rarely attended services there any more, and Amanda went only on Easter, Amanda felt she would be doing a disservice to her family by not holding the wedding ceremony there.

"Oh, those holy charismatics," Mother Wentworth had scornfully spouted off. She had no time for anyone who didn't have her beliefs or ideals on any issue. "If you get married in Robert's church, I swear I'll have heart palpitations. Everything they say and do is so absurd. Let's have a nice civilized wedding. I don't care what Ed and Belle think."

Zoe had never had heart palpitations, as far as Amanda knew, but just to shut her up, Amanda went along with her mother's wishes. She did like Robert's church, though. She got caught up in the emotion and the singing. She'd always had a flair for dramatics, which was in sharp contrast to her practical serious side. Actually, there were several sides to Amanda Wentworth Shaw.

"The pictures are great, Mandy. Wish I could take them all with me," Robert mused, as he quickly flipped through the black and whites one more time. He was the only person who got away with calling her "Mandy."

They finished opening their presents. A small jewelry box held a pair of red earrings that matched the wool dress, and Robert opened a small package that contained one little wedding picture and another that had a copy of the New Testament that he could carry with him.

Shopping had been difficult. What do you buy a man who will soon be shipped out somewhere overseas? Finally, in desperation, Amanda had talked to Belle, and she suggested something he could take with him. "I feel bad. That's all I got for you," Amanda blurted out, when the last little gift had been opened.

"Hon, it's O.K. Just being home and with you on our first Christmas is a gift. You're a gift, Mandy, the best gift of all."

"Yeah, but I wanted to give you more. I just didn't know what you could use right now," Amanda sighed.

"Next year will be different. It's O.K. I'm happy." Again Robert was the cheerful one.

If there is a next year for us, Amanda thought.

The long, hot bubble bath that Amanda treated herself to on Christmas morning relaxed her tense muscles and brought a rosy glow to her cheeks. She lay back in the tub reflecting over the days that Robert had been home. There was really no tension between the two of them, but, after all, a war was going on, so everyone was anxious and stressed out, especially if they had family overseas or about to go there. She had tried to discourage Robert from enlisting.

A man in his late thirties didn't need to enlist, but Robert, like his father before him, insisted on fighting for his country.

As she bathed and dressed for the day, Robert read the morning paper. There was no way to ignore the news of the war. It was on every page. *Battles Escalate In South Pacific.* The headlines hit Robert like a tank. He read on, knowing full well that the Pacific would be his destination and the battles there might soon be joined by his Division. He buried the newspaper under the crumpled Christmas wrappings in the kitchen wastebasket just as Amanda stepped into the room in her new red Christmas dress. No need to upset her, he mused. The smile he gave her was full of pure love and pleasure. His heart nearly broke as his mind told him this could be their last Christmas together.

Robert swooped Mandy up in his arms and spun her around. His six-foot-one-inch body seemed to tower over her five-foot-five-inch frame. In his strong arms her lithe body felt as delicate as a single snowflake that had fallen overnight. The hot bath had brought rosiness to her cheeks, now even more accentuated by the bright red dress. Her dark brown hair was bluntly cut straight across the bottom and hung just above her shoulders. She snuggled against his body, as her feet touched the floor.

All was right in Robert's world, if he ignored the news of the war.

All was right in Amanda's world, as long as her secret was invisible.

If you press me to say why I loved him,
I can say no more than it was because
He was he, and I was I.
                    —Montaigne

Chapter II

It was a few minutes before eleven that morning when Robert and Amanda departed for the Wentworth home. Their apartment was just down the hill and one block over to the east on the main street of the town of Wheatland. It was a short but refreshing walk, and the couple held hands as they sloshed through the melting snow up the hill.

The big yellow house where Amanda had grown up looked better than usual. The snow seemed to cleanse and decorate the yard. Robert unlatched the front gate, and they entered the Wentworth property. The large front porch with its white pillars had always reminded Amanda of pictures she'd seen of colonial houses in the South, but the welcoming committee stopped short of Southern hospitality. The front door was off limits, and the doorbell there was rung only by unsuspecting solicitors or those "uninformed nincompoops," as Mother Wentworth called Jehovah Witnesses, who were consistently ignored by the Wentworth women residing there. The untouched skiff of snow on the front porch was so pristine and perfect; Amanda could hardly resist messing it up.

As Amanda and Robert walked around the house on the south side, Amanda glanced up at the bedroom window on the main floor and noticed a single string of red and green Christmas lights had been placed around the glass. That room had been Amanda's for a time, but when she went away to college Margie had taken it over, so Amanda was shuffled off to a room upstairs. When she came home for the summer between her junior and senior years, she'd been moved to the "blue room" because her room was being renovated. She never did get her downstairs room back. She told the neighbors she was "sleeping around." They wondered if she knew what she was saying.

"Someone shoveled the sidewalk," Robert said, as they rounded the corner and approached the back porch. The snow had been cleaned from the wooden porch steps and the gray floor boards of the porch.

"That's Margie's job, now that I'm gone," Amanda answered. "I suppose she threw her back out like she usually does when she shovels, even though it snowed about one-sixteenth of an inch!" Amanda had hated the shoveling job. Nails stuck up through the old wooden sidewalk, and the metal snow shovel would "twang" as it hit the nails. Amanda had better luck using the broom, but Margie insisted on using the shovel. The boards were showing their age and buckling and needed to be replaced.

"Be careful," a voice called out as a gnarled hand reached out to push open the screen door.

Amanda sucked in one long, deep breath of fresh, cold December air before they entered the stuffy kitchen with its smothering combination of liniment odors and Christmas scents.

"Margie is on the couch," Mother Wentworth greeted them, as they shed their coats and boots inside the kitchen door. "It's nothing, really. She is just a little sore from all the shoveling."

How many times have I heard this? Amanda thought.

Margie sat up as they entered the dining room. Most families didn't have a sofa in the dining room, but the room was so large that it doubled as a living room. The furniture was eclectic and misplaced. The large mirrored and intricately carved sideboard was at one end of the part that was used as a living room. It contained the silverware, some of the family linens, and the antique silver service that had come from Papa Wentworth's family in New York. Amanda had always thought it belonged at the other end of the room near the dining room table, and she was surprised that her practical mother hadn't agreed with her. It was hard to change the ideas of a stubborn, unswerving mind, so Amanda had given up and gone with the flow—well, most of the time.

As Robert entered the room, Margie jumped up and threw her arms around him. Because it was Christmas, she felt she could kiss him on the cheek in front of God, her sister, and even her mother, who in her eyes was even more formidable and awesome than God Himself. "Merry Christmas, Robert," Margie whispered in his ear, just before she reluctantly let go of him.

Amanda wasn't surprised about her sister's display of affection. That was just her emotional, demonstrative older sister. Robert smiled rather sheepishly as he slowly disengaged himself from Margie's arms and looked furtively first at Mother Wentworth and then Amanda.

Oh, it's just Christmas, and Margie's in the spirit, Amanda thought to herself.

For once the double doors between the dining room/living room and the parlor were open, and as Amanda stepped into the parlor, a blast of heat from the floor vents hit her bare legs. It was unheard of to use this room, let alone heat it, unless the bridge club was coming, as it did once a year.

At the east end of the parlor where the window looked out on the front porch stood a Christmas tree, the tallest, fullest one the Wentworths had decorated in years. They'd always had a beautiful tree when Papa was alive, but since his death four years ago, a table-top tree had been placed on a desk in the north window of the dining room.

"We THOUGHT you'd be spending ALL Christmas day with us, so Margie decorated this beautiful tree for all of us to enjoy together," Mother said sarcastically.

Just bite your tongue, don't say anything critical, be nice, smile, it's Christmas, peace on earth, goodwill toward men. Amanda had this little two second talk with herself. Smiling at all of them, Amanda finally sweetly said (and, oh, she could be so sugary sweet), "As I tried to explain to you both last week, we just felt since Robert's been away and will be leaving again soon for duty, we should spend the day at his parent's house. But here we are now, so let's enjoy each other's company, and Margie, it IS a gorgeous tree!" Oh, the sugar was dripping now; Amanda was so sweet! Inside she felt like she was going to be sick. Margie, meanwhile, had tuned her out and was smiling at Robert, and Mother was scowling at all of them. Robert just looked bewildered.

"Let's have a nice hot cup of tea," Mother finally smiled, but her face almost cracked. Amanda had never liked tea, and her mother knew it, but it was the panacea for everything in this household. Amanda thought a nice hot toddy sounded good—a little Christmas cheer.

They drank their tea and ate some finger sandwiches that Margie had made. Amanda kept stealing glances at her watch. Time was marching on, but very slowly. They still had a few small packages to unwrap.

Finally Robert spoke up. "Here's a little gift for you, Mother Wentworth," he said, as he handed her a package from both of them. The white cardboard box about the size of a shoe box was full of an assortment of various shades of thread, darning floss, and a shiny, white darning egg. Mother Wentworth was the consummate seamstress. She was always bent over some piece of clothing, strengthening the buttonholes, reinforcing a seam, or darning stockings.

Happily, she smiled and said, "Well, bless you both for such a practical and useful gift." She was an undemonstrative woman. A few well-chosen words said it all. "No use babbling on like the brook," she had preached to her family over the years.

The two sisters exchanged gifts of books. They both loved to read, had always read a lot, and had shared some books over the years, although their tastes were different. Margie, the romantic, had penned a book of poetry for Amanda with her own pen and ink drawings to illustrate each page.

"It really is a work of art, Margie," Amanda said with admiration, as she quickly thumbed through all twenty-five pages. It wasn't her favorite kind of reading. She could be romantic in real life, but she didn't enjoy reading someone else's mush!

She had to admit, though, that Margie had a real talent for expressing her deep feelings in rhyming patterns and using her artistic skills to add appeal in pictures. She'd often tried to encourage Margie to get published, but Margie was content to dreamily sit for hours in the window seat in her bedroom to write and draw, then hide her creations from the world in the hope chest at the foot of her bed. On rare occasions, she would share one or two poems with Amanda, but only when they were younger and in one of their rare sisterly moods.

Amanda, the more studious one and the realist, who saw the world's issues in black and white, opened another book from Margie. It was a large world atlas. No one could tell that Margie had gleaned it from the shelves of the local library's used book sale. It looked brand new and was even a fairly recent publication.

"What a great book!" Amanda was genuinely pleased. She almost felt like hugging her sister, but caught herself just in time. There was not much display of affection in the family, except for Margie, who loved to be hugged and kissed and would offer her own displays of love unabashedly on everyone. She loved animals, children, and the older citizens of society.

Amanda, likewise, had two books for Margie. One was a book of poetry by Emily Dickinson and the other was a book of artistic sketches by several rather recent new artists. Amanda, too, had found mint condition second-hand books in a used book store in Spokane.

They were all happy with their gifts, so far. The last to receive a present was Robert. Margie reached under the Christmas tree and pulled out a flat box wrapped in green tissue paper and decorated with tiny pine cones she had collected herself from under the trees in the back yard. The cones were tied delicately with green string to the green ribbon encircling the box. She'd made the little card, using an old recycled Christmas card received last year and cut down with pinking shears.

The contents of the package was the real treasure. Handed down from Margie's grandfather to her Papa was a green paisley scarf. Amanda had seen it in her father's dresser drawer, but she had never seen him wear it. Margie had saved it for four years in her hope chest. She thought it was the most beautiful piece of material she'd ever seen and begged her mother to let Robert have it to keep it in the family.

Amanda covered her mouth and stifled a cough to cover up her disgust. She'd almost snorted through her nose and quickly pulled a tissue out of the small pocket in the skirt of her dress and wiped her nose to mask her sounds of amazement. What would Robert do with such a God-awful rag? She'd never liked it.

Robert, always the gracious gentleman, looped it around his neck and tied it just once, and patted it down in front.

"Thank you both," he said pleasantly to Mrs. Wentworth and Margie. Amanda couldn't tell if his pleasure was genuine or not, but she hoped he had better taste. Maybe they thought he could wear it in the line of duty to ward off a sore throat in the high seas. A silk scarf? No, they couldn't be that stupid! Thankfully, at that moment Robert stepped into the kitchen to grab their coats.

"We hate to have to run off, but we're expected soon out at Mom and Dad's." He was still wearing the paisley scarf, and he buttoned his coat over it.

Mother Wentworth arose slowly from her rocking chair. Her arthritis was really bothering her due to the weather.

"Merry Christmas," Robert and Amanda said cheerfully and almost in unison, as they gathered up their gifts and headed for the door.

"We'll see you two before I leave," Robert added.

At that statement, Margie started blinking rapidly. The tears were damming up behind her eyes. "Thanks again for the books and . . . and for coming," she said as clearly as she could, but her voice cracked on the last two words. She dashed to the window to watch them descend the back porch steps.

"Christmas is over; All's well that ends . . . ," was all that Mother Wentworth could utter.

At that very moment, the ground shook near the Stratford parish church in England. It was not an earthquake as some thought—just Shakespeare turning over in his grave.

Robert and Amanda were lost in their own separate thoughts as they bounced along the country road out to the Shaws for Christmas dinner. Robert was dwelling on the war and his uncertain future, and Amanda was thinking that Christmas afternoon at the Shaws would no doubt be a pleasant time. Amanda loved to visit their farm any time of the year.

Twelve miles north of Wheatland amidst what was becoming some of the most fertile and productive farmland in the Pacific Northwest stood the stately farmhouse. The two-story, reddish-brown structure was surrounded by a large yard with evergreen and blue spruce trees. The house had started out with just three rooms, but was added onto over the years. A large red barn off to the southeast completed the typical picture-perfect farm.

As they left the road and drove up the lane to the farmhouse, Amanda began to have the nice warm feelings she always experienced coming to the Shaws. "I love to come here," she said to Robert. She had a big smile and a rosy glow to her cheeks again.

"Yeah, it's home, sweet home," Robert answered with sincerity, as he shifted the pickup down into first gear and swerved to miss two bantam hens that ran in front of the pickup. "What are they doing out in this kind of weather? Run on in, Mandy, and I'll chase them back home." Robert turned into the circular gravel driveway, shut off the engine, and jumped out. He ran toward the banties, flapping his arms and clapping his hands—a grand escort back to the chicken coop that was attached to the barn. He'd done this so many times before that the chickens all knew the routine.

Amanda looked up at the kitchen window as she got out of the pickup and saw her mother-in-law's smiling face, then as she hurried up the steps and onto the porch, the same chubby face appeared at the front door.

"Come on in, child," Belle Shaw said, as she wrapped her arms around Amanda in a warm embrace.

Amanda laughed at the word "child." After all, she was forty years old! She hugged Belle tightly. Belle was just one of those cuddly, teddy bear types a person wanted to hug. Belle's gray hair was cut short in the back with curls all over the top. Her home perm looked recently done. Belle always smelled so good with just a hint of cologne and a light touch of rouge on her cheek.

"It's nice to be here. Merry Christmas! Oh, the house is so warm and cozy and smells so good," Amanda said happily.

"Take off your things, and we'll put them on the bed. Where did Robert go?"

Amanda explained the chicken story, as she gave Belle her coat and set her snow boots on a newspaper by the door.

"Ed will have to find some wire and fix that coop. They've been getting out a lot lately."

Just then Robert appeared. Belle was still holding the coat.

"Hi, Mom. Merry Christmas," he said, as he scooped her up and spun her around. At just five-feet-two-inches, she barely came up to Robert's chin, but with every passing year (and sixty-five of them had passed) there was more of Belle otherwise to scoop up and spin.

Robert gently set his mother down. Amanda noticed that he had quickly pulled off the paisley scarf and shoved it into his deep coat pocket. Shedding his coat, he handed it to his mom, who bustled off to lay their wraps on the bed.

"Go on in. Dad's in the living room," she called over her shoulder.

Ed was bent over the hearth, poking at the fresh log he'd just thrown in the fireplace.

"Need some help, Dad?" Robert asked, being the polite son, but knowing that Dad had everything under control.

"Just finishing up here," Dad answered, as the two men embraced.

"Welcome to our home, again, Amanda." Ed hugged Amanda, too, who was actually not minding the warmth of a loving family and a happy home.

"It really looks Christmasy in here," Amanda remarked, as she looked around the room. It was similar to the Wentworth home in that the dining room was at one end of the large living room, but different in the way it was arranged. Belle had the china cabinet where it belonged, near the dining room table. The large table had room for eight chairs and plenty of room for the harvest crew in the summer. Two of the chairs had been placed by the wall for the winter. The table was already set with Belle's good silver and dishes. Star-shaped crystal candle holders held two red tapers, ready to be lit.

At the other end of the living room, a nativity scene graced the fireplace mantle, and a large home-grown blue spruce tree stood decorated in front of the picture window. Several comfortable chairs, a sofa, a coffee table, and a Victrola completed the living room.

Amanda excused herself to help Belle, who was hurrying around in the kitchen doing all the last minute things: basting the turkey one last time, tasting the stuffing, and washing the lettuce to decorate the salad plates. She stopped just long enough to admire Amanda's new red Christmas dress, which Amanda proudly modeled.

"It fits perfectly," Belle complimented Amanda, as she tied an apron around her waist to protect the new red dress.

"The earrings match so well, too," Belle added, with a twinkle in her eye.

"Oh, yes. Robert got the earrings to go with the dress."

At Belle's request, Amanda began to unmold the large red gelatin salad to cut and place individual servings on each salad plate. As she ran the knife in a circular motion around the ringed mold and watched the shimmering jello loosen from the sides, Amanda began to perspire. She felt the dizziness again.

Belle stopped talking about her Bible study at church when she saw Amanda wiping her brow on her apron. "Are you all right, dear?" Belle asked.

"I think so, just a little warm. Maybe I'll sit down for a minute." Amanda rested herself on a kitchen chair.

"The kitchen is warm," Belle agreed with her.

Soon Amanda was up again and the "storm" had passed. She helped by mashing the potatoes and carrying the steaming bowls of vegetables, the gravy boat, the salad plates, and the bread basket to the table. Much of the food was home-grown and had been brought up from the root cellar earlier in the week.

The kitchen clock said 3:00 p.m. Dinner was ready, right on time. Belle dashed into the dining room at the very last minute to fill the water glasses and light the candles.

"Boys, it's time. Christmas dinner is now served in the dining room," she announced to Ed and Robert. This was her domain, and she was proud of it. They thought she was the best cook in the county, and Amanda agreed.

Robert seated his mother first, then Amanda, as Ed made his traditional entry into the kitchen. He soon appeared in the doorway, bearing a sixteen pound golden brown turkey, which he placed on the table ready for carving.

"He's a beauty, Dad," Robert said approvingly.

"Oh, I just raised him. Your mom cooked him so he'd look pretty."

At every meal the Shaws held hands, while Ed asked the blessings, not just on the food, but on everyone and everything. Belle prayed silently that the potatoes wouldn't get cold, and she kept saying "Amen," which led Amanda to believe that the praying was over, but Ed went on and on. Amanda sent up her own silent request that Belle wouldn't talk about that little spell she'd had in the kitchen.

"Amen," Robert, Belle, and Ed finally said, in unison, and they were through praying.

Amanda almost said, "Hallelujah! Let's eat." All of a sudden, she was famished.

Everyone oohed and aahed over all the good food, and Belle ate up the compliments, as well as two helpings of everything but the jello salad.

"One of my new-found goals in life is to be half as good a cook as my mother-in-law," Amanda announced, as she and Belle began to clear the main course away.

"Bless you, dear." Belle had a twinkle in her eye, and she winked at Robert as she thanked Amanda for her generous compliment.

The men leaned back in their chairs, as the women waited on them. They were resting while they could; they planned to help with the dishes, then fix the chicken coop, if it wasn't dark by then.

By the time they'd each had a slice of pumpkin pie, no one wanted to move, but Belle thought they could surely make it to the living room couch first and open their Christmas presents, letting the indoor and outdoor chores wait.

"You boys can fix the chicken coop, and Amanda and I'll do up the dishes, but first let's have Christmas. Robert, crank up the Victrola. Let's hear some carols."

Belle was so excited to give Amanda her gift that she was bubbling like a tea kettle.

"Oh, Ed, give Amanda that square one," she gushed.

Belle couldn't wait. She had put in long hours preparing this special gift for her new daughter-in-law. Amanda hurried and threw the ribbon and paper on the floor. She couldn't imagine what all the excitement was about.

Belle jumped up, ran to Amanda and looked over her shoulder, as she opened a cookbook that Belle had compiled herself, writing in longhand on recipe cards all her family's favorite recipes. They were all organized and catalogued. The black gummed triangular corners used to mount photographs held each card in place, in case she wanted to remove one when using it or maybe even copying it for someone else in the future. Belle had also cut out pictures of food items and glued them onto each appropriate page to make it look more decorative.

Amanda was speechless, as she perused the recipes. She knew Belle had lovingly spent many long hours putting it together, just for her.

> "To Amanda—Merry Christmas, 1944.
> May you enjoy cooking as much as I do.
>   Mother Belle"

Belle had printed this in gold ink on the first page.

Stoic, unemotional Amanda actually got a tear in her eye. She stood and hugged Belle, thanking her quite profusely.

"Now I can learn to cook like you do, Mother Belle. With college and teaching as my whole life, I've never bothered with it much, but thank you. Look Robert," she said, as she passed the book to him. He actually had seen it one day earlier in the week when he'd been out to visit Dad and talk about the war.

Belle winked again at Robert as she sat down. Ed was grinning broadly. He was proud of his plump little wife. Not only was she a good cook, but she knew how to make each person feel special.

Ed, too, had made something special for the kids. It wasn't wrapped, but was hidden under the tree.

"Robert, since you can bend over better than I, can you reach that item behind the green box?" he asked, as he pointed under the tree.

"Be careful and try to grab it by each end," Belle admonished. She was excited again and stood with her hands on her broad hips.

Ed proudly presented a wooden manger scene to Robert and Amanda, just like the one Mandy had seen on the mantle.

"He made it himself," Belle gushed, and went over and planted a kiss on the forehead of her talented husband.

"It's great, Dad. When did you find the time?" Robert was pleased.

"Oh, I worked on it here and there, whenever I had a few moments."

"Look, Mandy," Robert had her hold one end, as he pointed out each whittled wooden figure.

"It's a work of art, Dad, and we'll treasure it forever because you made it." This was the first time Amanda had actually called him "Dad." She felt comfortable doing it. They had always called her own father "Papa."

Amanda had taken an art class while Robert was away at Camp Pendleton, and she'd made Belle a mosaic tile. It was about eight inches by four inches. In the center was a mosaic bell done exclusively in a light gray color. It was supposed to be silver in color, but it was as close as Amanda could come. The other tiles were various shades of light pinks and cream colors. She had placed a hanger on the back. Amanda was quite pleased with the way it had turned out.

"Did you make it, dear, at your art class? Every time I asked you what you were making, you said, 'Oh, some water colors.'"

"I did try some water colors. They were fun, I guess. I brought some home, tacked a few up on the bedroom wall, and stashed the rest under the bed. Oops, Robert, you weren't supposed to hear that." She covered her mouth, and everyone laughed.

"But, yes, I did do the mosaic. It's sort of different. I discovered I like art better than I thought I would. This kind of art is a form of expression I like without being too abstract. I can be realistic."

Belle liked anything creative. "I love my silver bell, and I'd like to see your water colors, my dear."

"A bell for my Belle," Ed said, smiling at Amanda, as he slowly arose to crank up the Victrola again.

Well, somebody caught on, Amanda thought to herself. She was getting tired and a little cranky. She stifled a yawn.

"One more package, and it's for you, Dad," Robert said, as he grabbed it from under the tree.

On that same trip of used-book buying where she'd acquired books for Margie, Amanda had found one for Ed. He was interested in American Indians, and she luckily found a large book of American Indian tribes and customs with some photos of Northwest chiefs and their horses.

Ed seemed pleased with the book and tucked it under his arm as they all headed out to the kitchen. Dusk was settling in, and Belle wanted the kids to start back to town, but Robert took over.

"Dad, I'll come out soon and help with the chicken coop and whatever else you need done. You just sit there and look at your new book. We'll help Mom with the dishes and be done in no time."

Belle's protests went unheard as Robert filled the sink with hot sudsy water.

"Mandy, you dry, and Mom, you can put them away." There, it was settled, and Belle obliged. As they quickly worked, Belle asked sweetly, "Amanda, what are Zoe and Margie doing today? Did they have folks in for dinner?"

Amanda nearly dropped the good china dinner plate she was drying. Folks in? she thought to herself. She couldn't remember the last time they'd had folks in.

"No, they're just home alone," Mandy answered.

"Oh, really? I invited them to join us out here, and when Zoe said 'No,' I had the feeling they were busy," Belle said with a question mark in her voice.

Amanda tried to think of excuses. "They just don't like going out much in the winter. We stopped in this morning. Mother's arthritis was acting up, and Margie had hurt her back shoveling snow, so everything was pretty much normal."

Belle raised an eyebrow at that statement, but Amanda couldn't help it. She couldn't tell Belle that Mother felt she was just a little more aristocratic and well-educated than the farmer and his wife.

Ed had dozed off with the open book in his lap, but he awoke when Robert announced, "Well, that was quick. Time to hit the road."

Amanda hung up the wet dish towel to dry over the cookstove and handed Belle the apron. "I'll get the coats," she called over her shoulder, as she made her way down the hall, stopping first at the bathroom and then the spare bedroom. Amanda glanced around the room. It had been Robert's room, and although his bed and a chest of drawers were still there, it had become a sewing room and catch-all for Belle's projects.

Amanda passed by the treadle sewing machine on her way to retrieve the coats. A swatch of red wool material caught her eye. She picked it up and held it up to her dress. It was the same material, and then she noticed the pattern pieces folded and laying by the pattern envelope. A slender woman was pictured there, modeling the very dress Amanda was wearing.

So Belle made my dress! Amanda thought. She hadn't noticed that there was no brand name sewn into it anywhere.

Gathering up the coats, she hurried back out to the kitchen. Not knowing whether to thank Belle and ruin her little secret or say nothing and pretend she hadn't seen the evidence, Amanda thanked Belle for the wonderful afternoon, the tasty Christmas dinner, and the very special cookbook.

I have to say something. The next time she goes into the bedroom, she'll put two and two together, and she'll know I saw the pattern and material. Hugging Belle good-bye, she whispered in her ear, "Red is my favorite color. Thank you."

Belle gave Amanda an extra pat. "I know it is, and you're so very welcome. I'm glad it's the right size," she whispered back.

Robert was carrying the gifts out from the living room. He set them on the counter and helped Amanda on with her coat.

You're not half as glad as I am, Amanda thought, as they said their good-byes. It covers all my sins today, but maybe not by next week!

"Deep in her heart lives the silent wound"
—Virgil

Chapter III

Robert said his good-byes to Mother Wentworth and Margie and also to his parents right before the New Year. No one could predict if these farewells were just for the time being or forever. Granted, no one ever knows that for sure, but during war time the uncertainties of life put even the calmest person on edge. Robert knew that Amanda was becoming more upset with every passing hour and the thoughts of his leaving were showing in her face every time he looked at her. He admonished her to stay home and rest.

"I'll go, Mandy, and get it over with. You don't have to come. I have to help Dad with some chores anyway, and Mom is having her Bible study group out at the house today."

She looked relieved, as she kissed him passionately. She knew Margie would have tears, and she didn't need the emotional upheaval. She'd have her own tears soon enough.

"O.K., that's fine. I'll fix a surprise for you. Be sure to be home in time for dinner."

He didn't want to leave her even for a couple of hours. He stroked her cheek and tucked her hair back behind her ears. Taking her face in his hands, he looked into her hazel eyes for a long time, as if he were memorizing her beauty. "Where are the keys?" he asked, as he let her go.

"On the dresser where they always are." He can never find anything. She was still trying to figure out how two opposites could be so attracted to each other.

*   *   *

Amanda and Robert had known each other virtually all of their lives, having gone through twelve grades together in the Wheatland School system, but they barely knew each other existed.

Robert was deeply involved in his two family interests—the farm and the Assembly of God Church—all through his younger years and again when he'd come home from college. He'd been on the farm as W.W. II erupted and had felt an overwhelming compulsion to serve his country, even though he was thirty-nine years old.

Amanda, on the other hand, was entrenched in her books, school assignments, college studies, research, and teaching. She was a popular girl in spite of being studious, but rarely had time or interest to date. In high school she had attended Presbyterian Church Youth Group, but it was more of a social outlet and a chance to be away from home than a religious experience.

In October 1943, Robert and Amanda had met up again on the Washington State College campus. Amanda was enrolled in the Master's Degree program, working on an advanced degree in chemistry. Robert had returned to his alma mater for a football game, and he and his other unmarried buddies, who'd come down from Wheatland for the weekend, set out to find dates for the big game. The only person Robert knew on campus who was close to his age was Amanda Wentworth, and she consented to go with him. Amanda later said it was luck, pure and simple. Robert vowed it was part of God's great master plan.

Whatever it was, it worked. Robert met her criteria, the list of prerequisites Amanda had drawn up. Robert had stability, intelligence, and security. He was from a good family, and he was a genuinely nice man. Most importantly, he was not controlling. Amanda would NOT be controlled! Fortunately, he wanted Amanda to pursue her dreams.

So Amanda had found love with Robert. Their dating was sporadic and long distance. Mostly they fell in love by mail and on her breaks from college when she went home.

On April 10, 1944, Robert asked Amanda to marry him as soon as harvest was over in August. That fit in with her plans, too. She would have her Masters degree by then. They set the date for August 30, and the weatherman (according to Amanda) and God (according to Robert) had cooperated. Harvest was finished and the kerneled crop of wheat was safely tucked away in the local grain elevators long before the wedding bells rang.

They'd had so little time together as man and wife before he'd left for Camp Pendleton, and now it was their last night together until . . . well, who knew when?

*   *   *

Amanda had found a recipe she wanted to try in her new cookbook from Mother Belle, so she decided to make a special candlelight dinner for the two of them. It wasn't anything fancy— just shepherd's pie, but by the time Robert had returned around 5:00 p.m., she had managed to fill the apartment with the appetizing aromas of a good casserole, French bread, and freshly perked coffee. There was nothing for a salad and no dessert, but Amanda couldn't help it, and she really didn't care. She wasn't very hungry anyway.

The drop-leaf table in the kitchen was just right for two people, and she'd put on a fresh red linen tablecloth and even matching linen napkins. In the center was the bayberry candle she'd borrowed from the living room coffee table. She'd tried to drag the kitchen table into the living room, so they could enjoy the Christmas tree lights one more time and stretch the holidays out as long as possible, but the table was too heavy.

Robert was surprised at all her extra efforts and admitted the shepherd's pie tasted every bit as good as his mother's.

"Are you just being polite?" she asked, hoping he really did like it.

"No, really. It's perfect." He was a meat and potatoes man, so she had been right in thinking this would be a good hearty dish to master.

They sat for a long time over dinner and talked over his day. His stop at the Wentworth's was uneventful. Margie was downtown, running errands, so he didn't see her, which they both agreed was probably just as well.

"How was Mother?" Amanda wondered.

"She was cordial. She seemed surprised to see me. Didn't I tell her I'd stop by?"

"She probably forgot when you were leaving. You know she's not remembering things like she used to. Did she mention anything about Christmas Day?"

"No, not really. I thanked her again for the scarf. I suppose she could see I wasn't wearing it, but she didn't say anything. As I was leaving, I told her to give my regards to Margie, and that was it. She waved good-bye and told me to be careful."

"Don't take her coolness personally. She's that way with everyone, and she probably really is concerned about your safety." Amanda stuck up for her mother for once. She cleared the table and sat down again. They held hands over the table and drank a second cup of coffee, as Robert told her about seeing Ed and Belle.

"I'm sorta worried about Dad. He seemed really slow and old today. I helped him outside, and then we sat in the kitchen for awhile and talked, but he seemed so tired. If . . . I mean, when I come home from the war, they'll probably be ready to move to town and let us take over the farm. So, think about that while I'm gone, O.K.?" He cocked his head to one side, as if that would help her think about it. She knew this was coming before she and Robert married, but she had hoped it would be many years before she became a farm "girl."

Robert went on with the story of his day. "Mom's Bible study broke up about 3:30, so I had to talk to all the ladies, but that was good. They all said they'd be praying for me." Robert had known most of these ladies all his life, so he was used to all the attention they gave him.

"Your mom's lucky to have such good friends."

"It's not luck, Mandy. It's God's blessings." Mandy still didn't seem to see the difference, and they could have gotten into a messy argument over chance versus theology, but not tonight. She left the dishes in the sink. There weren't many, as she'd cleaned up while she cooked. She blew out the candle. Robert turned out the lights in the kitchen and living room and locked the front door. Not wanting any interruptions tonight, he slipped the phone off the hook.

It was early for bedtime, but they wanted to be close to each other. They talked far into the night and held each other, as though nothing could separate them. Their lovemaking was long and intense. Sleep overtook them for awhile, but they both awoke again to the touch and rapture of each other's bodies.

They were awake when the first light of dawn broke through the darkness. A snowstorm had blown through during the night, but once more it didn't amount to much. The sky, however, looked like it could blanket the area with a thick covering.

"I'll race you to the shower," Robert said, trying to be full of fun. They both ended up there at the same time, which was just the way they wanted it. They stepped in, one after the other, and Robert let the warm water stream down his body.

"It's cold back here in the back of the bus," Amanda said through chattering teeth. No one bothered to turn on the bathroom heater.

"Well, come on. Get up here under the water," Robert said, as he pulled her near him. They washed and rinsed each other, and the passions began again.

It was over all too soon, and they had to hurry to get dressed, have a little breakfast, and get Robert downtown to meet his ride to Spokane.

"Look, I'm wearing my red dress again." It seemed a little snug in the waist, but Robert probably hadn't noticed. But he did notice when she didn't want any breakfast. She insisted that it was just nerves. On the sly, she slipped a few soda crackers into her handbag.

Then it was time to leave the apartment to meet Bill, another Leatherneck, whose father was going to drive the two Marines to the city to catch the train. Robert replaced the phone on its cradle, turned, and gave one final look over their first home before he locked the apartment door behind him. As Robert and Amanda walked down the steps from the upstairs apartment, the phone rang endlessly.

Not giving up easily, Margie dialed the number again. "I guess I'm too late to say good-bye," she said sadly to herself, as she finally gave up and wiped the tears from her cheeks.

Later that night Amanda unplugged the lights on the little dried up Christmas tree and sat staring into the darkness. She wouldn't let Robert throw out the tree before he left, but now she wished she had. She felt as shattered and stripped as the branches where the needles were falling from the tree. She rocked back and forth and drew the fringed cream-colored afghan tightly over her knees. A sudden numbing chill went through her thin body clear to the bone. It was like the numbing of her heart and soul that she now felt. Forty years old and alone, with a husband who in a few days would ship out from Camp Pendleton to join the Fifth Marine Division in war, and then what?

The holidays had been so wonderful with Robert home and their great Christmas out at the Shaws. Belle had made her feel like a child again, full of wonder and excitement, but it was over. It was time to face reality again.

This wasn't like Amanda. She had always prided herself on her independent spirit. She was in many ways like her mother—strong, determined, brave, and stoic. One of her mother's bridge club ladies had called her "precocious" as a young child, and her high school teachers had told her she was ahead of her time.

Her college degrees were in chemistry and education, and she had always looked to the future, not just for her own life, but for the world, knowing that man's answers to the all-important questions of life could be found in science. Amanda knew that the universe was basically untapped. So much scientific research needed to be done and discoveries taught to others. The possibilities had always excited her, but not tonight. Her thoughts and life had taken a different turn. The tree was still up because she didn't want the holidays to be over.

She hadn't wanted Robert to leave, and yet, in her heart, she knew it was for the best that he was gone during this time. There was no way she could stop the clock or alter the past or remedy her mistake. Her logical mind told her that all she could do was go on and face her uncertain future.

The nausea was greeting her every morning now, and the last few mornings that Robert was home, she'd tried to blame it on something she'd eaten. "Too much rich holiday food, perhaps," she'd tried to convince him. Actually, with the sugar rationing, she'd eaten far fewer Christmas goodies than usual, but, thank goodness, Robert didn't seem to catch on.

Now that Robert was gone, she must know the truth and plan a course of action.

I must find a doctor and make an appointment, but I'll have to go out of town. The Wentworth's family doctor in Wheatland was old Dr. Petersen. They'd gone to him for years. In fact, he'd delivered Margie and Amanda and treated them all for everything from colic to Mother's menopause. The Shaw's doctor in town was Dr. Baker, a young new general practitioner, who was a member of their church, and whose wife attended the Bible Study with Belle.

"Well, I certainly can't go to him either," Amanda said out loud with disgust, as if it were his fault she was in such a mess. She was getting some of her old spunk back already!

Remembering a Spokane phone directory she had on a bookcase, Amanda stumbled through the darkness into the bedroom and turned on the bedside lamp. She sprawled across the bed and found the "Physicians" column in the Yellow Pages. They were all just names to her. She had no idea which one to choose.

Amanda was exhausted and decided she could figure it out the next day. Sleep came easily, in spite of her worries, and she dreamt that she and her husband were on a big ship out in the Pacific Ocean. There were over one hundred passengers, and they were all babies under the age of one. She was constantly calling her husband to come and hold a bottle, change a diaper, or cuddle a crying baby, but every time he came to her assistance, he didn't look at all like Robert. This man had a goatee, wore little round glasses, and distinctly resembled her art teacher from the evening class.

"I had a little sorrow
Born of a little sin."
—Millay

Chapter IV

Amanda awoke with a start and looked around the bedroom. She sat up and shook her head to clear her mind. "Oh, my gosh. It was only a dream," she sighed in relief.

She wiped the perspiration from her forehead, turned on the lamp, and looked at the clock. Six-thirty a.m. She dashed to the bathroom—it was always an urgent call these days—and then she returned to the safety of the bed. Nothing could really hurt a person under the covers. As a child, she'd learned that the boogie man couldn't attack, and no other harm could even come close. The sheets and blankets were a safety shield. Ha! What a lie that is! She snuggled down under the comforter. This is where all my problems began!

This was Amanda's first full day alone since Robert had boarded the train for his return to California, and already she could tell it was going to be a long one. She knew her mother or Margie would be calling to check on her, and she really didn't want to face either one of them just yet. She also needed to find a doctor and make an appointment.

Last night's feeling of intense panic had subsided.

Things always seem worse at night, was the thought Amanda clung to as she tried to plan her day.

The Spokane phone directory was still lying open on the bed, and as Amanda scanned the list of physicians, they were just names to her. "Dr. Randolph Bennett. That's a nice name, or how about Roderick McKay, General Physician? Now that has a nice ring to it. Dr. Roderick McKay." Amanda said the names out loud. This wasn't a very scientific way of finding a doctor, but it was Amanda's only choice. She couldn't ask anyone's opinion or acquire a referral.

O.K. At nine, I'll call for an appointment. His office should be open by then. Her stomach started churning, more from nervousness this time than anything else. She put her hand under the sheet and rubbed her abdomen. "I wonder what the doctor will have to say," she whispered. "Oh, Lord, what have I done?"

The line was busy at 9:00, but at 9:13 Amanda got through.

"Dr. McKay's office. May I help you?" The receptionist sounded pleasant enough.

"Yes, I need to make an appointment to see Dr. McKay," Amanda tried to sound sure of herself and in control.

"Are you a patient of Doctor's?"

"No, I don't have a doctor."

"So you don't have a referral?" The receptionist questioned Amanda.

"No, I don't."

"Fortunately, Dr. McKay is taking new patients. Why do you need to see Doctor?"

"Um, uh, I need to have a physical exam. I'm having some stomach problems," Amanda thought that was close enough to the truth.

The appointment was scheduled for 2:00 p.m. on Friday. Amanda had two days to find a ride to Spokane. If it were better weather, she'd drive Robert's old pickup, but not with snow on the ground. There was always the train. She'd taken it many times. It was convenient and reliable, and she knew the schedule was just right for her appointment. "O.K. That's settled," Amanda said out loud and felt somewhat better. She was in control again and had made some decisions.

She'd barely put the phone down when its shrill ring pierced the silence.

"Your line's been busy. Who called so early?" Her mother's voice sliced through her like a knife slicing a tomato.

"Oh, it was a friend from school. She's in Spokane and wants me to visit," Amanda's brain was working on double-speed to come up with that line! She hated lying to her mother, but sometimes she just had to. This wasn't the first time, nor would it be the last.

"Ooooooh," her mother drug out the word as if it had four syllables. "When are you going?"

"Not until Friday," Amanda answered truthfully. "I'll probably stay overnight."

"Well, would you possibly have time to come up here before you go and help Margie take the tree down and put away the decorations? Since you were elsewhere on Christmas, I thought maybe we could at least box up the holidays and end it together."

"Is Margie feeling poorly again?" Amanda tried to ignore Mother's sarcasm and offer some of her own. No one had any idea how SHE had been feeling lately.

"Physically, she's been doing pretty well, but she's been a little sad with the holidays being over and all."

AND ALL? You'd think they'd hosted holiday guests for two weeks straight. Amanda answered without hesitation. She'd learned over the years to think quickly on her feet, and she'd mastered it as well as if she'd taken an impromptu speaking class in college. "I'm keeping busy, but I'll come up this afternoon. Will that do?"

"Yes, come up around two. Margie should be home from the post office by then."

Mother liked to keep to a schedule. Margie slept in, often until eleven or so, and after a noontime meal, she'd make her daily trek to the post office. Margie was a night owl. It was nothing for her to start baking a batch of cookies at ten o'clock at night. Mother often went to bed with the sound of Margie beating eggs or the oven timer ringing in her ears. Oh, yes, I remember it well. I was usually up, too, when I was home, but I was studying.

At 2:00 p.m. promptly, Amanda entered the back door of the Wentworth home. Margie and Mother had already convened on the black velvet couch in the parlor by the tree, but no one had removed even one icicle or ornament.

"I'm here," Amanda announced as she shrugged out of her coat and deposited her boots by the door. It was normal not to be greeted warmly at the door, especially when there was big business, such as this tree defrocking.

The project went quickly and smoothly and was highly organized and overseen by Mother. They all knew the procedure. Amanda gently removed each ornament and carefully handed it to Margie, who delicately wrapped each individual one in a facial tissue and placed it in a suitably labeled box. Each type of decoration had its own special niche—bells in one box, balls in another, ornaments that had been received as gifts in a special round metal container, and those purchased over the years in a gray cardboard box.

Next, off came the icicles. Margie held the cardboard holder, while Amanda deftly lifted one foil strand at a time and placed it with precision over the holder.

With Mother's approval, the girls removed the lights, placing each string on a bed of tissue paper in a long, narrow, well-worn box.

Margie was full of questions as they worked.

"Did Robert get off to Spokane all right? Have you heard from him yet? When will he arrive in California? What are your plans while he's gone?"

Amanda's answers were brief and to the point. The last question threw her for a loop.

How in the world can I have any plans? She wanted to scream at Margie, but she calmly answered, "Well, my name's still on the substitute list at school, so maybe I'll get some calls to teach."

Now that the serious business was over and the tree was stripped of its trimmings, Mother could join the conversation and talk of other things. She too had a question.

"Did you ever hear from that college in Iowa about that fellowship you applied for?"

"No, not yet," Amanda answered quickly. How strange that Mother would think of that today and ask me when it just could be my salvation, Amanda thought with astonishment.

The girls dragged the tree out and placed it near the alley fence. Mother watched them, hurrying from window to window to follow their progression. Apparently it met with her approval. She offered them a "nice cup of tea" and a wafer as their reward when they reentered the house through the back door.

"I'll have the wafer, and then I must be going," Amanda said. "You know I hate tea."

"You're always in such a hurry. What is so important that you can't spend a little time with us? I suppose you're going out to Belle's again for supper."

"No, no, no," Amanda tried to smooth her mother's ruffled feathers. "I want to get a letter in the mail to Robert, and it's getting late."

Margie bubbled with excitement. "Oh, next time just let me know. I could pick up your letter and mail it to Robert on my way downtown."

"Well, I don't even have it written yet!" Margie just smiled and instructed Amanda to "say hello from us." Then Amanda was off.

The first letter to arrive at the Wheatland Post Office from Robert came the same day that Amanda traveled to Spokane for her doctor's appointment. It was postmarked Portland, Oregon. There was no return in the upper left-hand corner, but its writer was no secret; Margie would recognize his writing anywhere.

MARGIE WENTWORTH
BOX 21
WHEATLAND, WASH.

This was printed in all capital letters on a long business envelope, which Margie clutched to her breast as she went outside.

Not wanting to go home, she skirted the business district and ended up in the deserted city park. The benches were covered with the whiteness of winter snow, which she carefully brushed off with her gloved right hand. In the left hand she was tenderly clutching the white envelope as if it were a butterfly that would surely fly away.

Opening it, she began to read:

Dear Margie,

It was great being home for the holidays, but time went so quickly. I'm sorry I missed you before I went away. I did want to thank you again for the scarf. I have it with me, but doubt if I'll have the chance to wear it any time soon. I still don't know exactly where I'll be when I ship out. Take care of yourself, dear one, and please try to spend some time with Amanda. She seemed almost sick with worry the last few days I was home. Family is important with uncertainties like we have during wartime, but we can't let our feelings control our lives. Faith and prayer and hope and common sense must rule, and, Margie, we must put these matters of the mind over our weak and vulnerable human hearts. We both know how we feel. So, dry your tears (I'm sure you must have some fresh ones) and watch for my return. God is in control, and He will help us sort out our lives, one way or the other.

Good-bye for now.

Love in Christ,
Robert

Margie sighed. Robert was right; there were fresh tears to wipe away. The tears kept coming, and she could not control them. Through the blur, she tried to read the letter again and again—what did it mean? Was he speaking generally of all mankind and their human hearts or of just the two of them personally? Should she read into his words a love for her that she so desperately wanted—even at her sister's expense? Even the closing left question marks in her mind. "Love in Christ." What did it mean? That Robert loved her in a special way or that, as Christ loved the church, then we should all love one another? It boggled her mind. She loved puzzles and word games, and she loved reading the poetry of the English writers, who had deeper meanings in their writings than what appeared on the surface. However, Robert's words seemed so personal, but should she read more into them or just accept them in a general way? Oh, she wanted so much more. She knew Robert was a Christian, but he was also a man with a vulnerable human heart.

She slipped the letter back into the envelope, folded it in half, and thrust it deep into her coat pocket. She shoved her gloves into her other pocket. Her left hand caressed the envelope in her pocket, as she slowly made her way out of the park.

Normally she walked down the main street toward home and looked in all the store windows and talked and smiled at friends she encountered. In a town of 1,600 people, she easily knew everyone. Today, however, confusion directed her pathway, and she took the back way that angled through several alleys and took her directly to the residential district. She was anxious to reach the safety and security of her bedroom, her sanctuary where she dealt with the big and little issues of life, and where now, hopefully, word by word, she could dissect Robert's letter and figure out the meanings.

As she ducked through the alley and caught sight of home, she knew the deciphering would have to wait. Belle Shaw was just stepping down from the running board of her 1942 Plymouth in front of the Wentworth house. She rarely stopped by, but when she did, she always had some home-cooked food for Margie and her mother. Margie liked Belle, and her casseroles were delicious, but today when Margie saw her pull a covered dish from the car seat, she felt a migraine coming on and knew she wouldn't be able to swallow a bite!

Perhaps someday it will be pleasant
To remember even this.
　　　　　—The Aeneid

Chapter V

The strong smell of medicine took Amanda's breath away as she entered the Paulsen Medical-Dental Building through the revolving front doors. Located on Riverside Avenue in downtown Spokane, the building was home to a pharmacy on the main floor, doctor's and dentist's offices on many levels, and even a small hospital. Ordinarily, Amanda loved the medley of medical concoctions and the odors that emanated from them, but today the mixtures of drugs were too overpowering for even a chemistry lover's nostrils. The nausea hit her harder than ever before, her nerves were at the breaking point, and her heart was pounding as she entered the elevator and whispered in a barely audible voice to the operator, "Ninth floor, please."

Thank goodness! Dr. Roderick McKay's office was directly across from the elevator. Amanda took a deep breath and sighed heavily as she turned the golden doorknob and entered the office. The news she'd learn here today would confirm that her life was changed forever.

Dr. Roderick McKay was middle-aged, short in stature, and slight of frame. Dark beady eyes stared at Amanda from behind round wire-rimmed glasses as he read her chart, which she'd filled out in the waiting room. He was no speed-reader, Amanda decided as she nervously watched his little eyes dart from line to line.

"Now, your chart says you're suffering from nausea. How often does this happen?"

"Every morning," Amanda replied.

"Now, your chart says . . . Now, your chart says . . ." He droned on and on with questions.

Suddenly he jumped up from his swivel chair.

"It's time for the examination. I'll get the nurse. Just relax."

Oh sure. That's like telling the wind to stop blowing. She rolled her eyes and watched him go out the door. She was still squirming around, trying to find a comfortable spot on the table, when Dr. McKay reentered the room with a starched white uniformed lady in tow.

"This is Nurse Jo."

"Yes, we met when she weighed me," Amanda informed the doctor of facts he should have already known.

Nurse Jo bustled around, lining up Dr.'s instruments and getting the stirrups ready for Amanda's feet. She helped Amanda move her body down farther on the table and, as she calmly worked, she smiled the whole time. The twinkle in her eye was in sharp contrast to the doctor's serious demeanor and nervousness. As she helped put Amanda somewhat at ease, she reminded Amanda of Belle Shaw with her round hips, rouged cheeks, and pleasant personality. Of course, Belle must never know of this episode or the comparison.

Now it was time. Dr. McKay positioned his stool and took a seat. With Nurse Jo at his side, the examination went quickly.

"Hmmm." Dr. McKay sighed.

"Hmmm." He repeated.

"Is anything wrong?" Amanda asked with fear in her voice.

"Oh, no. It's just as I thought. You can get dressed, and I'll be back in a few minutes with your instructions," and then he was out the door.

Nurse Jo helped Amanda to a sitting position.

"Now, dear, just put your gown here in this basket when you finish dressing and open the door just slightly, so Dr. will know you are ready."

"Thank you." Amanda said, as she smiled for the first time that day. "Well, that part's over and now for the verdict." Amanda added.

"Now, now, dear. It will be all right. Doctor will take good care of you," Nurse Jo encouraged, as she hurried out to prepare another patient.

Soon the doctor was back with his prescription pad and Amanda's chart. He sat down on the stool and wrote on the pad, dramatically filling in her chart. Head cocked to one side and then the other, he held his pen in the air and wrote with big flourishes of the wrist and the fingers, as if he were illustrating it.

Come on, doctor. Amanda was silently screaming.

"O.K. Here we go," he announced, as he handed her the prescription. "Get these vitamins, don't lift anything heavy, rest as much as you can, and come back in one month. Make an appointment with the receptionist as you leave," and he got up to go.

"But, Doctor, what is wrong with me?" Amanda implored.

"Oh, I thought you knew. You're two months pregnant," and he was gone.

Amanda glared at the back of his head, as he callously went on his way.

"But when is my due date?" she hollered into an empty hallway.

No one answered and no one seemed to be around. All the other doors were closed. Amanda heard a phone ring and a door slam, but it was eerily quiet for a doctor's office. No wonder. He probably doesn't have any other patients. I sure picked a doozie! Amanda followed the arrows to the front desk and paid for her visit in cash, wanting no outstanding bills or paper trails to disclose her secret and follow her path, wherever that was going to lead. Clutching her statement marked "Paid in Full," and shoving it into her purse, she made an appointment for the next month (only because it was expected of her), while knowing full well she would not keep it.

The elevator soon whisked her down to the main floor, where the pharmacy was handy, so she got her prenatal vitamins before even leaving the building. Then she was out the door and walking down the sidewalk into a world of hell that she'd created for herself. Calendars formed in her head and possible delivery dates loomed in front of her eyes. Amanda would just have to sit down and try to figure it out herself at the hotel.

Plodding west on Riverside Avenue, then south on Post Street with the icy breath of winter's north wind at her back, she trudged over the slushy sidewalk and curbs. Suddenly exhausted and hungry, Amanda was almost too tired to think of lifting a fork to her mouth.

"I'm eating for two now," other pregnant women had said, and now it applied to her—to Amanda Wentworth Shaw, the scholar, the teacher, the sibling, who, unlike Margie, had never wanted to waste her time bearing and rearing children. *I do have options.* She clung to that thought as she reached the corner of Sprague and Post and the hotel where she would spend the night.

Designed for Louis Davenport by Spokane's mansion builder, Kirkland Cutter, the Davenport Hotel opened in 1914 as one of the nation's best hotels. Mr. Davenport was a perfectionist, and it showed in his staff. He demanded perfectly set tables, absolute obedience, and training even in body language, so that guests would not be offended.

Amanda passed by the Italian Gardens, the opulent restaurant that adjoined the Davenport. Abundant in fresh flowers from the Davenport's own flower shop, it had the finest menu in town and was a wonderful place to celebrate a night out in downtown Spokane, especially now if a loved one came home alive from service overseas.

For Amanda it was not a time for that. She had nothing to celebrate and wanted only the intimate warmth and coziness of the hotel coffee shop on this cold January day. As she was shown to a small table, she almost felt normal again. It was like coming home, away from the sterile, cold doctor's office and the noisy streetcars of the bustling city.

She ordered a cup of coffee and then realized she should have had milk, but it would be so cold. A bowl of hot vegetable soup and a buttered roll sounded filling and soothing, and waiting for her late lunch to arrive, she closed her eyes and breathed deeply. It was hard to stay awake, and she let her mind drift to the last night Robert was home. She was sleeping in his arms and nearly jumped out of her skin when she heard a deep voice say, "Ma'am, your lunch has arrived." Amanda smiled dreamily at the waiter as he set a large bowl of steaming soup in front of her. A wicker basket of various kinds of crackers and a hot crescent roll with butter completed her lunch.

Amanda looked around at the other tables as she slathered butter on her roll and waited for her soup to cool. Thank goodness, she saw no one she knew, as she didn't feel like explaining her presence to anyone from home.

Amanda glanced at her watch as she finished her meal and paid the bill. It was 4:30. Well, I'll get my room, and then maybe take a long hot bath. This could be a fun adventure, if I didn't have so much on my mind.

The lobby of the hotel was an entertainment center in itself. Lavishly decorated, it contained tropical plants, singing birds, and glass pillars filled with swimming goldfish. After securing a room and getting a key, Amanda wandered around for a few minutes. At the west end of the lobby, the large fireplace was blazing, and the winged chairs nearby were so inviting. Amanda had rested here many times before when she had to kill time making connections between home and college. She'd often watched the man in charge of the fireplace on a particular shift keep the fire going, as it blazed around the clock during the winter months.

The elevator soon swallowed her up and whisked her up to her room. The carpeted hallway and dim lights were soothing, and Amanda was soon locked away in the safety of her room, throwing her small black bag on the bed. She traveled lightly with just a few necessities to get her through a couple of nights with clean underwear and a change of clothes for the morning. She took care of things in the bathroom, but she was too tired for that long hot bath. Maybe later. Maybe I'll just take a little nap. She pulled back the bedspread and rearranged the pillows on the bed. Then I'll try to figure things out. I think tomorrow I'll call . . .

A Woman Takes Off Her Claim To
Respect Along With Her Garments
—Herodotus

Chapter VI

The black phone on the kitchen wall rang at precisely 9:00 a.m. at the Wentworth home. Margie, not ready to talk to anyone after a long wakeful and painful night, staggered through the living room and caught it on the fifth ring. Hearing the operator's voice ask if she would accept a collect call after spending the night so totally absorbed in thoughts of Robert made Margie's stomach jump.

"Yes, I'll accept the charges," she blurted out when she heard it was from her sister.

"Are you all right?" she cried.

"Well, of course I am. Why wouldn't I be?" Amanda's defenses hadn't waned with her condition or dilemma. She went on without giving Margie any time for an answer. "Tell Mother I've decided to stay another night in Spokane. I'm having an interesting time, and there's no reason to hurry home with Robert gone. So, I'll be home tomorrow on the train, and then we'll get together and have a chat."

"What have you girls been do . . . ?" But the phone went dead, and Amanda was gone. "Always in a hurry," Margie mumbled to herself, as her mother appeared in the bathroom doorway.

"Was that Amanda? I heard you say 'you girls.'" Mother never missed anything, even though she was getting deaf. Amanda called it "selective hearing"—Mother heard what she wanted to hear.

Margie relayed the message with each nuance and tone and word emphasis, mimicking Amanda's speech delivery in every way, just as she'd been taught in her elocution lessons. Then the two of them examined the message over their cups of morning tea. The questions bounced back and forth over the tea cups like balls on a tennis court.

"What is Amanda doing? Why would she spend another night? What does she mean by an "interesting" time? Get together for a chat?"

Mother Wentworth set her china tea cup down on the saucer and moved her body around on the seat cushion of the kitchen chair like a hen settling into a nesting position, ready to lay an egg. She was ready to present her final thoughts on the matter like a lawyer giving a summation to the jury. "It doesn't appear to me that Amanda is missing Robert too much. There she is, gallivanting all over Spokane with her girl friend, and it's probably that wild one from Hillyard. I wish I'd answered the phone, but now I'm going to have to quiz her when she gets home."

Margie said nothing, but nodded her head in agreement. She was missing Robert even if her sister wasn't.

Mother gave two sniffs of her nose and then another. Usually two were sufficient. The third one was saved for greater effect and for a larger audience, but today's disturbing phone call from Amanda really did deserve three!

Amanda's next phone call was to the front desk in the lobby of the Davenport Hotel, where she made arrangements to spend another night. "I'll be down soon to sign the papers," Amanda told the desk clerk. She could hear the birds chirping and singing in their cages in the lobby.

"Oh, no hurry, Mrs. Shaw. Your reservation is secure. In fact, you don't have to do anything until you check out," the clerk assured her. She'd been on duty for two decades, had known the

Wentworth and Shaw families for years, and had recognized Amanda immediately the day before. Now her voice was familiar on the phone.

That was a relief. Amanda was in no hurry to go anywhere today. She had a due date to figure out and a future to plan. Retrieving her purse from the chair where she'd tossed it late yesterday afternoon, she began searching for a small calendar. Like the rest of her life, her purse was meticulously organized, but now in her nervous state, she couldn't remember in which compartment she'd stored the little engagement calendar. She soon found it just where it belonged along with a notepad and pen. She was equipped to be a secretary, although she'd never stoop to such a menial job.

Seating herself in a leather chair in front of a massive desk, she began thumbing through the pages. It was really quite easy to figure out. She'd known all along that she was pregnant. She had all the symptoms, like it was a disease. Over Christmas she'd tried to hide it from Robert, and she didn't think he'd suspected anything.

The month of the baby's arrival was easy to figure out. In all of her studying of science, she'd learned that forty weeks was the magic number from conception to birth. If I'm two months along now, then it'll be due in July. The exact day was harder to figure out, and Amanda contemplated calling Dr. McKay's office, but then she quickly came to her senses, and remembered that she never wanted anything to do with him again.

Oh well, I'll just pick a date and maybe the next doctor I see will be able to tell me. Babies aren't always on time anyway. Deep down she knew this baby would be punctual like she always was in her daily life. In fact, she usually was early for any appointment or engagement.

The next question in her mind had already been answered too; the baby could not possibly be Robert's. "Oh, help," Amanda cried to no one in particular. "What do I do now?" It was time to face facts head on and weigh her options. Abortion was NOT an option. Amanda was not the most religious person in the world, but she did believe that life began at conception and that the little form developing in her womb was a part of her with her genes. Its little body parts were a real live human being, and it would be murder to deprive this little person of life.

There were two other choices. One was hardly an option at all and not worth wasting the time mulling it over. There was no way she could pretend it was Robert's baby. The other was a possibility, but one that would require dramatic changes, upheaval, and secrecy.

Suddenly Amanda knew what she wanted to do—what she had to do. She thought of her mother, holding up to the light a glass jar of red currant jelly that she made every year. After Margie and Amanda picked the currants, Mother ran the juice through the stained cheesecloth and filled the sterilized jars. It was a common procedure, undoubtedly done in households wherever currants were available, but Mother Wentworth's currant jelly was the most perfect and clear of them all. It was with the distinct clarity rivaling the clear currant jelly that Amanda came to know the answer for the future of her baby.

Yes, of course, it will work. I must get home immediately and put my cards on the table and implement my plan of action. I hope I'm not too late to cancel my reservation here and get on the next train to Wheatland. There's really no need to stay another day. She quickly gathered up her few cosmetic items and articles of clothing, shoved her calendar, pen, and paper in her purse, and grabbed her coat. Suddenly she was ravenously hungry. Glancing at her watch, she figured she'd have time for a quick bite of brunch in the dining room. She patted her tummy as she closed the door of the hotel room and the door on options that just wouldn't work.

"Don't you worry, little baby. You'll be loved and have the best of everything. I'll see to that."

"Oh, what a tangled web we weave,
When first we practice to deceive"
—Scott

Chapter VII

Mother Wentworth was beside herself with worry, and Margie couldn't quite understand that. After all, Amanda was an adult, a college graduate, and even a married woman. She had good common sense, and if she wanted to go away for a couple of days surely she was entitled to that. She must be lonely with Robert gone, so a little shopping and lunch with a couple of girl friends did not seem so bad.

"Lord only knows how I wish I could have gone," Margie sighed, as she washed up the breakfast dishes. Mother fidgeted with the newspaper, and Margie knew she wasn't getting a thing out of the paragraphs she was scanning.

"Why don't we have some girls in for cards?" suggested Margie. This was totally unheard of. Mother looked at Margie over her glasses as if Margie had just lost her mind.

"Today?"

"Yes, this afternoon. It will take your mind off of Amanda, and it would be fun." Mother shook her head in utter disbelief.

"Where do you get such ideas, Margie? We haven't planned it. The house needs a good thorough cleaning, we have no dessert made up, and who would we invite—the bridge club?"

"Oh, no, just a couple of ladies like Hilda or Dottie or even Belle. We could have just one table and play Hearts. I could run downtown to the bakery and get some scones, do a little dusting, and all you'd have to do would be make a pot of tea. Come on, call around and see who's available, say for around 2:00 o'clock."

"Totally unheard of and utterly impossible. This conversation is over." Mother declared sniffing again, and that normally would have been the end of it, but Margie decided it was going to happen. She didn't want to sit around all day and think about Robert and his letter, and she certainly didn't want to watch her mother stew and suffer over Amanda's freedom to do what she wanted.

She went to the phone, made a few calls, and promptly at 2:00 the girls arrived for a game or two of hearts. They, of course, were surprised to get a call out of the blue to go to the Wentworth home for an impromptu game.

Belle was not available, as it was her day to help out as a volunteer at the hospital, but Dottie and Hilda accepted with alacrity. Dottie Nelson lived just across the street, and Hilda Johnson lived right behind the Nelson's, so it was really just a gathering of the neighborhood friends, and there was no need to worry or fuss over frills; but, of course, Zoe Wentworth did. Her best china appeared from behind the glass breakfront and the silverware she'd gotten for a wedding present was resurrected from the purple felt-covered lining of the silver chest. It was kept polished at all times for emergencies like this, even though none had ever happened before.

Dottie was married with two children and belonged to the local bridge group of which Zoe was a member. She was used to sitting around Zoe's card tables whenever it was her turn to entertain. Margie didn't play with the group just yet, but she was learning the game, and as soon as there was an opening, Margie expected to be asked to join the group. That meant that someone had to move away or pass on, so it could be some time before she was a member. Hilda usually didn't have time for cards. With four healthy teenagers still at home, she was busy with their activities, her church work, and her job as "society columnist" for the local weekly newspaper. Today, however, she was free.

"We should get together more often," they all agreed, as the afternoon sun faded to a dull gray and cast shadows on the cream-colored walls of the living room. They had stopped the game for the raspberry scones and tea, and Hilda entertained them with all the gossip that wouldn't be printed in the next paper.

"I do have a nose for news, don't you think?" she bragged, as she wound up her story of Betty Moore's accident out on Highway 2 west of Wheatland. "You know, she was traveling too fast for the road conditions, and, of course, she'd been drinking again. Oh, look at the time. I must get home and write up this party before the noon deadline tomorrow."

Zoe didn't like to have her name in the paper or have the whole town know her business, so she protested futilely, knowing full well that Hilda would go ahead anyway. She liked to see her own name, in addition to her byline, in the society section. Hilda pulled her pen out of her purse in preparation as she went out the door. Dottie, who liked to smooth things over and leave on a congenial note, patted Zoe and then Margie.

"Don't worry; it will just be a little paragraph about the wonderful time we had." She turned and blew a little kiss to them as she descended the wooden steps.

"You know, it was a good afternoon, Margie. I have to thank you." This was undoubtedly the greatest compliment Margie had received from her mother since she won the poetry writing contest in high school. A tea cup slipped out of her hands and fell to the floor, and then the phone rang.

Zoe rushed to grab the phone, just in case it was important. She certainly didn't want to miss out on any more news, especially if it should happen to be Amanda calling, and sure enough, it was.

"Mother, I'm home. I'm coming up to talk to you and Margie right now."

"What in the world is going on? Has something happened to Robert?"

"No, Mother, but sit down. I'll be there in a few minutes."

Margie gasped as she heard her mother's query about Robert. "Who was that?" Margie demanded as her mother hung the phone on the hook angrily.

"That was Amanda. All hell has broken loose. You broke a tea cup, Amanda is home, and she sounds upset. She even told me to sit down. I knew she shouldn't have gone running off to Spokane. I could see the handwriting on the wall."

"Now, Mother, just calm down. The tea cup fell on the carpet and didn't break, and I'm sure there is nothing wrong with Amanda. She's probably just excited about her trip."

Zoe sat down quickly on the hard yellow kitchen chair, not because she was ordered to do it; she just needed to sit. She sat stiffly, rigid, and upright as a figurine on a wooden shelf. Occasionally she smoothed each gray eyebrow with her left hand and rubbed her abdomen with her other hand.

"Get me my peppermints, Margie. My stomach is terribly upset."

Amanda appeared ten minutes later, somewhat flushed and flustered, but she bustled in as usual and tossed her jacket over the hook on the kitchen wall behind the door.

"Why is the card table set up in the living room?" She never missed anything. Mother often said she should have been a detective.

Margie casually said, "Oh, we had Dottie and Hilda over to play cards."

Mother still hadn't moved a muscle.

"My goodness, I go away for a day and a night and you have a party. What brought this on?"

Margie looked to her mother for an answer, but her face was made of stone.

"It wasn't really a party. We just played a few hands of Hearts," Margie said aloud, but thought, Why does everything have to be such a big deal?

Mother finally spoke. "What's that envelope in your hand? Did you hear from Robert?"

"That's what I need to talk to you about."

Margie's hand automatically shot to her forehead, as it often did during times of stress and migraines. She rubbed her temples as she tried to crane her neck to see the return address on the envelope. It was typewritten and looked quite official. She was looking, too, for a postmark, when suddenly Amanda jerked a white sheet of paper from the already-opened envelope and stuffed the envelope into the pocket of her skirt.

"Is it from Robert?" Mother repeated her question with aggravation in her voice. When she wanted an answer, she expected it immediately.

Amanda seated herself on a wooden kitchen chair and, although she drew the chair up to the table, she was careful to place the sheet of paper so neither Mother or Margie could make out its sender or its contents.

"No, it's not from Robert. This letter came today from a college in Iowa actually. I had applied for a teaching position there before Robert and I were married, and I'd almost forgotten about it what with the wedding, the war, and everything else going on. I had never heard a word from them, but now they want me to come immediately and join their faculty on an interim basis for the remainder of the school year. Isn't that great news?"

Mother still had her hand on her upset stomach, and Margie was still rubbing her temples.

"But why now?" Margie asked. "There's a war going on."

"That's the very reason. So many men have been called away that there's a real shortage of profs right now." Whew! Amanda had to muster all her forces to come up with that reasoning so quickly. She knew she would be bombarded with questions from the two of them, so she hastily scribbled her ideas for the letter on her way home on the train and hurriedly banged it out on her typewriter when she'd gotten home just ninety minutes ago. Just in case they'd somehow get close enough to read it, she'd tried to make it look as official as possible. She'd even cut out a seal from an old letter from the college and glued it onto the sheet of paper, so it would appear authentic, at least from a distance.

"I'll have to pack and make arrangements and leave next week. The spring term starts in February."

The color in Mother's cheeks was nearly gone. "You mean you would go away and leave us at a time like this?" Mother glumly said, as she glared at Amanda through squinted eyes.

Amanda had gotten through it, pulled it off, and made it believable with a demure demeanor, too, but with her that could only last so long. The old defiance crept back as she answered. "What do you mean 'at a time like this?' Robert's gone to fight for his country and now I'm going to do what I can to help. Education must go on, my life must go on, and there's nothing I can do by sitting around here moping and waiting. This is a great opportunity."

"But what about us?" Margie wondered aloud. "We'll be so all alone with you and Robert both gone."

Now Amanda was totally disgusted. "Well, then do something, Margie. The country is crying for help, for volunteers. Even in this little town there are things you can do to help others. Look around, ask around, and find out what is needed to be done and do it." All of a sudden, Amanda had donned the role of a warrior, a champion for causes, and was trying to make her teaching sound like a service project.

"Well, I never." Mother spoke at last.

"Never what?" Amanda retorted.

"Never thought I'd see the day when you became so caring for others and so civic-minded. You've always put yourself first."

"Haven't we all done that?" Amanda said under breath. She was still doing it, but apparently she'd pulled that off, too, and even she believed in her own goodwill and care and concern for mankind. "Oh, I have so much to do," Amanda brought the subject back to the reality that she was leaving soon.

"What can we do to help you get ready?" Margie was already taking Amanda's advice to heart and was ready to assist her.

"Gosh, I don't know. I haven't had time to think. It's all happened so suddenly. Let me go home and think and jot down some plans. I'll let you know." Amanda sounded like she would appreciate their help, but she knew in her heart they'd just be a nuisance with all their questions and old-fashioned ways. Margie would be no help in packing; she'd barely been around the block! She wouldn't be taking too many clothes anyway; soon none of them would fit. All she knew was she had to get out of town.

"Stay for dinner, and we'll help you figure things out. Margie, warm up the stew and cut some cornbread." Mother was back to normal now, giving out orders like a commanding officer.

"Stew does sound good." The hungry wolves were pounding on the door of her stomach again. "Let me wash my hands and help you," she said over her shoulder, as she entered the bathroom and closed the door. Amanda sighed heavily as she washed her hands in warm water and then splashed cool water on her face. It was refreshing and cleansing, although it washed away none of her sins. Her reflection in the mirror reminded her that she hadn't put her cards on the table at all. She'd taken the advice she'd heard the ladies say so often around the card tables in the front room. So no one would see their bridge hands or know who held the most hearts or the "old biddy" in the game of Hearts, they'd hastily hide their hands close to their chests, and one of them would say, "Breast your cards, girls!"

I have played the fool.

—I Samuel 26:21

Chapter VIII

Like the calm lapping of the waves on the ocean beach, the hum-drum rhythm of Engine #700 was steady and smooth and relaxing enough to lull the most unruly child to sleep or calm the nerves of a frazzled traveler. It did nothing of the kind for Robert. He was scared, and as the miles from Spokane to Portland put distance between his family and himself, he grew even more tense and apprehensive. This was not an ordinary feeling for a man who had practiced self-control and who maintained a deep and abiding faith in God.

Who wasn't scared of the future in a time of war? That was a natural reaction, and even though Robert felt well-trained as a Marine and battle-ready, all the training in the world couldn't guarantee he'd escape alive or uninjured from WWII.

Now, however, in addition to all that, Robert felt a different kind of fear. Never before had he had to fight the enemies of lust and infidelity that were bombarding him. All the good moral values that he'd been taught at home and at church, and all the biblical knowledge of God's principles, couldn't seem to suppress the emotions and feelings for another woman that he was trying to deny. That woman was Margie.

In some ways, he was greatly relieved to be away from home. The ache in his heart that he felt for Amanda as he kissed her goodbye was compounded by an internal longing for Margie. This was so odd, because he'd never dated her or thought too much about her, but over the holidays somehow she began to capture a portion of his heart. She seemed so lonely and sensitive and vulnerable, and he regretted that he hadn't been able to tell her goodbye. That regret resulted in the letter.

Robert had many long, quiet hours to think on the steam locomotive to Portland, and by the time they reached the depot there, he could only hope that he'd written a discreet, friendly note. He dropped it in the mailbox and transferred to a Greyhound bus for the final leg of the journey to Camp Pendleton. He tried to sleep, and dozed off and on, but he kept awakening to the fact that he'd made a grave mistake.

"The letter—of all the stupid things to do," he chided himself. As he thought of Margie, the sensitive, lonely spinster with the furtive glances and her heart worn on her sleeve, he knew that Margie would embellish it and romanticize his words and make even more out of what he was trying NOT to say. I'm a hypocrite, and I've always despised hypocrites. He beat himself up inside.

In the past, Robert had felt secure within himself, knowing that when he was troubled or had questions or problems, he had family and friends to pray with him and help him sort out the albatross around his neck. He knew also that the ultimate answers were from God Himself.

Now he felt so unsure of himself. Maybe he shouldn't have married Amanda, or at least maybe they should have waited until the war was over. Who wants to wait when they're in love? Most of all, why did he have these feelings for Margie? Was it pity, because she was the weaker of the sisters and was stuck at home with her over-bearing elderly mother? He could pretend it was pity, because he was a sensitive man, but in reality he knew it was more than that and a much different and intense feeling—a feeling of love. This can't be happening! I can't be in love with two women at the same time, and if that's not bad enough, they're sisters!

He was dreaming of both women as the bus finally pulled into Oceanside, California. He'd written letters in the dream to both

Amanda and Margie, but as dreams go, they'd gotten mixed up somehow, and Amanda knew all about his feelings for her sister. He awoke with a start. It all seemed so real. He *had* written to Margie, but as yet not one word to his bride. What must she be thinking? Oh, what a fool I've been. I tried to be vague about my feelings, but Margie, being the romantic that she is, could probably read between the lines. I hope she can hide her emotions and not create a big chasm between the two of them.

He was almost getting irrational in his thinking, but seeing the main gate at Camp Pendleton brought him back to reality. He knew he had a bigger worry looming over him in the days ahead. The war-front battle was more awesome than anything at home, and he would just have to trust God to keep peace within the family, to keep secrets hidden, and to protect all those he loved, as well as himself.

"God, you've got an awful lot to do," he muttered prayerfully, as he staggered off the bus.

"Hey, buddy, you O.K.?" Another Marine named Rick, whom they'd picked up in Eugene, slapped him on the back

"Oh, yeah, I'm fine," Robert lied. "Just had a weird dream, though."

The two men had talked some shortly after Rick had boarded the bus. He, too, had left a recent bride waiting by the train tracks and wondering about the future.

"Man, that was a long trip," Robert groaned, as he stretched his long legs and muscular arms. "Too much time to think."

Rick agreed, but added, "It may be the last time that we have much time to do anything for ourselves. I'm not looking forward to receiving our orders."

"Yeah, I did appreciate the freedom, but that's over now. We'll soon know where we're headed."

Robert and Rick both reported to the Fifth Marine Division Headquarters and were ordered to ship out in four days. Robert would be leaving on a Navy PBY with "special priority status" to report ASAP to his unit in the South Pacific, carrying with him special revised landing information for the battle of Iwo Jima. He swallowed hard when he heard the news.

It really came as no surprise, and yet his responsibilities were awesome. It certainly snapped him back to the real world and the life and death situations that he would soon face. The cockiness that was uncharacteristic of Robert, but which had been instilled in him as a Marine, came back to him. I am a Marine; I can do it. God will spare me.

The days passed quickly, and there was very little free time except in the evenings. All the final preparations were jammed into those four days, and Robert had absolutely no time during the day to think of Amanda or Margie.

Day one was consumed with a final physical exam, shots, and paperwork. It went smoothly but took all day. Robert passed the physical with flying colors, endured the battery of shots and then, under the commander's watchful eye, reviewed his paperwork and records. He studied all the details of his will, making sure that Amanda was his beneficiary. This was the only time that the slightest thought of Margie entered his head, but, no, he couldn't leave her anything! Amanda also would be given "power of attorney" in the event that he didn't return. The pay records were reviewed, and everything seemed to be in order, much to Robert's relief. He wasn't in the mood to deal with changes or problems, and he was relieved when the day was over. Tomorrow would be a grueling day with training in the field.

After dinner he was free to relax in the officers' quarters. He'd been looking forward to that all day. Maybe he could get his thoughts together and write that long overdue letter to his wife.

"Oh, no you don't, Shaw. Don't just mope around. Come on. Go to Oceanside and have some beers with us," cajoled Rick.

"Maybe tomorrow night. I've got some stuff to do." Robert sounded so busy, and he hoped they'd leave him alone.

"Come on. Live it up a little. What's so important? Oh, I know. I suppose you have to write a mushy letter to your wife. Come on. You can give her a quick call from Oceanside."

Robert tried to get rid of them. "Actually I do need to write her a long letter. She hasn't heard from me since I left home."

"O.K., Shaw. Have fun. *We* will. That's for sure!" Rick laughed and joined the others for a night out in Oceanside.

"Yeah, I bet you will," Robert muttered, as he started to write.

> "Dear Amanda,
>
>   I haven't had much time to write."

No, that was a lie. He'd had plenty of time to write to Margie on the trip down.

> "Dear Amanda,
>
>   Is it cold up there in Washington?"

No, that sounded stupid. Of course, it was cold. It was winter, and it was always cold there in the winter! Maybe I should just try to call her. No, if I can't write my thoughts, how could I say them?

After several more tries, and several sheets of paper wadded up and thrown across the room in disgust, he headed out the door and found a row of phones. He'd have to call collect, but she expected that. The operator tried more than once, but there was no one at the other end to accept the call. Maybe she was up at her mother's. Where else would she be on a January night? Knowing that he couldn't call there, he turned down the operator's request to call someone else, and as he loped back to his quarters, he convinced himself that he could write from the heart and get a letter ready to go out in the morning. He was worried about where she could be and if she was all right, and he tried once again to put his thoughts down on paper. It came easier this time.

> "Dear Amanda,
>
>   It's seven p.m. here at Camp Pendleton, and I just tried
> to call you, but no answer. Hope all is well. You're probably
> up visiting with your mother and Margie. We got in here

yesterday. The train and bus rides were long and boring, and it was actually a relief to finally get here. I got my orders and ship out in three days. Sounds like it's going to be a rough tour of duty. I can't tell you much else about it now, but will write whenever I can. What are you doing to fill in your time while I'm away? I'm sure you'll find some things to do—maybe substituting up at good old Wheatland High or taking another night class. I'm sure my mother would love to have you go with her to volunteer at the hospital. Whatever you do, try to keep busy and don't worry too much. O.K.?

The holidays sure went fast. It seems like a dream that I was there with you, and we had our first Christmas together, and now it's over.

Are you feeling all right, dear? You didn't seem to be yourself over the holidays. The guys wanted me to go out for some beers tonight, but that's not my thing, and I wanted to write to you. Will try to call you again before we leave, but wanted you to get some mail too.

Mandy, you are in my heart and on my mind all the time. I love you so much.

Always, Robert"

There, now, that wasn't so hard after all, Robert consoled himself. He did miss Amanda, and he did love her. He felt lonely tonight. He'd accomplished what he needed to do, but now he also wished he was out with the men. After all, he was used to their ribbing about his abstinence, and he could always have a soda. Oh, well, maybe tomorrow night.

It wasn't long before Robert was sound asleep, and then suddenly it was morning. Day two had dawned, and he had to hurry out to chow and then to the field for a grueling day of training.

Captain J.D. Carlson was in charge, and he was a demanding buzzard. Well, they all were; that was their job. Weapons Training took most of the day, and by the end of the afternoon, the sounds of the Thompson Sub-machine gun and the M1 Carbine were ringing in their ears.

By nightfall they were all exhausted, but after chow and showers, they convinced Robert to join them for a good time.

He tried to call Amanda again—this time from a noisy bar in Oceanside, but all he got was a busy signal. They were on a party line back home, so it didn't necessarily mean that Amanda was talking to someone. The phone could be tied up for hours, and with Hilda Johnson on the same line, it often was. As a reporter she had requested her own line, and her name was first on the waiting list for that to happen. Robert had only one more evening to catch Amanda from stateside.

Day three brought with it a cool drizzle that lasted most of the morning.

"Great weather," barked Gunnery Sgt. S. Butterfield. He believed that a little mud in the morning and a muggy, humid afternoon made the jungle survival training just that much more authentic. Gunny Butterfield was just as sweaty and smelly as his troops at day's end.

"What are you doing tonight?" Robert asked the guys, as they walked back to their quarters after chow.

"Packing my gear, calling home, writing a letter, sleeping . . ." They all had different answers, and none of them sounded like fun.

"Thank goodness," Robert was relieved. He hated to be a party-pooper, but he had no desire to party on his last night.

He wondered if the others were experiencing the gnawing pain that stabbed him deep in the pit of his stomach every time he thought of the future. "Fear" was not in the Marine Corps vocabulary or mind set, but how could one deny it?

One more time he tried to call his wife, finally reaching her. She sounded so far away and a little strange.

"Hi, honey, it's me, Robert."

"Well, it's about time," she retorted. "I've looked for letters and waited for the phone to ring every day."

"There's a letter on the way, and I have tried to call, but the line was always busy. You know how that goes, Mandy."

They continued to visit, both of them quite formally at first about what each other had been doing. Little did they know that they each had secrets that were not for sharing. Robert actually found it easier to converse than Amanda did. Maybe he didn't have quite so much to hide.

It was soon time to say good bye.

"I'll send you my APO address as soon as I can, Mandy. I think it will be San Francisco."

Little did he know that she wouldn't be in Wheatland and would be working out her own postal arrangements in a matter of days.

"Good bye. I love you so much, Margie."

"Margie?" Amanda questioned, but he was gone.

"Margie?"

There is no animal more invincible
Than a woman, no fire either, nor any
Wildcat so ruthless.
　　　　　　　—Aristophanes

Chapter IX

"Margie?" Amanda still continued to question the final word Robert had spoken over the phone the night before.

She finally had to shove it to the back of her mind; she had too much to do and too many plans to work out before she left for Iowa to worry about his obvious slip of the tongue.

"Iowa, Why didn't I choose a destination closer to home? It is so far away. Oh well, we'll be O.K., little baby. We can take care of ourselves." Amanda patted her abdomen, trying to reassure herself.

The phone rang before she was out of bed, and, as usual, it was her well-meaning but annoying mother wanting to help her get ready for her travels. Mother Wentworth had reconciled herself to the fact that Amanda was leaving and was even beginning to feel a sense of great pride for her determined and intellectual daughter.

"Is this the professor?" Mother's attempts at humor were few and far between and because of her lack of practice, one rarely knew if she was being facetious or truthful.

"Yes, this is Dr. Shaw, and how may I help you?" Amanda loved to pick up the ball and run with it, especially if she could upset her mother. Today, however, Mother Wentworth was in rare and unusual form.

"What is our assignment for today? How can we help you get ready for your trip?"

"Oh, just stay there and do your homework. I have lots to do—go to the bank, make travel arrangements and plans, and squeeze in a trip out to see Belle and Ed. Oh, and one thing, Mother, don't tell Hilda about this, or she'll want to do a human interest story, and I don't want to be splashed all over the front page of the *Wheatland Times* right now."

"Well, we'll try to keep it quiet, but you know how it is, Amanda. We all know when each other flushes the toilet in a small town."

"Wow, Mother! What did you put in your tea? Two jokes in one morning."

"It's true, and you know it. Well, you run on and tend to business. Let me know when you are going out to Belle's. Maybe I'll ride along. I need to return her casserole dish."

CLICK and she was gone. Amanda shook her head in amazement. She never wanted to go out to the Shaws. Amanda had invited her many times. Margie had bounced along in the truck several times, but not Mother.

"She must have something up her sleeve," Amanda mused as she pulled on some baggy black slacks and an over-sized red sweater. She ran her fingers through her hair several times, brushed her teeth, and added a hint of red lipstick for color.

"Oh, yes, the pill." Amanda could do most things well. She could do difficult things, like understand and teach chemistry to college students, drive a wheat truck (although she hated it) and do most things on her own, but she could not swallow pills. If an aspirin would stick in her throat, how could Dr. McKay possibly expect her to swallow a vitamin that was almost as big as a Vienna sausage? She had to put as much water in her mouth as it would hold and then throw her head back and swallow. More often than not, it wouldn't go down, and she'd choke and sputter. Her determination to have a healthy baby was the only thing that made her not give up.

"What in the world am I doing?" Amanda said out loud to the whole world. "Sooner or later, I'm going to have to tell Mother, or as Margie would dramatically say, 'I'll have to bare my soul,' or otherwise my plan won't work . . . but not today."

She fixed a bowl of oatmeal and flipped on the radio, thinking of Robert and wondering where he was. At that very moment he was riding in a staff car to San Diego driven by the base commander's driver to board a DC3 with "special priority status orders" to report ASAP to his unit in the South Pacific. Amanda just thought of him as a Marine—her husband who was going far away, and, just as she knew nothing of his future location or orders, he knew nothing of her troubles or plans either. Mesmerized by her thoughts, she dropped a spoonful of cereal on her red sweater when the doorbell rang.

Who in the world? She dabbed at her soiled sweater. "Well, for heaven's sake, it's you, Belle." Amanda beamed at the plump little lady standing in the hallway of the apartment complex. "Come on in."

"I just thought I'd pop around with some cinnamon rolls I made early this morning." Belle marched into the kitchen and set the still-warm pan on top of the stove.

"What a nice surprise!" Amanda said with genuine warmth. "Can I get you some coffee or a glass of juice?"

"No, I can't stay but just a minute. I'm on my way up to the hospital to visit Eva Barth. She fell and broke her hip and has been at the Deaconess Hospital in Spokane, but was finally able to come here. Her daughter called from Iowa to see if I could go up and see how she is really doing. The nurses don't give her much information, you know."

But all Amanda heard was *Iowa*. She suddenly remembered her planned trip to the Shaw farm later that day and the news she had to share. She didn't have her speech ready yet, and so she sat in a stupor.

"Are you all right, dear?" Belle noticed her sudden change of demeanor and her tomato-red face. Amanda fanned herself and tried to regain her composure.

"I was going to call and come out to see you today. I have
so much to tell you, but I'll make it quick, since you're in a
hurry."

"Oh, no, take your time. I always have time for you, dear."
That was just like Belle. She had such a calming spirit.

Amanda was sitting close to Belle at the dining table, and she
grabbed Belle's hands and clasped them hard as she began her
story. Belle beamed and settled into her chair like a plump setting
hen, feeling the urge to lay an egg.

"You will probably be surprised to hear this, but since Robert
is gone, I've decided to pursue my teaching career."

Belle was not surprised. "That's wonderful, dear! Are you
substituting? Oh, I bet you'll be filling in for Susan Anderson; I
hear she's taking maternity leave."

Amanda gulped at the word *maternity* and went on to explain
that it would not be a job at good old Wheatland High, but rather
at a long-distance location.

"No, Belle, I'm going to Iowa, to the University of Iowa,
actually. I've been accepted to fill out the spring term there in the
Chemistry Department." She hated lying to Belle, who was so
good and pure and had probably never shaded the truth in her
whole life.

Belle let go of Amanda's handclasp and her right hand flew to
her chest, as if her heart was acting up—one of Mother Wentworth's
tricks.

"Oh, my goodness, you'll be so far away. What about your
mother and Margie? And Robert, does he know?" She was visibly
upset.

This was not the reaction Amanda had expected from Belle,
who usually thought everything Amanda did was wonderful. Now
it was Amanda's turn to try to smooth things over and calm Belle
down.

"It's all happened rather suddenly, and I'm surprised myself,
but it's a wonderful opportunity, and with Robert away, I jumped
at the chance."

She hadn't answered any of Belle's questions, and while she

hadn't really meant to be evasive, she said what had come to be her pat little speech on the subject.

"Have you told Robert?" Belle persisted.

"Yes, I've written about it." Well, she *had* planned to and still would, so it was just a little white lie.

"Mother is quite proud of me, of course. She's happy I'm using my education."

Belle managed a wan little smile. "Well, if you're happy with the idea, Amanda, then I guess we should all support you. I know you love your profession, and you might as well pursue your dreams. Everything will change when Robert gets home and you start your little family." The always hopeful Belle was getting back to normal now, and she patted Amanda on the arm.

That last remark upset Amanda, and she fluffed up her sweater over her abdomen. She gave a nervous little laugh and felt very warm again. "It's a little soon to think about that."

"Yes, for now, but time goes fast." Belle glanced at her watch. "And it's going fast now," she added. "I must be going. When are you leaving, dear?"

"Classes start in two weeks, so I'll need to go early next week to get settled in." With that, she kissed Belle on the cheek. "Don't worry; I'll see you again before I go."

Belle squeezed her tightly. Such affection was uncommon for Amanda, but she welcomed it from Belle.

"Oh, I hope so. I know you have a lot to do, and if there's anything I can do to help, please call me."

"I will," Amanda lied again.

Sixty minutes later, while Amanda was calling her best friend, Jenny, in Iowa, Belle was tapping on Zoe Wentworth's back door. Margie peeked out between the kitchen curtains. She, too, liked Belle, so she dashed to the door to let her in even before forewarning her mother of impending company.

Belle took them by surprise. Zoe wasn't used to having people just drop in, but she looked presentable. Margie was up and dressed, too, after a long night thinking about Robert. It was nearly time for her daily trip downtown, but with Belle here to visit, that could wait.

"Let me take your coat," Margie offered. "What are you doing out on this cold day, Belle?" The temperature on the north side of the house had registered just twenty six degrees just moments ago when Margie had checked it and written it in her journal.

"Oh, I'm just running a few errands. I went up to see Eva at the hospital. Rachel called me last night from Iowa and was so concerned about her mother."

"Sit here by me," Margie begged, as she and Belle settled into the deep cushions of the couch. Zoe liked the rocking chair, so she could sit up straighter and face her guests.

"How is she doing?" Zoe tried to show some interest, although Eva was not one of her bosom buddies. She thought Eva was a whiney old lady, who believed the world should revolve around her.

"Coming along, coming along. At her age, it takes a long time to heal, you know."

"Why doesn't she go and live with Rachel? She could take care of her," Zoe said coldly.

"I'm sure they'd both like that, but Eva couldn't travel now." Belle tried to like everybody and find good qualities in each person. She could never understand why Zoe would get so down on people.

Zoe was tired of hearing about Eva, so she changed the subject.

"Amanda and I were talking about coming out to see you today. I wanted to return your casserole, so she said she'd drive me out." Zoe made it sound as if it was all her idea and her mission.

"Yes, I stopped and saw Amanda a little bit ago. She told me of her teaching plans in Iowa. I was so surprised!"

"Weren't we all?" Zoe put her hand on her chest, and Margie massaged her forehead. "We knew she had applied, but had no idea the job would really materialize," Zoe continued.

"We're all so proud of her, aren't we?" Belle hoped for agreement, and Zoe and Margie both nodded, although Margie looked like she might be ill. She felt like it too.

"I told her she might as well do it before Robert gets home and they want to start a family."

Margie excused herself on that statement and headed for the bathroom.

"We'll all miss her," Zoe finalized the conversation.

"Well, I have one more stop to make, and then I must get on home." Belle struggled to extricate herself from the soft enveloping cushion of the couch. It seemed to swallow up her short plump body, but she was finally able to twist and turn and push herself up. Zoe had almost as much trouble getting up from the rocking chair, but at least she had sturdy chair arms to help thrust her arthritic body up and out.

Margie came out of the bathroom just in time to shove the empty casserole dish in Belle's hands before she headed for the door. "Have you heard from Robert?" She blurted out.

"Yes, dear, he called last night, and he's shipping out today. We don't know his destination, of course. Be sure to pray for him." Belle didn't know if Zoe and Margie ever lifted their hearts in supplication to the Lord, but she believed it never hurt to nudge people in that direction.

"Oh, yes, we will," Margie promised in all sincerity, "and if you hear any more, let us know."

"I will, dear, and now I really must run." Belle waddled across the porch, down the wooden steps, and around the corner to her car. Just as she opened the back door of the Plymouth, so as to set the casserole dish on the back seat, her left foot hit an icy patch, and she fell, hitting the back of her head on the car door. Right before she passed out, the sad face of Eva Barth, lying in the hospital bed with her broken hip, flashed before her eyes.

Scurrying through the dining room and hallway like a little mouse, Margie stationed herself to watch Belle through one of the narrow rectangular windows on the front door. She saw her fall and watched for just a moment or two. Belle lay perfectly still. "Mother!" Margie screamed, "Belle's fallen, and I think she hurt herself. She's not moving!"

"Get your coat on and go out and see to her. I'll call someone," Mother ordered from her command post near the kitchen phone.

"Oh, dear, what will I do?" Margie mumbled to herself, as she wrung her hands and then slipped her thin arms into her heavy winter coat. She grabbed a kitchen towel in desperation and ran through the house to the front door. It took her a few moments to unlock the three locks and to remove the heavy toweling that had been shoved up against the bottom of the door to keep out the cold.

Belle was coming to just as Margie reached her.

"Oh, Belle, are you all right?" Margie asked, as she bent over the crumpled lady in the snow.

"I don't know; wh . . . wh . . . What happened?" Belle stammered and looked around with glazed eyes.

"You fell. It's very icy right here."

"Oh, my head." Belle gingerly put her hand on the back of her head. Her short gray hair was becoming matted with blood.

Margie was glad she'd grabbed the dish towel as she wiped Belle's fingers, and then tried to dab at the blood in her hair.

"Do you hurt anywhere else?"

"I don't know. I'm so dizzy and so cold!"

Meanwhile, Zoe was frantically dialing phone numbers. Amanda's line was busy, and no one answered at Dr. Peterson's office or at Dr. Baker's. It was the noon hour, and everyone was out to lunch. She was so frustrated and at her wit's end. She finally called Dottie across the street, and she agreed to run over and help Margie.

Margie was so surprised and relieved to see Dottie when she suddenly appeared. Between the two of them, they got Belle to her feet and eased her into the back seat of Belle's Plymouth. She didn't seem to be in pain anywhere else. Margie ran back to the front door, got a blanket from her mother, and tucked it around Belle's shaking body.

"I'll drive her up to the hospital," Margie informed Dottie.

"Do you want me to go along with you?" Dottie questioned her.

"No, we'll be all right, but thank you so much for helping us." Belle nodded in agreement with Margie's thanks, but the throbbing pain made her wince once again.

Margie found the car keys in Belle's coat pocket, and drove her across town and up the hill to the hospital. It was only a mile, but it seemed like an eternity for both of them. Margie wasn't used to driving in the winter, but thankfully the main roads were clear of snow. Belle held the towel to her head and shivered and shook and moaned a few times.

Zoe had called and reached a nurse's station at the hospital, and although there was no specific emergency room, a nurse was alerted and came out a side door with a wheelchair just as Margie pulled up. The nurse was surprised to see that the patient was Belle, who just a couple of hours ago had been a visitor.

"Dr. Baker will be on his way up to check on you in just a few minutes, Belle." The nurse consoled her, as she wheeled her behind a curtained partition. Belle had little to say and continued to shake, as the nurse helped her out of her wet clothes and into a clean gown. She found a soft warm blanket and wrapped Belle in it.

Margie was pacing the floor and wringing her hands. She wondered what else she should be doing. She felt so helpless.

Soon the nurse popped her head out from behind the curtain. "Margie, could you come here for a minute? Belle needs to ask you something."

In a shaking voice, Belle said, "Margie, could you . . . um . . . could you please call . . ." But she couldn't think of the name. Finally she came up with it. "Ed, and tell him what happened."

"Of course, why didn't I think of that?" Margie said and nodded her head.

"What *did* happen?" the nurse queried Belle, but Belle couldn't get the words out. She shrugged her shoulders and looked pleadingly at Margie for answers. Margie explained what she had observed and what she'd done, and the nurse jotted down a few notes on a clip board.

There was a phone on the wall in a small waiting room, so Margie tiptoed out and called Ed and then her mother. Zoe still hadn't reached Amanda, and, of course, there was no way to reach Robert.

About the time Dr. Baker entered the back door of the hospital, Belle grabbed the edge of the bed, as the room went spinning out of control and her world went black again.

The Face is the mirror of the mind,
And eyes, without speaking,
confess the secrets of the heart.
—St. Jerome

Chapter X

Amanda spent the rest of the morning trying to reach Jennifer Hollis in Iowa. Jenny had been Amanda's roommate and best friend in college, and, in spite of the distance in miles between them, they were still close friends.

Sophomore year they had been placed together in Stevens Hall, and it was an almost instant friendship. They had so much in common and got along so well. They were both from small farming communities, and they were both science majors. They were serious students, who never caused the house mother any trouble—well, almost never.

Jenny was the only person that Amanda knew who she felt would really listen to her and advise her without lecturing. Amanda could be herself. She could be who she wanted to be and not who her mother wanted her to be.

"Don't be afraid to be your own person." That was Jenny's motto, and Amanda believed that, too. It was easier now to practice it, and she adopted that as her lifeline.

Amanda had a few friends growing up, but she didn't really feel close to any of them. She usually felt she was better and smarter than they. She tried not to show it too much, but she couldn't be phony. The silly little cheerleader types annoyed her to no end, and they thought she was an intellectual snob. Jenny was her first true friend, and they were still more like sisters than she and Margie were.

When Amanda had called Jenny when she first suspected she was pregnant, Jenny assured her that if she could do anything to help, just to call her.

Jenny was a science teacher, too, and just happened to be home recovering from bronchitis when Amanda called.

"Where have you been?" Amanda asked in desperation when she finally reached her.

Jenny's voice cracked with hoarseness. "I've been to the doctor, Mandy." She coughed and sputtered. "I"m trying to get over this bug."

"You sound terrible!" Amanda admonished.

"Actually, I'm a lot better, but how are *you* doing?"

"Physically, I'm feeling better, as far as the morning sickness, but I've got to get out of here soon. Do you still have that spare bedroom you offered me earlier?"

"Of course, I do. You come any time. I've been hoping you'd call. I've been so worried about you. Is Robert gone?"

"Oh, yeah, he left right after New Year's Day, and now he's on his way from Camp Pendleton to who knows where. Well, actually some place in the South Pacific, I guess. You know, Jen, in a way it was a relief when he left; I was so afraid he'd suspect something was wrong."

"You've always been good at keeping secrets, Mandy. Remember that one and only time we tried to pull the wool over Mrs. Merrill's face and almost got caught? We could have gotten kicked out of the dorm." Jen laughed, then started coughing again.

"That was nothing compared to this. I've got a big secret now," Amanda inserted in-between Jenny's coughs. She added, "Get over that bug so I don't catch it!"

"When are you coming?" Jenny questioned.

"Next week, if it's O.K. I'm telling the family that my teaching position starts in two weeks, so I need to get there and get settled in."

"You're sure this is what you want to do?"

"It's what I *have* to do."

"I suppose so. Just let me know when you're arriving, so I can pick you up. You'll be all right here, and Amanda, I can't wait to see you. It will be like old times."

"I'll let you know, and thanks."

"Don't mention it, kiddo. See ya."

"Bye, I'll call you," and Amanda hung up the phone. She didn't hear the click that followed when some busybody on the party line hung up the phone a second later.

The clock had ticked off the minutes of the morning and was inching its way toward 1:30. Amanda had several errands to run before the afternoon slipped into the shadows. She was just putting her coat on to go out when the phone rang. Her mother's voice was sharp and businesslike.

"Who in the world have you been talking to? Well, never mind." She didn't wait for an answer, but cut right to the chase. "Belle is in the hospital."

"No, she was just here," Amanda said in disbelief.

"I know. She was here, too, and she fell out in front on the ice. She hit her head on the car door, and then passed out. I hope she doesn't sue us!"

Amanda was shocked. "Did you call someone?"

"Of course, but it was lunch time, so Margie took care of her and got her to the hospital."

"Margie?"

"Yes, you know—your sister! You should really give her more credit, Amanda. She did a marvelous job and was very efficient. She drove Belle to the hospital, and she's still there with her."

Amanda couldn't quite believe it all. "Is Belle going to be all right? Did someone call Ed?"

"The doctor was just going in to see Belle when Margie called from the hospital, and, yes, Amanda, Margie called Ed."

"For heaven's sake. Margie did all that?" Amanda seemed more shocked at Margie's efficiency than at the accident that had happened to Belle. It surprised and pleased her to know that Margie was able to handle a crisis. It was good practice for the future.

"Here comes Margie now. I'll call you back when I know more."

Her mother's abruptness disturbed Amanda. It seemed she never got all her questions answered or got enough information. But she had things to do, too, and a couple of lives to get in order, so she bustled out the door and briskly walked the three blocks down the street to the bank.

The sidewalks were as dry as her mother's meatloaf, but the huge white banks of cottony snow on the side of the road were frozen monuments that testified that this was indeed January in the Pacific Northwest. It would be no different in Iowa, and Jen's stories of long, cold winters came to Amanda's mind as the wind pushed her toward the business center of Wheatland.

The bank was busy, so she had to stand in line and wait. Patience was not one of Amanda's shining attributes, but luckily today the lines moved quickly. She cordially greeted everyone as they finished their business and walked past her and out the door. If the people were friendly, she could cope with it, and she did enjoy watching people, even those she'd known all her life. She cashed a sizeable check of five hundred dollars. Money was one thing that wasn't a worry. She needed to make sure there was enough for several weeks in advance.

Because Robert farmed with his dad and earned a goodly amount from the sale of the crop each fall, their joint checking account was adequate enough to pay the few bills they had each month, and some was stored away in a savings account.

Today, however, Amanda was withdrawing the money from another account in which she had secretly squirreled away a little bit each month. It never hurt to have your own resources, she believed, in case of emergency, and this would certainly classify as an emergency. This wouldn't be enough to last her through the doctor bills, the expenses she would have at Jen's place, and the hospital bill, but she could always cash another check. So much to think about! As Mildred, the teller, was getting her money, she decided she'd be paying her local Wheatland bills through their joint account as usual. They'd have to be sent to her at Jen's post office box. So many details to work out, and as Mildred was counting out the bills in front of her, Amanda felt an odd sensation in her abdomen—just a little reminder that someone had taken up residence there, and this was what the trip to the bank was really all about. There it was again, like someone had the hiccups.

She said, "Excuse me," to the teller, and put her hand over her mouth. When Mildred looked at her quizzically, Amanda remembered that no one knew what was going on.

I have a lot to learn about this motherhood business. Smiling at everyone and no one in particular, she walked out the door into the dismal day.

As she hurried along to do her business at the post office, the clouds looked down upon her as if to say, "We're trying not to dump another load on you just yet. Hurry up and get home," but a few snowflakes eked out and spun around in the wind as she entered the post office, and in the few short minutes it took to tend to business there, the clouds could no longer hold back, and the white stuff was descending like big white feathers from a tear in Mother's pillows.

Amanda shivered as she hurried back to the apartment. Luckily, she hadn't run into Margie at the post office. Her schedule had probably gotten all fouled up because of Belle.

"Oh, dear, what should I do about Belle? Should I go see her? No, I'll call Mother first, but . . . not right this minute," Amanda thought.

She was so exhausted from her trip downtown, battling the elements, and all of her monumental decisions, that five minutes after she sat down to read her mail, she was sound asleep. The mail slid off her lap and onto the floor, and her head bobbed up and down until her chin finally rested on her chest. She didn't hear the gentle tapping on the door, but suddenly she awoke with a start, and there was Margie standing in front of her, staring at her.

"What's the matter? Haven't you ever seen anyone sleeping before?" Amanda snarled at her, as she blinked her eyes and then rubbed the sleep away. "How long have you been gawking at me?"

"Just for a minute or two. I love to watch people sleeping. They look so peaceful and vulnerable. They're like different people when they're sleeping, like they could never be mad at anyone and . . ."

"O.K. O.K. You don't have to present a whole monologue on the subject. What do you want anyway?" she snapped at Margie.

"See, that's what I mean. You were so quiet and calm when you were asleep, and now listen to you. You should just listen to how you sound and look in the mirror at yourself and see the mean expressions you get on your face. Are you mad at me?"

"No, I'm not mad; I'm just tired and have a lot on my mind."

"I just wanted to tell you about Belle. I have her car parked out in front if you want to go up and see her."

"I thought about going, but how is she doing?"

"Well, she does have a concussion and a deep cut on the back of the head and a few bruises, but she will be all right. She has to stay in the hospital overnight. I guess I'll be taking her home, because Ed came in from the farm in the pickup. He's staying just a little longer and then will try to get home before dark."

"Is it still snowing?" Amanda hoped Ed didn't have to drive in a blizzard, but Margie assured her that it was tapering off. Amanda rubbed her eyes again and realized she was still feeling exhausted.

"How about if I go with you tomorrow when you take Belle home? That way I can see her and be with you in case you have any trouble."

Margie clapped her hands in childlike delight. She thought that was a great idea.

"The nurse told me to call around nine in the morning just to be sure she can be released, and then she'll tell me when to come and get her."

"Gosh, you'll have to get up before breakfast tomorrow, Margie," Amanda teased.

"Yeah, that will be early for me," Margie admitted, "but I can do it for Belle."

"Of course you can; you can do anything you set your mind to, and Mother said you did a terrific job taking care of Belle today. It's not often that Mother praises us, you know, Margie, so you must have been very efficient."

For once, the sisters were aligned, and Margie even blushed with the unheard of attention such as this from her sister.

"I felt so sorry for Belle and just did what had to be done," Margie said matter-of-factly, and got up to go.

"Call me in the morning then, Florence Nightingale."

"Oh, by the way, I found this envelope addressed to you out in the hallway. You must have dropped it."

Amanda took the envelope and glanced quickly at the return. Doctor Roderick McKay. What does he want?

Thank goodness Margie didn't question the letter. Blowing her sister a kiss, she went out the door. Amanda just waved her away. That was going too far!

"What a day!" Amanda said out loud, as if she'd been the one who'd fallen and been hospitalized. It *had* been busy, and she had gotten some important things accomplished, but still needed to make travel arrangements and pack for her "teaching career." Picking up the mail from the floor, and walking into the bedroom, she tossed it on the bedspread, including the one from Doctor McKay. The blanket of darkness was beginning to descend and smother the light of day. Amanda flipped on the bedside light and then looked in the mirror. Belle had picked up the cheap mirror for them at the church bazaar, and Amanda had always felt it didn't give a true image. Today the reflections were distorted for sure.

The greatest conflicts are not
between two people, but between
one person and himself.
—Garth Brooks
In *Country Magazine*

Chapter XI

Amanda fell asleep again before reading her mail or thinking
about dinner. The bed was warm and cozy, and when she awakened
around 6:30 p.m., the shades of night had been drawn all around
the town. The table lamp with the pink shade cast a warm and
comforting glow over the bedroom. The cavernous emptiness in
her stomach reminded her that she hadn't eaten for hours. "I bet
you're hungry, too." She rubbed her tummy. "Let's go and see
what we can find to eat." Belle's cinnamon rolls were still sitting
on the stove. Amanda pulled two apart and put them on a plate.
After devouring them and drinking half a glass of cold milk, some
warm food sounded soothing, and as she waited for a can of chicken
soup to heat on the stove, she went back into the bedroom to
retrieve and finally read the mail. The first envelope grabbing her
attention was from Dr. Roderick McKay. What does *he* want? I
paid the bill. It was merely a reminder for her next appointment.

Gosh, they send these out early. I was just there. Oh well, you
won't see me ever again. She tore the note into shreds and buried it
in the kitchen waste container under the soup can, wondering if
Margie had read the return on the envelope. I've tried to be so
careful, but I can't worry about it; she'll find out in due time
anyway.

The rest of the mail was of little importance. There were no personal letters and not even any bills, so all the rest of the mail went in the garbage as well, but on top of the soup can.

Her dinner was boiling, and she spooned it into a bowl, wondering what to do for the rest of the evening. Her nap had refreshed her, and she felt ambitious. Sorting and packing had to be done, but there were still a few more days for that. What she wanted was to do something fun, but what can a pregnant woman with a husband gone to war do in Wheatland on a cold January night? Not much. The theater didn't show movies during the middle of the week, her art class had ended before Christmas, and she didn't feel like running up to Mother's and Margie's. They weren't much fun to be around. *Poor Belle is in the hospital, and here I am wanting to have fun. Maybe I should call and check on her.*

Her hand was on the phone when it rang.

"Hello, Amanda." It was Margie. "You know, I've been thinking," she went on. "Our plan to take Belle home isn't going to work."

"Oh, why not?" Amanda was puzzled.

"Well, if we both take her home in her car, how are we going to get back home here? We'll be stranded out there!"

"I hardly think we'll be stranded. Margie, you're being dramatic again."

"Whatever word you would like me to use, it all means the same thing, Amanda, so we need to come up with another plan."

"It's pretty simple, Margie. I'll just follow you out to the farm in our pickup. That's the best I can do, unless you want me to dig out Mother's driveway to the garage, charge up the battery somehow, and take her car!"

"No, the pickup will be fine." Margie said quietly. She felt chagrined, as once again Amanda had put her in her place.

"All right, then. See how easy that was? Just call me when you're ready to leave town, and I'll meet you by the cemetery road and follow you on out to the farm."

"Fine. I'll call you tomorrow from the hospital, Amanda. Good night."

"Bye," and they both hung up.

Now I know I don't want to get together with them tonight. Margie will be worrying about something or other. *Stranded.* Now wouldn't that be terrible? She must get home to her mother. Well, not me. I can't wait to get away, even though my adventure this time will be vastly different.

And with that in mind, she went into the bedroom, dragged out two suitcases and tore into the closet and chest of drawers like a burglar ransacking a house. She loved a challenge even in adversity, and she tackled this job as if her life depended on it, which, in fact, it did—and so did someone else's.

"I need to find a name for you, little one," she chatted with the baby while packing. "Are you a boy or a girl? Oh, I hope you're a girl. How do you like the name *Claire?* It's always been my favorite name for a boy or girl. It sounds like it stands for something, like clear and not muddied up and not complicated or like the word *declare,* a strong, bold word, like a declaration. We'll think about that name. We sure can't name you Robert or Roberta. Robert. I must write to him."

She worked even faster, sorting and packing. Actually, there wasn't too much to take and one large suitcase would suffice. Nothing would fit her in the coming months, so shopping for a maternity wardrobe would be on the agenda as soon as she hit Iowa.

Jennifer was always on the go, and Amanda hoped to tag along to some of her activities, and have some fun, if her body would cooperate. There would be no reason to hide or cover up her secret there in Iowa.

Amanda was famished again. Scouring the refrigerator and cupboards for something substantial to tide her over until morning, she finally decided to eat up the perishable items, since they wouldn't keep too well until July or August. It never entered her mind to cart them up to Mother's.

Two brown scrambled eggs from the Shaw chicken coop, another cinnamon roll from Belle's kitchen, and a glass of milk tasted like a gourmet meal.

"Did you find that tasty, Claire?" She talked to the baby again. Another little series of hiccups must have been a positive answer.

With nothing else to do, Amanda wandered toward the bedroom. The warmth of the covers and the firm but comfortable mattress seemed to be calling to her again, but it was only 9:00 p.m. She looked out the window from their second floor apartment and down on the peaceful main street. In the distance she could see the hulk of the local movie theater, the Marquee Lights. It loomed in the air like a dark shadow, but Saturday night it would light up the corner of the block. She had noticed that afternoon while running her errands that "Gaslight" with Ingrid Bergman, Charles Boyer, and Joseph Cotten was advertised for that particular weekend. She loved suspense thrillers and also loved Charles Boyer, so she decided right then and there that she would see one last movie Saturday night before she headed off for Iowa.

Across the street was Charley's service station, where every spring, along about April 15, the Wentworth Plymouth rolled in for its annual check-up and servicing. Charley himself would drive it out of the garage for its first spring outing. Then it was ready for the summer travels. The Plymouth's longest trip was to Spokane when the Wentworth mother and daughter team drove to the big city for doctor's appointments and shopping at the Crescent Department Store, the Palace Dress Shop, or Kress's Five and Dime. Those trips also included at least one night's stay at the Davenport Hotel. Margie did the driving and Mother told her where to go and how to get there.

Their other long-distance trip was the opposite direction from Wheatland, when they headed west to bask in the healing mineral waters of Soap Lake, Washington. They also visited the local chiropractor there and made a day out of it. Maybe once every two years they would extend their stay and rent one of the small cabins and take mineral baths right in their room. Mother's arthritis would be so much better, and Margie didn't complain of headaches so often after they'd been to Soap Lake. Amanda thought it was all in their heads and couldn't be convinced otherwise. Of course, she'd

never been there herself, so all she could do was scoff in disbelief at
their "healings."

Amanda had to admit she would miss seeing the familiar sights
and faces of her hometown, but even more so of Spokane. She was
really a big city girl at heart and liked the sounds and smells of
traffic, of movement. She loved progress and the bustling city
seemed to excite her. How Margie could be content to sit and spin
her wheels in Wheatland was a concept that Amanda could not
fathom. It was a friendly little farming community with neighbor
helping neighbor, but Amanda was glad she had expanded her
horizons and looked beyond the city limits of Wheatland. Her
"teaching" in Iowa seemed so real that for a moment she almost
believed it herself. She wished it were true. *I could be teaching if
that man hadn't come to town and fouled me up!* Then she felt
guilty as if the baby could really hear and understand her derogatory
remarks.

"A few more days and a few more plans, and we'll be there,"
she said softly to Claire, as she tended to her bathroom duties,
donned the warmest flannel nightgown she owned, and slipped
under the covers once again. She was making a mental list of
tomorrow's activities when sleep closed her eyes. If not, she would
have had to face the biggest decision left to be resolved—when to
tell Mother and Margie her secret, and then it would have been a
very restless night. Should she tell them now or in four or five
months?

Up on the south hill, Belle was getting settled for the night.
Dr. Baker had been over two more times to check on her. He lived
just across the street from the hospital, so he was in and out several
times daily to see his patients. Belle was improving, and when he
checked her over at 7:00 p.m., he assured her that if she continued
to get better, she could go home in a day or two, but a severe
headache was still a complaint. "That's to be expected, Belle. You
really cracked your head on the car door and then hit it hard again
when you fell," Dr. Baker tried to reassure her as he shined a light
into each eye. "You will be very stiff and sore and bruised tomorrow,

but that's normal, too. You know, you are very fortunate that bones weren't broken."

"Yes, praise the Lord! He was watching over me," Belle answered, as she gazed heavenward.

Dr. Baker patted her arm. "Get some rest now, and I'll see you in the morning."

"Thank you, Doctor. You are so kind."

"That's part of my job," and Belle knew he really believed that.

Meanwhile up on the north side of town, the neighborhood was all tucked in for the night. Dottie's three-year-old twins had finally settled down after a restless evening. They wanted to stay up and play, and then made a mess of water and soap in the bathroom during their bath time. They loved their story times in the bedroom, and tonight they had wanted the Mother Goose rhymes to go on for hours. Dottie finally left them chanting "Jack and Jill" to each other and tiptoed down the stairs.

Her husband, Steve, who rarely paid any attention to what the neighbors were doing, had pulled back the living room curtains just a crack and was staring across the street.

"Hey, Dot, what in the world is Belle's car doing over at Zoe's at this time of night?" He'd heard the stairs creak as she came down.

"Oh, I guess the car was just too tired to go home," she teased.

"No, really, come on, Dot. Why is it there?"

Dottie explained to him what had happened earlier in the day and what Hilda had told her later in the afternoon. Any traffic in and out of Zoe's after dark or cars left out at night raised questions in the neighborhood. It was so out of the ordinary.

Hilda had inquired about Belle from Zoe after she'd heard some gossip downtown. With the investigation completed on Hilda's part, and the kids in bed, she wrote up a detailed report for the paper. It wouldn't come out again until next week, and by then it would be old news, but at least it would be an accurate account of Belle's accident to counteract the rumors that would have circulated the town many times around.

Over at the Wentworth home, Zoe and Margie were exhausted. The confusion and disharmony of the day had worn them both out. Zoe dozed in her rocking chair. Her teeth were soaking in the bathroom and with the pins out of her gray bun, the hair flowed down her back like a waterfall frozen in time. The even predictable rhythm of her snoring was punctuated every so often by a snort. Her eyelids fluttered, and she rocked a few times, and then dozed off again. She'd get up and go to bed if she wasn't so tired!

9:00 pm was too early for Margie to think about going to bed, even tonight after her mind had been racing since Belle had fallen, and so much had been expected of her. The mother of all migraines should have been jabbing behind the eyes, but surprisingly her head didn't hurt a bit. The warm bubble bath had been relaxing after dinner, and she would have loved to be up in her bedroom reading right now.

Zoe snorted again, and they both jumped.

"Mother, why don't you go to bed?" Margie implored.

"What? Why? What time is it?" Zoe awakened to full attention.

"It's only a little after nine, but you'd be more comfortable in bed."

"All right. Let's go," Zoe agreed readily, for a change. She was used to being escorted to her room every night and expected Margie to pull back the covers, fluff up the pillows, and remove her slippers. She also demanded that Margie kiss her on the cheek, just a little brush of the lips, as she sat on the edge of the bed. The peck of affection was not returned, which hurt Margie deeply. She was a loving person who couldn't understand why Mother couldn't show a little love. They'd been over it many times, and it was always the same.

"It's a matter of respect for me, Margie, and that is all. This conversation is over!"

Margie had no choice but to accept that statement and had stopped bothering to even broach the subject.

Zoe settled her arthritic body under the sheet. She slept on her back under one woolen blanket and a white down comforter. Margie tucked her in like a mother would tend to a child.

Amanda often showed her sarcasm to Margie by saying, "I'm surprised you don't have to read her a bedtime story!"

"Well, I would if she wanted it," was always Margie's reply. "It's a good thing one of us is a dutiful daughter."

Margie turned out the light. "I'll be up early tomorrow, Mother. I have to call the hospital by 9:00 a.m."

"Yes, I remember. I was proud of you today, Margie. Good night."

"Thanks, Mother. Good night."

That compliment was almost as good as a kiss, and it helped Margie's tired body sail up the stairs on a cloud. She hoped to do as well the next day.

Out on the farm, Ed was worried about his Belle. He'd hurried home to feed the chickens and the pigs before dark, and he'd eaten a few bites of a casserole from the refrigerator. He wasn't very hungry and didn't even bother to warm it up. Dr. Baker had called to reassure him.

"Your wife will be fine when the swelling goes down and the headache lets up. She took quite a blow to the head, but will be fine in a day or so."

Ed was not usually a person who worried. He left that up to Belle, and she left it up to God.

"God doesn't need my help," she'd often say to Ed.

It was rare for Ed to be lonely, but with Belle in the hospital and Robert so far away, he felt like a lost sheep. Then there was Michael, the younger son.

"If only Michael was more like a son than a stranger . . . I'm going to call him anyway; he needs to know about his mother," Ed thought, as he rummaged around in the desk drawer trying to find Belle's address book. Ed finally found the number, but, as usual, there was no answer.

Michael Edward Shaw was three years younger than Robert, and they were as different as steak and chocolate pudding. Michael was independent from day one. He wouldn't even take his mother's milk. Growing up, they had to force or bribe him to go to Sunday School, and he hated the farm. When his dad would chop a chicken's head off or butcher a cow for meat, Michael would become physically sick. Killing any living thing, even a spider, was repulsive to him, so it came as no surprise to Ed and Belle, and to Robert, too, that Michael was totally opposed to the war. Michael had tried to talk Robert out of going. "Become a conscientious objector like me," he had begged Robert over and over again. "It's not your duty or mine to kill or be killed. It is so wrong."

Robert came very close to calling his brother names. "Chicken" came to mind, but he gave up arguing with Michael over a person's duty, just as he'd given up talking to him about Christianity. As a dedicated Christian, Robert hated to give up on that, but finally decided someone else might have more success trying to get it through his head that God was continually knocking on the door of his heart.

Michael tagged along with Robert to Sunday School when they were growing up, but refused to make any commitments, even as a child. In high school, he vehemently began to vocally question his family's beliefs.

"I can't believe in something I can't see or reach out to and touch," and he thought evolution was the only way that man could possibly have come into being. They finally stopped making him go to church.

After college at Washington State College, Michael went into the field of photojournalism. He liked to capture reality, and the only way he'd shoot anything would be with a camera. Settling in Seattle, he worked for a major newspaper there and did some freelancing on the side—shot some weddings, some children's portraits, and some still life around Puget Sound.

He liked his beer and his parties. He had never married, but he liked his women. Even when visiting in Wheatland, Michael would either bring some gal along from Seattle, or he'd call up an old friend in the area for a date. The visits home were short and far between.

He liked to capture the fall colors of the trees before the last leaf fell to herald the advent of winter, so he usually came in October or early November. This last time he came, Robert was at Camp Pendleton.

Michael liked to stay at Carlson's Motel on the east end of town. It was quiet and secluded with huge maple trees lining the driveway up to the office, and he could come and go as he pleased without being under the watchful eye of his mother. This year with Robert gone, he definitely didn't want all the attention from his parents. He just couldn't stand it. He avoided discussions of those subjects where they differed. What was the use? They would not change him. A quick meal at the farm was enough, and then he had to get back to the camera before the light changed too much or a girl was waiting. Busy, busy, busy, with lots of excuses. He couldn't and wouldn't let his parents get too close and personal.

Michael stopped once to see Zoe and Margie. He thought Zoe was a witch and that Margie was a nut case, but now they were part of the family, and it pleased his mother when she heard that they had enjoyed a visit from her son. He was not so hard-hearted that he couldn't please his mother once in awhile.

One whole evening was reserved for Amanda. Now, here was one family member with whom Michael could relate! He brought some beer, which Amanda enjoyed. Robert would not allow it in the house. She and Michael talked for hours about all kinds of things—science and evolution, art and photography, and even some of their personal feelings about the family and relationships. Finally, late at night the beer ran out, and Michael was tired. The light of dawn found him still at Amanda's, and he extended his visit in Wheatland for one more day.

The Human Heart has hidden treasures,
In secret kept, In silence sealed.
—Charlotte Bronte

Chapter XII

The long, clammy arm of winter was still wrapped around the shoulders of Eastern Washington. It was only the middle of January, so it would be many more weeks before the green sprigs in the fields of wheat and barley would have the courage to penetrate the fertile soil to announce the arrival of spring.

Margie shivered as she sat on the edge of her bed. As tired as she was from the stress of Belle's fall and all of her responsibilities from the day before, she'd had a restless night, tossing and turning and dozing and worrying. She thought of Robert and wondered where he was and what he was feeling. She worried about Belle and her injuries and getting her home safely. She was also in turmoil about Amanda's leaving but, surprisingly, she didn't have a migraine headache.

"I hope it didn't snow again," she thought, gingerly pulling back the pink lace curtain, "or how will I drive up the hill and out to the farm?" She looked down on Belle's car. There was a dusting of frost covering the car, especially the windows, but she knew Belle carried an ice scraper and a brush for that purpose, and she was relieved to see that there was not a fresh snowflake anywhere, and the road was bare and dry.

"Thank goodness," she whispered with a grateful heart.

It was only 8:00 a.m., so she had some time before the call to the hospital. Her favorite morning ritual was to wrap herself up in the extra blanket that was at the foot of her bed and sit on the window seat. She was rarely up this early, so she saw neighborhood activities that she didn't witness very often. Today she watched Steve back his truck out of the garage across the street and leave for his job at the hardware store. The twins were up, and Margie could see their blond curly heads in the kitchen window, as they waved to him.

Time passed quickly as Margie was lost in her reverie. She recited to herself from memory Robert's letter, truly feeling in the deepest depths of her heart that he was in love with her. She couldn't figure out why he had married Amanda, and if he could possibly be in love with two sisters at the same time. It was all such a confusing mystery, and yet the possibilities warmed her lonely heart at the same time. She smiled, thinking of how proud he would be of her if he knew how she'd taken care of his mother, while Amanda had been too busy on the phone making her stupid plans to leave town! Margie was not so naive that she couldn't tell it was an excuse so she wouldn't have to spend time with them while Robert was gone. She knew how desperately Amanda had wanted to get away and live her own life. Maybe that's why Amanda married him—just to escape.

The hands of the clock hurried around the circle of time, and it was 8:45 when Margie entered into the reality of the present day again. She threw the blanket on the bed, pulled on a pink robe, and stuffed her feet into pink corduroy slippers, loving the soft and feminine shades of pink, while Amanda loved the bold and courageous tones of red.

Tiptoeing down the stairs, Margie tried to avoid the squeaks of the old house. Her mother slept with her bedroom door open. Margie peered in, and Zoe was still asleep with her mouth as wide open as the door. There was no reason to wake her up just yet, so Margie went about her duties as she went on through the cold house. She stopped in the living room to turn up the heat and raise the shades. The thermometer on the north side registered twenty-five degrees, and Margie stopped at the desk to record it.

It was too early to put the tea kettle on, so she continued on to the bathroom, and plugged in a small electric heater to warm up the bathroom because Zoe liked a warm morning bath to start her day. As soon as Margie's bathroom duties were completed, it was 9:00 a.m. and time to call the hospital.

"Hansen Hospital. This is Emma speaking."

"Good morning, Emma. This is Margie Wentworth, and I'm calling to inquire about Belle Shaw."

"Oh, hello, Margie. It's nice to hear from you. How are you and your mother doing?"

"We're doing quite well, thank you, but what about Belle?" Margie persisted.

"The doctor was just here. She made a vast improvement overnight, so he released her to go home today. Belle said you'd be picking her up to drive her out to the farm."

"Oh, I'm glad she's so much better. Yes, that is the plan. When will she be ready to go?"

"Well, let's see here. Um . . . How about eleven? We need to do a few things, and then she'll be ready."

Margie was relieved that she had plenty of time to get ready herself and call Amanda.

"That's good for me, too. I'll see you then, Emma."

"I'll have her ready. Bye for now."

Just then Zoe shuffled into the kitchen on her way to the bathroom. "Who in the world were you talking to at this ungodly hour?"

"It's 9:00 a.m., Mother. Remember I had to call the hospital about taking Belle home."

"Is it that time already? I slept so soundly all night."

"Good. I'm glad someone did. I guess I slept off and on."

"Well, is Belle able to go home?" She ignored Margie's sleep problems.

"Yeah, she'll be ready at eleven. I need to call Amanda. I hope she hasn't changed her mind about following me out to the farm."

Amanda had been up since seven. She'd finally written that long overdue letter to Robert, but wasn't quite sure of his address. She'd ask Belle. After her bath and breakfast, she was listening to the radio when Margie called. "Call me about fifteen minutes before you are ready to leave the hospital." She'd need a few minutes to warm up the pickup.

The morning flew by quite smoothly, and they got Belle safely home. She was sore and bruised as the doctor had predicted, but so happy to get home. The trip seemed to wear her out, so she went right to bed. She still put others first, even in her misery, so she instructed Ed to warm up the casserole for lunch for the girls, but Amanda quickly spoke up and declined for both of them.

"Belle, we'd love to stay," she gushed, "but I have so much to do before I leave, so if you don't need anything else, we have to be going," she said rather abruptly.

Margie was astonished at her sister's urgency to get home. She would have loved to stay, but it was Amanda's wishes that she'd always bowed down to, so why would today be any different? Margie and Amanda both kissed Belle on the cheek and gave Ed a big hug. He was so grateful to them both that he was actually gushing with praise and thanks, though not usually a demonstrative man, but it was wonderful to have Belle home and on the mend.

So, off they went toward home—the two sisters rattling down the bumpy lane and out to the main road in Robert's old pickup. It was a beautiful, sunny mid-January day. Someone—God maybe—had sprinkled diamonds all over the snow. The girls were quiet for the first couple of miles. Margie was admiring the scenery and enjoying the drive, and Amanda's mind was going faster than the fan belt was turning on the pickup.

Amanda finally broke the silence. "Margie, have you ever wanted to have a baby?"

Margie turned her head so quickly that she almost cried out in pain, and she stared at her sister in shock. Glad she wasn't driving, she'd have put the truck in the ditch!

"Well, have you?" Amanda persisted.

"How could I? I'm not married!"

"Well, I know that. I'm not questioning your marital status. I'm just wondering if you ever had the desire to be a mother. You seem to like little kids so well."

"Of course, I would love to have a baby, several babies. I've always wanted to be married and have a family, but it just never happened, and now I'm getting too old. So I just take care of Mother and go on with my life, such as it is." Margie didn't know what else to say. If she really opened up her heart and let all her hopes and dreams fall out and talk about the love she had and lost, she would be in tears, and nothing made Amanda madder than seeing her sister snivel.

"What brought on this questioning, Amanda?" Margie finally put the burden of answers back on Amanda.

"Just wondering . . . just wondering. Have you ever thought of adopting? Right now, there are lots of babies needing homes."

"Adopting? Well, no, who ever heard of a single woman, especially at my age, being allowed to do that?" Margie was overwhelmed at these questions. What was causing them?

Amanda was walking on eggshells now. "Oh, it's just that I know a lady who is pregnant and wants, I mean needs, to put her baby up for adoption when it is born."

"Oh, really. Who is she? Is she from around here?"

Amanda's stomach was becoming upset. She either had to lie or blurt out the truth, and she just wasn't ready for that yet. So she lied one more time.

"You wouldn't know her. She's someone I know from college. Well, just forget it. It probably wouldn't work out anyway," and for the time being, the case was closed.

However, it opened up a whole new world of thinking for Margie. She just could not figure out her sister sometimes. Me? Adopt a baby? Margie had never entertained such a thought!

"The cemetery's right here. Shall we drive through and pay our respects to Dad?" Amanda changed the subject as quickly as she'd started it, but she'd had years of practice at that.

"Sure, if they've plowed the lanes," Margie agreed.

"It looks pretty clear," Amanda observed, as she shifted down into second and then first gear.

She had to stop completely so Margie could get out and open the big, black, wrought iron cemetery gates. They were heavy to pull back, and Margie feared she'd hurt her back, but she did it anyway. They swung fairly easily today. Maybe Margie had a sudden burst of energy from the adrenalin of their conversation just moments ago. She hopped back in the pickup, and they drove down the lane and turned left. Cemeteries seemed like such cold and lonely places to Margie, even in the summer months when the warm sun heated the stone and marble markers. Today, with the temperature hovering just below the freezing mark, she shivered, even though the heater in Robert's pickup was blasting out the heat like a furnace.

"We don't have to get out, do we?" Margie begged, as Amanda parked the truck in the lane.

"No, it's too cold, and the markers are all covered with snow. Dad would understand if we just stop here for a minute."

"I sure miss him," Margie said sadly.

Amanda wondered what he would think of her predicament. He would not be pleased, but he would probably try to be understanding. "Yeah, I miss him too." At least this was something they could both agree on.

Their dad, Frederick Wentworth, passed away in June 1942 of a heart attack. He'd had problems with his heart for several months and was in and out of the Deaconess Hospital in Spokane, so the family was forewarned, but not prepared for his eventual passing. No one ever is ready. Margie, as expected, took his death the hardest, as they were very close. They were so alike. He had a compassionate heart, a loving, gentle way about him, and a love of literature. He read Margie's poetry and encouraged her to publish and make her writing into a career. She hadn't done that, but she took his advice under consideration, and if she ever conquered her fears of letting others read her poetry, she'd have her dad to thank.

Of course, he tried to encourage Amanda in her endeavors too, but she was struggling to be her own person all through her growing up years. She had different interests and her scientific mind had little imagination. She had no fears and wouldn't accept defeat. Amanda was definitely more like her mother.

As for Frederick and Zoe's relationship, they tolerated each other. While Zoe wore a stern consternation and presented an authoritative persona, Frederick had an ever-ready smile and tried to smooth things over. They usually agreed to disagree. The girls rarely saw emotion or affection between them. They just did their own thing. He was busy with his teaching career as head of the English Department at Wheatland High and with his investments on the side. He believed buying property when it was cheap was a sound way to put any extra money aside, and he owned some land in Wheatland and a few plots in Spokane. He'd made some money, and Zoe inherited his investments. He had hoped she was set for the rest of her life, so she could continue to enjoy keeping house and having the bridge girls in for cards.

"Well, let's go," Amanda was anxious to leave the grave sites behind.

"Bye, Dad." Margie wiped her eyes on her coat sleeve and looked out the other direction toward the fields. Amanda shifted into first gear, and they slowly rolled down the road and out the gate.

"I'll close it," Amanda said quietly, as she parked the pickup and jumped out. As she returned, Margie noticed she was wiping her eyes. "It's the wind; it makes my eyes water," she said, and roared off toward town.

In four short minutes, they were back in town and had pulled up in front of the Wentworth home. Amanda put the pickup into first with one foot on the brake and one on the clutch.

"Are you coming in?" Margie questioned, but she knew from the roar of the engine that Amanda had no intention of turning off the motor and visiting her mother.

"No, I'll come up later. I have some important things to do. Tell Mother I'll be back later this afternoon."

"All right. Thanks for your help today, Amanda."

"It's O.K. See 'ya later or tomorrow." Amanda said the last two words as Margie slammed the door, and she was on her way down the hill, very thankful for an excuse, as the events of the morning did not need to be rehashed over a nice cup of tea.

Zoe had been watching the clock and wondering when Margie would be back—not that she needed her for anything but companionship, but she always worried when Margie was gone. Suddenly there she was, opening the back door and calling her name.

"Mother, I'm home."

"Heavens to Betsy. What took you so long? Pour yourself a cup of tea and sit down and tell me all about your trip." A person would think her daughters had just returned from a journey around the world!

Margie related the rescuing of Belle from the hospital, the ride out to the farm, and the settling of Belle into her home, all in great detail and in her dramatic style. Zoe listened intently. She enjoyed a one-act play once in awhile, but then Margie went off on a tangent.

"Mother, Amanda is off her noodle!"

"What? What does that mean? Where did you hear those words?"

"All right. To put it another way, Amanda has lost her marbles, she's way out on a limb, she's lost her mind. Do you need any more cliches about her mental state?"

Zoe smirked at Margie's choice of words, but she was still mystified as to why she sounded so sarcastic and was so upset with her sister. Sarcasm was not one of Margie's traits.

"You'll never believe what she asked me. You'll never believe it in a million years," Margie's voice was rising in her excitement. She pushed her saucer and tea cup away and stood up.

Mother's gray eyebrows shot up in amazement at Margie's upset attitude. "Sit down right now and talk to me and relax. It couldn't be all that bad. How will I believe it or not if you don't calm down and tell me what it is? Wait a minute; pour me some more tea first."

Margie poured the tea, and then went to the kitchen cupboard to get the glass jar of peppermints. She was sure Mother would need them for her stomach by the time she got through.

"Well, here goes. We were coming home, and I was really enjoying bouncing along in Robert's pickup. You know, he's taken such good care of it, and it runs so well for being so old.

The sun was brilliant and the snow just sparkled. It's one of the prettiest days we've had all winter, even though it's cold. I doubt if the temperature has gotten up to . . ."

Mother interrupted. "Come on, Margie. You don't have to set the stage. Just get to the point. You've always been one for long, rambling details. Sometimes they're interesting, but not when there's some drama to spill forth, like I am anticipating now."

Margie continued. "Well, anyway, all of a sudden, out of the clear blue sky, Amanda asked me if I'd ever wanted to have a baby."

"She was probably just making conversation, don't you think?" Mother was sure that was all it amounted to.

"But wait, Mother, there's more. I told her, yes, I had wanted children, but that it's too late now," Margie stopped for air.

"So, did that shut her up?"

"Oh, no, that was just the beginning. Then she wanted to know if I'd ever thought of adopting a baby."

"Oh, for heaven's sake! She *is* off her noodle. What in the world made her ask that?" Mother had been smoothing back her hair and checking her bun to make sure it was still intact. She was beginning to feel Margie's anxiety and dishevelment. Suddenly her hand flew to her stomach like a seagull diving for a fish in the ocean.

"See, I told you you'd never believe it in a million years. Here, have a peppermint. In fact, you'd better take two." Margie shook a couple out of the jar into Mother's hand.

"It is so hard to believe. Did you ever find out her reason for asking?"

Margie was about to wrap up her story. "Yes, she claims she knows someone who is pregnant and needs to put the baby up for adoption. She said it's no one I know, but someone she knows from college."

Mother frowned as she tried to figure out the mystery. "Well, the only one she really knows from college is Jennifer Hollis, and she's in Iowa."

"It could be Jennifer, but I just don't know what to think. I haven't really had time to figure it out. I was wondering about something even before Amanda brought up the subject today. Just yesterday I found an envelope out in the hallway of Amanda's apartment from a doctor in Spokane. When I gave it to her, she blushed, but didn't say anything."

Mother was shocked, "Maybe that's why she was just in Spokane."

"She's been so secretive lately and changes the subject so quickly."

"Oh, she does that all the time," Mother came to Amanda's defense.

Margie scratched her head, not because it itched, but to help her think. "You know, Mother, it seems to me that she sprung this teaching job on us awfully suddenly. Would there really be an opening now during wartime?"

Mother nodded, "Yes, I wondered about that myself. I suppose if the professor had to go to war, they'd need a replacement or they'd have to cancel the class."

"Hmm . . . I suppose. I just think Amanda's been acting weird lately—more evasive and even more in a hurry to get away and do her own thing than be with us."

"She *does* have to get ready to go to Iowa," Mother stuck up for her again. "Oh, I just had a thought; maybe she's going to help Jennifer, if she's the one who's pregnant."

Margie blurted out the rest of her thoughts, as the game of hearts was beginning to fall into place in her mind. The cards were lining up just right to be placed on the table, if not by Amanda, then by Margie.

"No, I've got it! Maybe Amanda is going to Iowa so Jennifer can help *her*. I think Amanda is the one who is pregnant, Mother."

Zoe and Margie stared at each other. What else was there to do? They'd never heard quiet so loud.

The heart is deceitful above all things,
And desperately wicked, who can know it?
—Jeremiah 17:9

Chapter XIII

Although 1:00 p.m. rolled around to 2:00 p.m., Zoe and Margie were still seated at the yellow kitchen table. They were nailed to the hard wooden chairs by their thoughts and their feelings—immovable in their discovery that perhaps Amanda had been cheating at the game of hearts.

So many thoughts had percolated through their minds, and so many possibilities had been poured out and watered down all because of one shocking question: "Margie, have you ever thought of adopting a baby?"

Was Margie's creative, imaginative mind working overtime? Was Amanda really going to Iowa to teach? If she was pregnant, was Robert the father or was someone else? Who could he be? Why the secrecy and lies?

Margie insisted that Amanda was gaining weight, and that she'd been even more distant and preoccupied than usual. And, of course, there was the envelope Margie had found from the doctor.

"What do we do now?" They both asked of each other. "Is she going to tell us or just go away?" They had no answers. They were both tired and running on empty. They weren't hungry, but they knew they should eat something. No one can solve the problems of the world on endless cups of tea and peppermints!

While Zoe went to freshen her face with warm water and a washcloth, Margie reheated some left-over macaroni and cheese and opened a jar of home-canned peaches. It was their favorite kind of comfort food—the macaroni and cheese warm and soothing and the peaches just cool and sweet enough to be refreshing.

Margie skipped her daily trip to the post office on the assumption that they would be blessed by Amanda's visit, but as the afternoon's brilliance faded into twilight, the promise of her presence faded as well. Just as they'd given up all hope and were beginning to relax, their nerves were jarred to attention by the jangling phone.

"Well, answer it," Mother commanded, as they sat and looked dumbfounded at each other.

"Margie? What are you doing?" It was Amanda, as nonchalant and unnerved as ever.

"Well, we've been waiting for you all afternoon. You said you'd come up and visit Mother today. So what in the world have *you* been doing?"

"I'm sure you wouldn't know, but it takes a lot of work to get ready to leave. I had to verify my travel arrangements and talk to Edna Grayson about the apartment, and, of course, call Jen. I'm staying with her, you know, in Iowa."

"No, I didn't know. How is Jen anyway?" Margie questioned. Her interest was at its peak now, and she was making faces at her mother, raising her eyebrows and then frowning. Zoe was opening her mouth and then closing it with unspoken questions.

"She's better now. She's had a bad siege of bronchitis."

Margie had more questions. "Is she married yet?"

"Heavens no! She's too dedicated to teaching to take the time to get involved with a man!"

That didn't prove anything to Margie. It could all be a lie.

Then, as usual, Amanda changed the subject. "Not to change the subject, but time's flying, Margie, and I was just wondering if you'd like to go to the movies tonight. Your favorite man will be on the screen."

"Oh, yes, Charles Boyer. I saw the marquee."

Amanda persisted, "Do you want to go?"

Margie glanced over at her mother who was tired and slumped down in her chair. Her eyes were sad, and she looked defeated.

"I'll go on one condition—that you'll promise to come and see Mother tomorrow and spend some time and not just run in and dash out."

"Why certainly, I intend to. Mother can come if she wants," Amanda generously threw out the invitation at the last minute, even though she knew it would be out of the question.

Margie felt she really shouldn't leave Mother alone, but maybe some last-minute bonding with her sister would shed some light on all the questions that were buzzing around in their heads like a swarm of agitated bees.

"I'll tell her you asked, but you should know Mother never goes out at night, especially in the winter, Amanda."

"I know that; I was just trying to be polite."

They made plans then for Margie to meet Amanda on the sidewalk in front of her apartment at 6:30, and they'd walk the two blocks for the 7:00 p.m. showing.

"Do you mind, Mother?" Margie asked, when she got off the phone.

"Heavens no! You go right ahead. I'll listen to the radio and probably doze off anyway."

"Just don't sit and worry. Maybe we'll have some answers tomorrow from Amanda."

Mother was skeptical. "Maybe we will and maybe we won't; but speaking of tomorrow, I wonder what time she'll come up. She is so unpredictable, but I thought if you could find out, we could cook up that leg of lamb. It takes up so much room in the freezer compartment."

"But, Mother, that's for company, plus we'd have to take it out now to thaw it, and then what if she didn't come?"

Mother nodded her head. "Well, try to find out anyway when she's coming, and we'll put something together for a meal. We can always make up a batch of tomato sauce in the morning and have spaghetti. We all like that, and we should send her off with a good hearty meal."

"Yeah, especially if she's eating for two," Margie added.

Like gold speckles of paint on a black canvas, the stars spattered the dark January sky, and although she was dressed warmly, Margie shivered as she trudged down the hill to meet her sister. She stopped for a moment at the corner of the block and found the North Star. She had so many things to wish for that it was hard to pick just one desire.

"I guess my greatest wish is for Robert to come home safely," she whispered toward the heavens.

At the very same moment, Amanda was standing on the sidewalk in front of the apartment building, looking up at the sky, wishing for the very same thing.

Margie's heart was racing as she reached the bottom of the hill and rounded the corner to meet her sister. It was pounding not from walking too fast but from thoughts of Robert.

"Oh, I'm out of breath," she gasped, as she reached Amanda.

"You didn't have to hurry; we have plenty of time, and soon you'll be swooning in your seat over Charles Boyer!"

"I think the cold night air just took my breath away. I hope I won't catch cold!"

"You won't, Margie, unless you've caught a germ from somebody else." Amanda could never convince Mother or Margie of the way that one gets sick. After all, with her science background, she ought to know!

They soon reached the theater and went inside out of the cold night air. Sara Fosberg was selling tickets. She lived kitty-corner from the Wentworths in a white two-story house. She was surprised to see the two sisters out together. Sara knew they led their own lives, and Amanda had her own agenda, although she had no idea of the course she was following now. Sara was closer to Margie than Amanda because of the bridge club.

"Well, I tell you true. It's good to see you girls out tonight," Sara gushed in her dramatic manner. Her big brown eyes glanced from one sister to the other as she tore off the tickets. Amanda insisted on paying for them both, so Margie jammed her money back in her coat pocket.

"This cold night air has really flushed your cheeks, Amanda. Gosh, you're just glowing. Oh, well, of course, you look good too, Margie." She threw that last sentence in just to appease Margie, but she really did think Amanda had a special unusual radiance about her, especially for someone who had just sent her husband off to war.

"I don't think I ever looked so good when I sent Jess to war. I know I sure never felt too great when he was away. My stomach was so . . ."

A line was forming behind Margie, but Sara prattled on. She loved to talk about everything and anything. She was well read and could carry on a conversation on just about any subject. The girls just wanted to get further into the theater out of the doorway, so they inched their way into the lobby.

"Come over and see me," Sara ended the conversation finally, just as she launched into greeting the next patron and visiting with her.

"We will," Margie and Amanda responded in unison. Of course, Amanda had no intention of running over there on her last day in Wheatland. Margie might go to visit when she had the time. She did like Sara and found her very entertaining when she came over for the bridge club.

There were just a few minutes to visit before *Gaslight* started, and as Amanda settled comfortably in her seat, Margie was nervous and squirmed and fidgeted like a two-year old.

"What is wrong with you?" Amanda soon asked in irritation. "Sit still."

"I'm just getting so nervous about you leaving, Amanda. Robert left, and now you're leaving. I can't handle it." The emotions of the day were finally catching up with her.

"Robert's leaving had nothing to do with you, and as for me, I"m just going to Iowa to have a . . ."

Just then the theater darkened, and the trailer of coming shows burst forth on the screen and drowned out the rest of Amanda's sentence.

"Baby, it's cold outside," someone was singing. Margie put her hand to her forehead and rubbed her temple.

Amanda rolled her eyes. I hope she's not getting a migraine, she thought.

I think I feel a migraine coming on, Margie brooded silently and rubbed her temple even more vigorously. But soon Charles Boyer took all her thoughts away from the troubles at home, and she settled back and fell into the emotion of the story on the screen.

It ended all too soon, and Amanda had to prod Margie to get her to vacate her seat. Movies always stayed with Margie for days. She would reenact scenes and recite words and continue to be swept up in the emotion of it all. She totally forgot everything else. Amanda flipped it off in her mind like turning off the radio and went on to the next subject at hand.

Sara tried to strike up another conversation as they went out, but Amanda hurried Margie along. Margie was oblivious anyway and was humming as they strode along the sidewalk toward home.

"Well, I'll see you tomorrow," Amanda broke the silence, as they neared her apartment.

"Tomorrow? Oh yes, tomorrow. What time are you coming up to visit? Mother thought you could have an early dinner with us, and you know how she likes to plan ahead when she entertains."

Amanda was irritated at having to be on a schedule and pinned down to a time. She'd just wanted to relax on her final day at home, and maybe wait around to see if Robert would call again, but promises were promises, so she'd be there.

"Oh, how about 3:00?" She picked a number out of the cold and dark thin air.

"We'll see you at 3:00 p.m. sharp, then, and oh, and thanks for the movie."

"Sure, see you tomorrow." Amanda turned into her apartment, and Margie trudged on down the sidewalk, turned the corner, and marched up the hill.

Mother was dozing in her chair and awakened with a start when she heard the back door open. Margie poured out the details of the evening and, although she had nothing startling to add to the day's events, Mother listened with rapt attention.

"She'll have to play her wild card tomorrow," Mother finalized the day with a yawn.

*   *   *

Amanda began her last day in Wheatland by going for an early morning walk. She bundled up and headed out around 7:45 a.m. She walked downtown—first up one side and then the other, looking in all the stores and offices. It was Sunday and absolutely nothing was open, so she could stand and gaze in the windows as long as she wanted. Sundays were so boring with no mail to read and nothing to do.

The churches would fill up around 9:30 for Sunday School followed by church at 11:00, but Amanda was not one bit interested in attending. She was trying to sort out her thoughts on religion on her own, and she didn't want some preacher shoving it down her throat!

Robert and his folks just seemed to take it all for granted and never questioned their trust in someone they couldn't see or prove.

"As a scientist, Mandy, can't you see that someone greater than you and I had to create all this harmony? Just think of the human body and how it all works together or the water cycle or the rotation of the earth." Robert had often gone into great detail trying to prove God to Amanda, but it was impossible. He'd tried to show her how the prophesies in the Old Testament were played out in the New Testament and tried to lead her to salvation with a child-like faith.

She wasn't going to be gullible. She needed more concrete proof and more evidence before she wasted her precious time worshiping every Sunday morning and night and even in the middle of the week.

She thought of all these things as she left the main street and saw the churches proudly standing to welcome their believers. The manger scene still placed in the snow in front of the Presbyterian Church made her think of all the hours that Ed had spent whittling away on the creche he made for them for Christmas.

"Sorry, Ed, it just doesn't mean that much to me. Who ever heard of a virgin having a baby?" she wondered out loud and shook her head in disbelief. "I'm certainly no virgin!" She laughed to herself.

As she trudged along toward home, she gathered her coat more tightly around her. The approaching time of her leaving Wheatland, where she was going and why, began to hit her hard. She tried to think of an excuse for not going up to Mother's at 3:00 p.m. *sharp*, but she knew she was trapped. What she didn't know, because she hadn't decided, was whether to tell them the truth and have her tarnished morality and virginity aired like dirty linen in front of them or to have them send her off proudly as the intelligent chemistry professor. They could always find out later about her improprieties. She would have to tell them soon, but she could always write a letter. That was the chicken way out, which stuck in Amanda's craw, but it just seemed easier in this case not to have to witness the reactions of Mother and Margie. There they'd be this afternoon—all three sitting around the dining room table, eating some dried-out concoction that Margie had over-cooked. That was enough to chew up and swallow down without them choking over her announcement!

They were waiting like two hens watching for the farmer's wife to come and gather the eggs. It had been a long morning for Zoe and Margie, and even though they'd been as busy as if they were entertaining folks outside the family, time passed slowly. They wanted everything to be just right on Amanda's last afternoon with them for a long while. Mother helped Margie roll the dining room table out from the wall. Thank goodness it was on little wheels, but it still was a heavy wooden table with intricately designed fretwork underneath.

"Set it with all the good dishes and silverware," Mother ordered, as she went about her business of placing the three chairs they would use and rearranging the fourth one by the east wall.

"Why?" Margie was astounded.

"Because this could be a momentous occasion," Mother retorted.

"Somehow I have my doubts," mumbled Margie. She may not have had exposure to the world like Amanda, nor was she up on all the latest whims and fashions of society, but she had an innate ability to figure people out and not take everything at face value or trust everybody who knocked on the door.

3:00 p.m. arrived promptly on schedule, but Amanda did not. Margie's eyebrows shot up and down at her mother who stood with her back to the stove and her hands on her hips.

Just as Margie was saying at 3:20, "I'm not surprised," they heard the unmistakable wrapping of Amanda's knuckles on the door—five sharp knocks, then a pause, and two more quick raps. She dashed in, as usual in a hurry, and threw her coat over the hook behind the kitchen door. She quickly pulled down her red sweater and then stretched it out in front to cover her increasing waistline.

"Sorry I'm late. I called Belle at the last minute to say 'Good-bye,' and you know how she rattles on."

Oh sure, criticize Belle and blame your tardiness on her, Margie thought, as she stirred the spaghetti sauce. She was going to have trouble being nice to Amanda today, but she really should try to treat her kindly since she was leaving.

Mother motioned for Amanda to sit down in the kitchen. "How is she feeling since her fall?" Mother wondered.

"She's still sore, but you know it takes time for bruises to heal. She says she's feeling better every day, and Ed is a good nurse."

"I doubt that! He can't cook a thing," Mother snorted.

"No, maybe not, but Belle had some things cooked up, so he just has to reheat them, and the ladies from church are running out to help him, too, so they're getting along fine."

"Oh yes, the ladies," Mother said sarcastically.

"So, is dinner ready? I'm famished," she said, as she glanced at the bare kitchen table. "Should I set the table?"

"We're eating in the dining room today," Mother announced with authority. "We're treating you like company—our chemist, going off to teach the world." She wanted to add, "Here's your first opening to tell us what's going on," but nothing more was said, as she ushered Amanda into the dining room.

"You dish up," she ordered Margie, who already had the spaghetti in one bowl and the sauce in another, and was following them into the dining room.

"I'll get the bread. Be right back. Sit here, Amanda." Now Margie was giving directions.

"The table looks elegant, Mother. I feel honored." Actually, she felt a little embarrassed, but they didn't need to know that.

So they began their last dinner together. Amanda commented on the interesting tasting tomato sauce.

"We didn't have much hamburg, so we used a lot of carrots, tomatoes, and onions," Margie tried to explain.

Amanda rolled her eyes. Why did they call it "hamburg?" That's a city in Germany. Was it so hard to put an 'er' on the word? That had always bothered Amanda immensely.

"Actually, it is quite tasty," Amanda had to admit. "This is the best meal I've had since Robert left."

"Will you be eating at the university cafeteria?" Mother quizzed her.

"Oh, I doubt it. You know how awful food is at college. Jen and I will probably do our own cooking most of the time."

Another opening, but it was dropped and Amanda moved on. "I must remember to scribble down Jen's address and phone number for you before I leave."

"Oh yes, we"ll want to correspond to hear all about your classes, the students, boarding with Jen, and you know, all about . . ." Mother hesitated and drew a deep breath.

"What?" Amanda grew alarmed.

"And all about what you hear from Robert," Margie blurted out.

Mother glared across the table. Another chance blown!

The afternoon wore on, the dishes were done and put away, but nothing earth-shaking transpired. Amanda kept looking at her watch. She was anxious to get out of there before it was too late.

Finally she voiced those very words. "Well, I'd better go before it's too late."

"Too late for what?" Margie asked frowning.

"You know, too late. I need to get to bed early tonight. My train leaves at 6:00 a.m."

"Oh, my goodness. So early. I thought we'd be able to see you off, but I suppose we'll have to say 'good-bye' tonight. How are you getting all your suitcases to the station?" Mother looked so worried.

"I don't have that much, but Earl Grayson—you know, Edna's husband—said he'd help me get there. They're so good. They'll keep an eye on my apartment while I'm gone. Of course, it's their apartment anyway," Amanda forced a little laugh. She felt like she was losing control.

Such babbling, Mother was thinking. "Is there anything else we need to know?"

"Oh yes, Jen's address and phone number. Margie, get me a pen and paper," and Margie jumped to the task.

Amanda quickly jotted them down and put the paper on the kitchen table. Grabbing her coat, she said, "Well, I'll write real soon."

"Is that all?" Mother persisted.

"Yes, of course." Amanda looked first at Margie whose eyes were filling with tears and then at her mother. "You take care of each other now," and that was as close to any sentimentality as Amanda could come.

Margie rushed towards her and threw her arms around her. Amanda gently patted Margie on the back and pulled away.

Mother was stoic and immovable, but Amanda knew she was worried.

"Oh, I'll be back before you know it. It will soon be spring, the semester will be over in May, and I'll be home, unless they want to keep me on for summer school," and she was out the door and gone.

"Summer school?" Margie and Mother unified their voices, but it was to a closed door. Margie locked it and secured the dead bolt.

"Do you want a cup of tea, Mother?"

"No, it's too late. Much too late."

If pregnancy were a book,
They'd cut the last two chapters.
—Nora Ephron

Chapter XIV

March blew through the streets and alleys of Wheatland on the coattails of February, and April drip-dropped her spongy rain clouds into puddle-jumping wonders of delight for the younger generation.

Zoe and Margie didn't pay much attention to the weather.

"What can we do about it anyway?" Zoe philosophized, and so they tried to keep busy through the winter and early spring with their mundane daily routines, boring to some, but satisfying to them. Zoe did some crocheting and knitting. She made baby booties and a pretty little yellow sweater, just in case someone might be having a baby.

Margie finally sent in one of her poems, which was accepted and published in the spring edition of *The Poet's Corner Magazine*. She received a five dollar check, but told no one about it. Her dad would be so very proud of her.

They tried not to fret over Amanda or over the war and Robert, but as the dreary days wore on, their storehouse of worries filled to overflowing.

Word came from Belle that Robert had been involved in combat at Iwo Jima in February. He was part of the Fifth Division that took part in the assault. Zoe watched the daily *Spokesman Review* newspaper for news of the war, but Margie was too scared and tried to ignore it, especially when she heard that more than nine thousand men had been killed, wounded, or were missing in action. She knew Robert would be next. She kept hoping that Robert would write again. When he would have had time to write again never entered her mind. After Iwo Jima had been secured, Robert sailed to Hawaii for rest and relaxation and for training for a planned landing on Japanese home islands in the fall.

Then in April came the letter they'd both been waiting for. Amanda had written short notes from time to time about living with Jen and what they'd been doing, but she'd never mentioned her health or her classes.

On the day the letter arrived, Margie flew up the sidewalks and dashed through the alley behind the old Christian Church. She couldn't wait to get home and open the long, white, business envelope that was addressed to them both.

"Sit down, Mother. We've heard from Amanda, and I think it is important. There's no time for tea."

Zoe set the boiling tea kettle back on the stove and settled herself on the kitchen chair.

"It looks very business-like," Margie said, as she examined the envelope.

"Would you please just open it!" Zoe begged.

Margie stood up to read it, as if it were a dramatic reading from her elocution lesson in high school.

Dear Mother and Margie,

I hope you are both together and sitting down when you read this. I have a very serious situation that I need to discuss with you both.

Margie lowered the paper and looked at her mother. "Should I be sitting?"

"Oh, for Pete's sake. Carry on as you are." Mother commanded.

You will no doubt think that I should have told you sooner, but I've had so many decisions to make. Last fall I managed to get pregnant. It can't possibly be Robert's, and so he must never know about this. So, here I am in Iowa. I had to get away and hide. Margie, do you remember when I asked you if you'd ever thought of adopting a baby? I'm sure you've never given that question a moment's worth of thought, but now I'm asking you again. I desperately want to keep the baby in the family. I chose you, Margie, because you have strong family ties, such a gentle spirit, and so much love to give. I know it is unheard of for a single woman and an older woman to adopt, but I've already done some investigating. As you know, Jen's dad is a judge, so he has connections and can pull some strings, and he feels it is possible for you to become an adoptive mother. So what do you think? It will change both your lives dramatically, but you can always count on me, inconspicuously and incognito, of course, to be on the sidelines to encourage, advise, and try to be the best "aunt" that is humanly possible. So, that's my dilemma—blunt and to the point. We can work out all the details, and nobody needs to know. I'll give you a few days to mull this all over. Try not to be upset!

Amanda

Margie nodded her head. "I was right."

Mother shook her head. "This is all wrong," but she knew what Margie's decision would be.

*   *   *

The back-breaking pains of hard labor tore through Amanda in the early hours of July 15. They were much worse than she could have ever imagined they could be, and once again and even more so, she regretted the mess in which she was involved. It was a long labor, and although the ether helped, she could hear a nurse encouraging her to bear down time after time. She never wanted to hear the word *push* again.

Finally at 7:32 a.m., Claire Maria Shaw uttered her first resounding cry. Amanda caught a glimpse of her little pink fists punching at the world, and Amanda knew she would be a fighter. Claire was whisked away to get cleaned up, and Amanda yawned and sighed with great relief. She vowed to herself right then and there that she would never go through that again.

And so it was done; but really it had all just begun. She'd weathered the nine months fairly well, with Jen's help, hidden out, and as far as she knew no one was the wiser. Now the game of hearts had a new player, a novice, as a result of a game that had gone all wrong. But Amanda pledged to herself and to her baby that Claire would be the winner.

Later in the day after most of the effects of the ether had worn off, Amanda summoned Jen to her bedside and helped her compose a short telegram to send home to Wheatland, rather than risk a phone call and have the little birds listening and twittering on the party line.

Mother and Margie received the telegram with trepidation. Margie was sure it was bad news about Robert.

WESTERN UNION

Claire Maria born July 15 *stop* Healthy and beautiful *stop*
Arrive in Spokane 3 weeks *stop*

Amanda

"What a horrible name!" That was Mother's first response. "Can you imagine the nicknames she'll have to endure? De clare, e clare, sin claire."

"Yes, it will have to be changed immediately," Margie agreed. "I've already chosen the name *Katharine Anne.* Do you like it, Mother?"

"Absolutely. They sound regal and elegant. Claire sounds like a man's name. I wonder where in the world she came up with it."

"Oh, well, it's settled. When the adoption papers are drawn up, we'll see that it is changed."

Margie had so many emotions surging through her body, crashing like waves on the ocean beaches. She felt sadness for Amanda for having to give up her baby and sadness for Robert, too, who would never know what his wife had just gone through. He would have wanted a baby, and now maybe Amanda would never give him one. She felt giddy with happiness that she was about to be a mother, but that was coupled with fear. What did she know about babies and rearing a child? She also felt relief, knowing that her mother would be there to help. Yes, motherhood would be the biggest challenge of Margie's life!

*   *   *

The three weeks passed quickly for Margie and Zoe. They made lists of what they would need to welcome the little girl home. Some of what they needed was upstairs and, although Zoe rarely climbed the polished wooden stairs to the second story of the old house, she made the supreme effort to help Margie go through the old trunks and dresser drawers and collect the baby items that had been stored away long ago after Amanda's birth. The smell of moth balls was heavy in the air as each trunk and drawer was opened. They found blankets and nightgowns and one tiny, pink dress, the one Amanda had worn for her christening. The binding on the blankets and the little dress itself were all hand-sewn by Zoe. Two sets of booties, one white and one pink, were tucked away in a corner of the trunk, and in another corner they found several fancy bibs, embroidered by Zoe. There was a stack of cloth diapers in a dresser drawer, but the pile had dwindled down to only a dozen.

"They sure make good cleaning rags. Run and get me a diaper, Margie." Zoe had often instructed Margie when they did major housecleaning before they had the girls in for the bridge club.

In just one trip upstairs they had found more than they could carry back down. Zoe needed her two hands for support on the bannister as she slowly made her way back down, but Margie had it all taken care of in two quick trips.

They washed it all in the kitchen sink, and Margie hung it up to dry on the lines in the basement, because they weren't ready yet to explain it to the neighbors. Their strategy had to be planned in accordance with Amanda's plans for their arrival and the adoption process.

Amanda finally wrote a long detailed letter of how it should all work out, and when the three weeks were up, Zoe and Margie had done everything they could think of to welcome a new baby into their home.

The yellow and orange dahlias under the kitchen window nodded their approval in the gentle August breeze, as Margie dashed down the sidewalk on her way to rev up the green Plymouth for the trip to Spokane.

August 6 was a typical, hot, summer day in Wheatland. Harvest was in full-swing and everyone was busy, so it was a good time to sneak away and act on their secret.

It was all arranged. Zoe and Margie had engaged a suite at the Davenport Hotel, and Amanda, Jennifer, and the baby would meet them there. Amanda had wanted Jennifer to come along to help her on the plane ride, plus they could always pretend it was Jen's baby in case of trouble.

Margie was a nervous wreck and could barely concentrate on her driving. Zoe bit her tongue; she was sure she could do no better. They slowed down for the wheat trucks, but other than that, traffic was light as they headed east on Highway Two.

They arrived about one hour before Amanda, Jen, and the baby, so they had time to settle in and freshen up. They had two bags—one for their own necessities and one full of baby needs.

Finally at 2:30 there was the old familiar knocking on the door, and they knew it was Amanda. Margie unlocked the heavy wooden door and threw it open, but then all she could do was stand there and stare.

From the background, the voice of authority rang out, "Margie, invite them in."

Margie stepped aside, and Amanda bustled in first, full of energy and excitement. She had gained a little weight, but didn't look or act like she'd just recently given birth.

"Well, here we are. You remember Jen?'

"Only from her pictures. You know we've never met her, Amanda," Zoe said, as she shook Jennifer's hand.

"How do you do. I am Zoe, Amanda's mother, and this is her sister, Margie."

"It is so nice to finally meet you. I've heard so much about both of you over the years," Jennifer said rather shyly. She was a blond with blue eyes and a sweet smile. Zoe liked her politeness and genuine demeanor immediately.

"And this is Claire," Amanda interrupted, as she pointed at the little bundle Jen was holding.

Jennifer pulled back the pink blanket, so Zoe and Margie could greet the baby.

"Well, I declare!" Zoe said, as she raised her eyebrows and looked at Margie. The jokes were already starting. Margie smirked, but no one else caught on.

"Do you want to hold her, Margie?' Jen asked, as she held the baby out to her.

"Oh, let's lay her here on the bed first, so we can all admire her at once," Margie was beside herself. She wasn't afraid to hold her, but it was all so sudden and overwhelming; she just needed a little more time.

Amanda was tired from the long trip, so she settled herself on an upholstered chair and let the others get acquainted with the new member of the family.

She was amazed at how quickly she had become attached to Claire, and that she enjoyed caring for her. It would be difficult to hand her over, even though she could soon see her every day.

"Well, what do you think of her?" She interrupted all of their oohs and aahs.

By now, Margie had picked Claire up and was snuggling her close to her breast.

"She's just beautiful, Amanda. She looks like you, but she has Robert's eyes."

"That's impossible, Margie. Don't ever say that again, and don't ask any questions," Amanda snapped at her sister.

"O.K., O.K.," Margie blushed and sat down on the bed.

Zoe tried to smooth the turbulent waters. "Babies just look like themselves for awhile."

The next day the attorney that Jennifer's father had recommended came to the hotel. The paperwork had already been started, and things went smoothly—all except for the name change. Amanda wanted it to be Claire, and she put up a big fight. For once, she didn't win.

On August 8, while Amanda and Jennifer stayed in Spokane for a few days, it was Katharine Anne Wentworth, or Katie, for short, who was sweetly sleeping in the back seat of the car with Grandma Zoe Wentworth by her side.

Where did you come from, baby dear?
Out of the everywhere, into the here.
—George McDonald

Chapter XV

T hree days later the phone rang at Hilda Johnson's in the latter part of the morning. She was tired and moved slowly to answer it. Wash days always wore her out.

"Hilda, it's Zoe."

"Well, hello, I haven't heard from you for days," Hilda said, and she sighed as she settled her big-boned frame on a dining room chair.

"Just busy as usual. Say, I was wondering if you could come over this afternoon; I have something to show you."

Hilda thought for a moment before she answered, "It would really be better if you could come over here. I think I am too tired to walk."

"Oh, please come. It's just down the alley. I MUST show you something," Zoe continued to beg her.

Finally Hilda acquiesced. "All right. I'll take a nap after lunch, and then run over around 2:00 before the kids get home from school."

"Oh, good," Zoe said with more enthusiasm than she'd shown in years, and they said their good byes.

Zoe did not think it wise that Margie take the baby out just yet, and especially not over to Hilda's house. Her home was like a square white package, tucked away in a maze of bending evergreen branches. It even looked like a tiny package. All it needed was a green bow on the top, but instead it was covered by a dull green shingled roof.

Four children, Hilda, and her husband, Ralph, called the little cottage home. No wonder they were a close-knit family; there was barely enough space in the nine-hundred-square-foot home for six people to move from room to room.

A visitor was always greeted warmly by Hilda's bear hug, and by the stifling heat in the little dining room. In summer, the air didn't seem to move, and in the fall and winter, the dull black oil stove overpowered the room as it pumped out heat like a blowtorch. The stuffiness left a person breathless.

The cluttered dining room table was the center of activity. All guests were invited to sit at Hilda's table, but not until a major reshuffling of old newspapers opened up an available seat. The papers bounced from chair to chair, depending upon how many guests had arrived.

Because of her newspaper job, Hilda had an assortment of pens, pencils, papers, phone books, and the phone with an extra long cord, scattered over the oilcloth-covered table. Other items included for easy access were a jar of Mentholatum, a box of tissues, a magnifying glass, scissors, stamps, and other correspondence. These were constantly being reorganized, moved a bit to find a spot for a cup of coffee or, during major cleaning, shifted to another chair.

The newspapers stacked around the dining room were suffocating, yet lent an air of history and knowledge. Hilda knew the news of the past and the present.

The kitchen spoke of antiquity. An old wringer washer was pulled out onto center stage to grind out the dirt on Monday wash day. A golden wicker basket waited patiently on the faded blue and white linoleum for the fragrant clean clothes to fall in heaps, then transported outside to wave in the breeze on the revolving clothesline.

Yellow wooden cupboards teemed with faded chipped plates

and cups and saucers. Often a dish would fall onto the cluttered counter, but it was usually lost among the canning jars, empty Wonder Bread wrappers, and pots and pans. Food was prepared and usually served on smooth slanted bread boards gaping from the counter.

One bathroom served the needs of six people, and the three small bedrooms were filled with teenagers and their belongings. The two boys shared one bedroom, overflowing with trophies, posters, and other things that boys collect. The two girls shared another bedroom. It was more orderly, decorated with ruffles and fluffy pillows. The pink walls were covered with pictures of their current boyfriends and movie stars. The doors were often closed to keep the heat in the busiest part of the house.

The clinging remnant that a visitor wore as he departed Hilda's house was the odor. There was no smell quite like it. Perhaps it was a combination of smells, none really offensive, but pungent and lingering, like walking into a chemistry classroom. A mustiness, the gaseous element of cooked cabbage, mothballs, and wintergreen liniment, gave one's clothes a certain aromatic air that made Zoe always say to Margie, "Oh, you've been to Hilda's house today!"

Yes, Zoe thought it best that the freshly bathed and sweet-smelling baby girl stay at home and not be bounced around town like a rubber ball. Others would want to see her, too, and they could come to the Wentworth home as well.

Margie was reluctant for Hilda to be the first visitor.

"Mother, she's a reporter. Think of the questions she'll ask. Why she, of all people?"

"First and foremost, she is a friend. Now, Margie, we've been over all this a hundred times," Mother admonished her daughter. "We'll say what we're going to be telling people over Katie's entire lifetime. You wanted a baby, and you had a chance to adopt one from Spokane. So don't get all nervous and red in the face; that's all there is to it."

Margie stood up tall and proud. "Oh, I can do it, Mother, but everyone will question how a single woman of my age is able to adopt a baby."

"It's none of their business. I suppose if they persist you can always say that you had a good lawyer."

Hilda appeared as promised promptly at 2:00 p.m. at the Wentworth's back door. All was quiet in the house as Zoe ushered her into the living room, where Margie sat rocking her baby.

"Hello, Margie. What do you have there?" Hilda's blue eyes widened, as she peered into the pink baby blanket that Margie was pulling back out of the way.

She answered her own question, "Oh, it's a little baby. Are you babysitting?" The interrogation had started.

"No, she's mine. I adopted her!" Margie proudly said, grinning from ear to ear.

"Oh, my stars! Zoe, I thought you invited me over to see some sewing or embroidery work you'd done."

Zoe laughed, "Well, she is a work of art."

"She's beautiful. Look at those big brown eyes. She's so alert. How old is she?"

"About three and a half weeks old now. Here, why don't you hold her? Sit right down here in the rocking chair." Margie rose slowly, and as soon as Hilda was seated, she gently placed the little bundle in her arms.

"I just can't believe it. Tell me, how did this all come about?"

Margie began, "Well, it did happen rather suddenly."

Zoe frowned at her. She was all ready deviating from her prepared speech, but she soon got back on track, and when she'd told the bare facts, Hilda was apparently satisfied. All she could say was, "I'm speechless. Can you believe that, coming from me?"

No, they couldn't, but a little laugh from Margie and Zoe was the only answer.

"Won't this make front page news?" The reporter had arrived for work.

"Oh no, not just yet, Hilda. Just give it a little time," Zoe tried to stifle the inevitable article, as she would every time Hilda would bring it up in the future.

"This is breaking news; but, of course, I would write it up as a feature article." Hilda obviously had it all planned out.

Margie came to her own defense. "Please, Hilda, like Mother said, we all need some time to adjust. I really just wish you'd keep it under your blotter, and let us announce it in our own time. Then maybe some day you can write that article."

Hilda said she'd try to contain herself, but Zoe and Margie both wondered who she'd call first when she got home.

"Won't Amanda be surprised? Does she know?" Hilda continued her questions.

"Oh, yes, it came as a shock to her as well, but she's happy for me. She'll be home from teaching next week, you know." As far as Margie was concerned, that subject was closed.

Katie came to the rescue of them all, as she squirmed and started to cry, and Hilda quickly handed her back to Margie. Hilda glanced at the clock on the wall over the radio.

"As much as I hate to leave, I'd better go before the kids get home. I just can't believe it, Margie. I am so happy for you. I will keep your little secret."

She gave Margie a quick hug, kissed Katie on the forehead, and was gone.

As Zoe and Margie walked into the kitchen to warm up a bottle, Zoe solemnly stated, "The news is out."

* * *

While in Spokane for five more days, Amanda and Jennifer were fortunate not to encounter anyone from Wheatland. They left the downtown area and found a cheap motel with a kitchenette on North Division, spending their time at the movies, riding the streetcars when Amanda felt up to it, and visiting Elaine Davis, Amanda's college friend. They got caught up on all the news, their teaching jobs, and their families, with one exception—Amanda's own little secret.

Jen flew back to Iowa on August 12, and Amanda returned home by bus to Wheatland the same day. She had sent most of her belongings back in the car with Mother and Margie, so was traveling lightly.

Her arrival back in Wheatland received little fanfare, which pleased her. She literally snuck into her apartment, locked the door, and collapsed on the sofa. All the fears and worries of the past ten months seemed to flood from her body in a wonderful freeing, cleansing relief. She rested her head on the back of the sofa. A nap would have been welcome, but a longing that had burned in her heart for five long days had to be fulfilled.

"I must see my baby."

So it's home again, and home again
America for me.
My heart is turning home again, and
There I long to be.

—Henry Van Dyke

Chapter XVI

A low steel-gray sky hung over Eastern Washington when Captain Robert Shaw returned home to Wheatland in late October. The naked locust and maple trees were stripped of their leaves, and the town looked dull and drab to the average person, but home had never looked more beautiful to Robert. He'd seen the bloody horrors of Iwo Jima and fought in the final great land battle of the Pacific—the invasion of Okinawa. In June, organized resistance on Okinawa had ended, and the first conquest of Japanese soil was completed.

Then Robert had been shipped back to Hawaii to prepare for the Japanese battle. Finally, it was all over, and on September 12, 1945, Japan surrendered. The 6th Marine Division, which included Robert, was sent to help disarm and repatriate the Japanese occupation forces in China.

Captain Shaw arrived at Camp Pendleton on October 15, 1945 and transferred from active duty to the Inactive Reserves. From there he went home.

He had no knowledge of all that had gone on with Amanda and Margie while he was away, but when Amanda met him in Spokane, he could tell that she had changed. Perhaps she had matured from living on her own or from teaching college students.

He couldn't pinpoint it, but he liked what he saw. She'd gained a little weight, and her brown bobbed hair was shorter, but she was still his Mandy. They clung to each other on the bus ride home and shut the rest of the world out. He didn't even notify his parents of his arrival.

Amanda thought he seemed different, too. He was much thinner, and his hair was turning gray. He was even more serious and somewhat nervous, but perhaps war did that to a person. The wind picked up in the night, and a tree branch repeatedly scratched across the screen of their bedroom window. Amanda was used to it, but Robert awakened with a start and sat straight up in bed, then was awake for hours. The war with all its sounds stayed with him and would haunt him for years.

It was strange, in a way, having him home. Although they'd written each other at every opportunity, they both had their little secrets. Robert would never forget the letter he'd written to Margie, and now he'd have to face her for the first time not knowing what her reaction had been or how she'd respond to him.

Just as he was thinking of her, Amanda piped up. "Robert, I can't wait for you to see Margie. She has quite a surprise for you!" He nearly choked on his mouthful of morning coffee.

"Oh, yeah? Tell me what it is."

"I can't. Then it wouldn't be a surprise, and she wants to tell you herself."

Robert pondered for a moment, "Hmmm . . . has she found herself a boy friend? Is she getting married?" Oh, how he hoped this was it!

"I can't tell you," Amanda teased with a sing-song lilt to her voice.

"Yeah, I bet that's it; she's finally found a beau."

"You can guess all day, but we'll just have to run up there so you can see for yourself."

Robert frowned, and there were deep furrows between his eyebrows that had never been there before. "Well, I really want to see Mom and Dad first."

"Oh, well, sure. You should," Amanda agreed. "We'll run out and see them and then stop by Mother's on the way home." She really wanted to be with him to see his reaction to Margie's little surprise package.

Robert had made Mandy promise that she wouldn't tell his folks when he was coming home, so when his old pickup rattled down the lane, Belle just thought it was Amanda coming to call. That in itself would have been a surprise, but when she came out on the porch and saw Robert, she put her hands over her heart, said a quiet "Praise the Lord," then in her loudest voice, she yelled at Ed, who was fast asleep on the couch, "Edward, get out here—quick!"

The homecoming was wonderful. Robert didn't want to talk much about the war, so they sat and listened to Ed talk about the farm, how harvest went, the yields of wheat, and all the help he had to hire.

"I'm so glad you are home, Son. Now I can think about retiring pretty soon," Ed said, with a tired voice and a weary look in his eyes. He, too, was thinner, and his hair was as white as the snow on the ridge beyond the barn.

"We'll talk about it, Dad. That's for sure." Robert assured him.

Then Belle regaled them with stories of her volunteer work and church activities. She had an entertaining way about her that made it all interesting and funny, but she never put anybody down or talked at the expense of hurting a person.

They stayed for lunch and into the afternoon. Robert hated to tear himself away. He had missed not only his folks, but the farm as well. He and his dad went out to the barn for awhile.

They finally left around 2:45. Belle didn't want to let him go. She held on to him for dear life.

"It's all right, Mom. I'm home, and I'm fine," he assured her.

"We need to stop and see Mother and Margie and . . ." Amanda explained.

"Oh, does he know the news?" Belle interrupted.

"No, it's a surprise. Now don't tell him," Amanda begged.

"I won't, but, oh Robert, you are going to be so surprised." Belle could hardly contain herself, her short little round body shaking with excitement.

"Well, let's go then," Robert said, as he opened the passenger door for Amanda and playfully swatted her on the rear as she got in.

On the way down the hill into town, Robert had a surprise for Amanda, too.

"Dad and I had quite a heart-to-heart talk out in the barn, Mandy. He really thinks it's time he gives up the farm."

"What do you mean 'give up the farm'?" Amanda inquired. "Do you mean sell it?"

"Oh, no, he'd never sell it. He wants me to take it over, which was always the plan; but he wants me to do it now. He's so tired, and Mom is worried about him. She wants him to go to the doctor, but he won't. He just thinks age has caught up with him and that he's been working too hard."

"That's probably it," Amanda said nonchalantly. She had other things on her mind.

Robert caught her blithe attitude. "This is serious, Amanda. They want to move to town, and we'll move out to the farmhouse. In fact, they could take over our apartment. We'll just switch places."

Amanda knew this was eventually coming, but so soon? Robert had just gotten home. The life on a farm was not what she wanted. It never had been and never would be, and although the possibility existed when they married, it seemed like a long time off, and the idea had been placed on the back burner. She'd worry about it when the time came. Now it had come.

Looking out the window as they passed the cemetery, she didn't answer. Moving clear out there now wouldn't work; she had to be near her daughter.

"What are your thoughts?" Robert persisted.

"Oh, Robert. We couldn't do that now; I just signed another year's lease on the apartment."

Robert mused to himself, I thought the war was over; am I entering another battle? He shut off the engine at the Wentworth house. Amanda grabbed his hand, as they walked around the south side of her mother's home. "It will all work out," she assured him." At least to my satisfaction, she added silently.

Zoe greeted them at the back door with no animation or surprise. Amanda had told Mother and Margie that he was coming home.

"Come on in. Margie is downtown. Let's sit in the living room." She was blunt and unemotional, as usual, and hoped Katie, who was asleep in a bassinet in her bedroom, wouldn't wake up until Margie got home. During the day Katie slept downstairs in Grandma Zoe's bedroom because it was handy, and at night she slept upstairs in Margie's room in a crib. It wasn't the best arrangement, but it worked, and there was no way that Zoe could handle the stairs morning and night if they switched bedrooms.

"Well, how are you, Robert? I bet you are glad to get home." Zoe broke the ice and showed some interest after all. Somebody had to say something.

"I'm O.K. It will just take a little time to adjust and get back to a normal life."

They talked for a few minutes about the weather and about what had been going on in Wheatland, and then they heard footsteps on the back porch. Margie had finally arrived with the mail.

Robert, always the gentleman, stood up when Margie entered the living room. Running to him and throwing her arms around him, she held him longer than she should have.

"I'm so glad you're home, Robert. Are you all right?" She finally let him go.

"Oh sure. I'm fine. I'm a tough old Marine, you know."

Margie grabbed his arm. "Before you sit down again, come on in the bedroom. I want to show you something. It's a surprise."

The bedroom? Why the bedroom? That blew away his idea that she had a boyfriend. He wouldn't be hiding out in the bedroom! Robert wasn't sure he should even go in a bedroom with Margie, but with Amanda and Zoe in the next room, there couldn't be anything immoral about it.

The bedroom door was slightly ajar, and as Margie pushed it open, she put her forefinger to her lips. "Shhh . . . She's sleeping."

At the foot of Zoe's bed was the white wicker bassinet. Katie was wide awake, just lying there looking around. She'd grown so fast in three months that she'd nearly outgrown her daytime sleeping quarters.

"Robert, this is Katie. I adopted her," she blurted out.

Robert was speechless, but Margie had plenty to say.

"Isn't she beautiful? She's three months old. Actually her real name is Katharine Anne."

She picked up Katie and kissed her on the forehead. "Would you like to hold her?"

Robert had no say in the matter, as she quickly held out Katie to him. He still hadn't spoken, but he really hadn't had a chance.

"Wow! This is a total surprise. How did it all come about?" He finally found an opening.

"Oh, it's a long story. I'll tell you all about it some day. Come on. Let's go out and join the others," and she took hold of his elbow and escorted him out the door and into the hallway.

"Look what I found, Mandy. This must have been the surprise you kept from me."

Amanda was grinning from ear to ear. "Yes, she's the surprise, all right." Amanda looked at her mother and Margie. They both looked very wise. Mother raised her eyebrows, and Margie left the room to heat a bottle.

When she returned, as he handed Katie over to her adoptive mother, Robert had a surprise, too.

"You know, Mandy, Katie's nearly outgrown her bassinet. Why don't we get her a crib as a baby gift?"

Nobody said a word.

"It's a wonderful idea, Robert. I wish I'd thought of it myself," Amanda finally said with enthusiasm. He didn't need to know that she'd purchased the brand new crib that Katie slept in every night upstairs.

Every man, as the saying goes,
Can tame a shrew, but he that
Hath her.

—Robert Burton

Chapter XVII

During harvest each summer and into the fall, the grain elevators and the mill were the busiest establishments in Wheatland, but the rumor mill was even more busy after Katie became Margie's adopted daughter. Questions were bouncing off the telephone lines, and those ladies who had rarely gossiped before, thinking that gossip was a sin, joined the ranks of the seasoned professionals. Of course, as Mildred Reynolds, a farmer's wife, would say. "I'm not nosy; I'm just interested."

Why would Margie adopt a baby and at her age? How was it even possible? Where did the baby come from? Even Amanda was under suspicion; but no, they all knew that she had gone away to teach. How would this child turn out with no father in the home and with two older ladies rearing her?

The gossip had just started to ease when Sara and Jess Fosberg adopted Elizabeth Anne. That was a more normal situation, so there wasn't really all that much to question, plus there were three other couples in town who adopted babies in the coming months, but the focus of interest kept coming back to little Katie.

"She is so precocious," praised the high school English teacher and librarian. Margie thought so, too, but this scholarly opinion sealed it as the gospel truth in her mind.

"She's such a happy child," observed Belle, as Katie grinned, deepening the dimples in her chubby cheeks into caverns. Belle wondered if she'd ever be blessed by a baby from Amanda and Robert. She doubted it, considering their ages and Amanda's other interests.

"There will never be a more loved child in this town," announced Margie, as she proudly reveled in these and other compliments, as if she had produced this prize herself. She didn't know or really care if Amanda heard any of the praise. This was *her* baby!

Grandma Zoe helped as much as she was needed. On election day both in September for the primary and in November for the general election, when Margie served on the board, Zoe had full charge. They were long days. Amanda made sure that she was available and "on call" to come to assist. When she hadn't heard anything from her mother by late afternoon on the November election day, she couldn't stand it any longer and popped in anyway.

"Is everything all right?" She quizzed her mother, who was changing a diaper with expert skill.

"Well, of course, why wouldn't it be?" snapped Mother. "I'm perfectly capable. After all, I reared three daughters, didn't I?"

"Well, yeah, but that was years ago, and don't forget the trouble you had with Camille. She escaped at an early age, and even now we never hear from her."

"Just be still, Amanda, about Camille. Her leaving home and going to Canada is a closed subject. We don't speak of her around here, and we're not going to argue in front of a child. This conversation is over!"

"It's always over." Amanda ended it by walking out and slamming the back door. I should have just moved out to the farm with Robert and slopped the pigs! But, of course, she didn't really mean that.

Belle and Ed had moved into town and were happy to get settled in a small two bedroom house on the south hill before winter set in. The living arrangement that Robert had hoped for was not in the cards. Amanda insisted on keeping the apartment, and Robert decided to live with the hand that was dealt him. A part-time wife was better than no wife at all.

Ed missed the farm and drove out a couple of times a week. He didn't need to keep an eye on Robert who was perfectly capable of maintaining it all. Ed trusted him implicitly to make the right decisions and to keep everything in good working order. Ed just needed to smell the hay on occasion and wander through the barn. It was like a tonic for his tired blood, and he needed it.

Belle absolutely loved living in town. She could visit more often with her friends and became even more involved in helping others, bustling from one church activity to another and helping at the school and the nursing home.

When she was volunteering at the school, she often ran into and sometimes even worked with Amanda, who was substituting in both the grade and high school. Belle could not understand how Amanda could leave Robert out there on the farm and spend so much time in town, but they tried to put the tension between them aside when they were thrown together in the classroom. Belle admired Amanda's teaching capabilities, even if she couldn't accept her lack of responsibilities as a wife to Robert.

Amanda decided that she should buy a car, and Robert was all for it, thinking that then she could drive out to the farm more often. As it was, he had to come to get her and take her back into town and, if she spent the night, she'd have to wait until he'd done the morning chores before he could drive her in. The few times that she'd kept the pickup in town hadn't worked out at all. He needed it and couldn't find her.

Amanda wanted a new car, but she finally settled on a used one that Dr. Baker had for sale. His wife had just driven it around town, so it had low mileage and had been treated well.

"It's fine," Amanda gave in, as Robert wrote out the check for Dr. Baker. She didn't really like the Army green color, but then decided she really didn't care what it looked like, if it would get her to the school, up to see the baby, out to the farm when Robert begged her to come, and into Spokane.

In her mind, their marriage situation was perfect. The freedom to come and go and do as she pleased made her happy and independent, and yet the warmth and love that Robert had for her was just a few minutes away at the farmhouse. She knew that most men would not put up with it, but Robert was a special guy. So it was the best of both worlds for Amanda.

Not so for Robert. He wanted a full-time wife and wondered why Amanda would spend so much time away in her own little world if she truly loved him as much as she said. It was a strange arrangement, which gave the folk in town another subject for gossip. Even Hilda, who thought she knew that whole family inside and out, could not understand it. As desperate as she was for news sometimes, she just couldn't write about their get-togethers.

Mrs. Robert Shaw drove out to the family farm late Friday afternoon. She spent the weekend with her husband and returned to Wheatland Monday morning.

No, that wouldn't sound quite right in the society column. To fill up space, she'd have to lengthen the blurb on the bridge club or enlarge the paragraphs on the trip to Spokane that Sara and Jess took for Elizabeth Anne to see the pediatrician.

Zoe and Margie were both baffled by Amanda's staying in town, but they had differing opinions on the subject. Zoe was more logical in her thinking, while Margie was guided by her feelings, emotions, and hidden, undying love for Robert. When the discussion first came up, they both agreed they couldn't understand how Amanda could do this to Robert, but, as time went by, and from all outward appearances it was working for them, Zoe and Margie argued about it more than just accepting it.

"Her marriage to him is just a sham. She always has to have everything she wants and do things her own way. I feel so sorry for Robert," Margie's heart was almost on her sleeve, and tears were in her eyes.

"Just calm down now, Margie. You know how she is. She always has been like that—a free spirit, and no one, not even I, can tame or dominate her, although I do think Robert could have more backbone. It seems to be working, though. They both seem happy to me." Zoe was decisive with her rebuttal.

Margie's feelings could not be changed. "He needs a full-time wife. Do you ever see them together? Oh, well, you wouldn't because you seldom go out, but I've never heard of them doing anything together."

"We don't know what goes on behind closed doors, Margie. The walls can't talk, so we just have to assume their arrangement satisfies them."

Margie was still not convinced that Robert was happy and, secretly, she hoped he wasn't.

She didn't have as much time to daydream now that she was a mother, but late at night when the last diaper had been changed, and Katie was asleep in her crib, Margie imagined that Robert would some day get so lonely that she and he could get together. She and Katie would move out to the farm in a heartbeat. Zoe could come too, although Margie knew that her mother would never leave her home. She pushed the thought aside that then Robert would be a father to his ex-wife's child, but they would be blissfully happy, and he would never know the truth. She entertained the idea that Amanda would then have a lot less contact with Katie; she just couldn't run out to the farm and interfere and criticize and hover over Katie like she was doing now. If Amanda saw Katie, it would have to be in town. It seemed all possible and plausible at night when Margie was imagining it could happen, but by light of day she knew it would never happen.

*   *   *

When Christmas rolled around, Amanda put on a big show and invited everyone in the family out to the Shaw farmhouse for gifts and dinner on Christmas day. She went all out with decorations, which she found in the basement. Belle had left them, and she encouraged her to use them. She wouldn't be doing much decorating any more. Their little house was too small to entertain a crowd. Belle did miss that part of living in town in a little "crackerbox," as she called it.

Everyone's motives for having a family Christmas together were different. Belle and Ed were happy to have the whole family at the farm where they'd spent so many happy years and holidays. It was a homecoming for them.

Robert was elated that Amanda was finally showing an interest in homemaking and strengthening family ties. She and Belle planned the menu and even the seating arrangement at the dining room table together. Now that was progress! Of course, Robert wouldn't think of spending Christmas without his mom and dad, so he was a happy man.

Amanda even got Michael's address from Belle and wrote him a quick note of invitation. She thought if she did the inviting, maybe he would come, but at the last minute he had an excuse. He and his buddies were going on a ski trip.

Even though she would understand none of it or even remember it down through the years, Katie deserved to have a special first Christmas, Amanda told herself.

Margie was thrilled to be going out to Robert's. She was tired of spending every Christmas year after year at home, and to be in Robert's home on that very special day would be like being in heaven.

Zoe was the only one who lacked enthusiasm. "Why all the fuss? Can't we just stay home like we always do? We'll have to pack up all the baby things, and then how will we get there? If it snows, Margie, you know very well you can't drive clear out there." Everything was negative.

Margie begged and pleaded and worked out all the details. When the big day arrived, snow-free, Belle and Ed picked them up around noon, and they all rode out together. Zoe decided to tolerate all the hullabaloo, and it turned out to be a wonderful day for them all. Without the war that had hung over their heads last year, they were relaxed and happy, and even Zoe got into the spirit as much as she would allow her stoic self to feel and interact.

Katie enjoyed the bright lights of the Christmas tree and clutched the soft brown teddy bear that Amanda and Robert had given her, but she was oblivious to the undercurrent of emotions that circulated throughout the farmhouse. She napped in the spare bedroom, where Margie went to check on her. Robert followed her into the bedroom, and together they gazed down at the little girl sleeping on the bed surrounded by big pillows.

Robert slipped his arm around Margie's waist but abruptly withdrew it.

"You look especially beautiful today, Margie. I think motherhood agrees with you, and that red dress really looks pretty on you."

Margie could have melted into his arms like a pool of butter. "Oh, yeah, well, um, I borrowed it from Amanda, but just for today. It's the one you gave her last year for Christmas."

"I thought it looked familiar. It looks even better on you than it did on Mandy. I thought it was a little tight on her," he added.

Just then Belle announced dinner. Margie didn't know if she'd be able to eat a bite. Her face was flushed, and her mother looked at her with raised eyebrows.

After dinner, Ed suggested a game of cards, but the women wanted to clean up the kitchen first. As Zoe and Margie cleared away the dessert dishes from the dining room table, Zoe muttered under her breath, "No need to sit around a card table; we've been playing the game of hearts all afternoon."

Who ran to help me when I fell,
And would some pretty story tell,
Or kiss the place to make it well?
My mother.

—Ann Taylor

Chapter XVIII

The next big celebration in Katie's life was her first birthday. Zoe thought they should celebrate on the Fourth of July and get the excitement over with all at once. Margie looked at her mother as if she were crazy.

"Why, I've been planning this for weeks in my mind, Mother. She needs to celebrate on her own natal day." Actually there wasn't all that much preparation. It was mostly a family affair, but Margie did mail invitations to Elizabeth and her mother, Sara; Dottie and her twins; and to Hilda. Hilda's children were teenagers, and Margie knew they wouldn't be interested in sitting around with some little kids and older ladies.

Margie wanted Katie to look just perfect on her birthday, but then Katie always did. She looked like a yellow jonquil in the pretty little yellow dress that Margie had found at Owen's Specialty Shop in Spokane.

Margie wanted the cake and presents to be special, too, and knew Amanda would want the same. She felt so threatened and intimidated by Amanda—even more so now than before. She knew that even though she was older than Amanda, she walked in Amanda's shadow, in the penumbra of the one who was always right and perfect and smarter and more ambitious, or at least that's the image that Amanda wanted to present.

Ha, Margie often laughed to herself. *She wasn't so perfect; she made a big mistake, and now it's to my benefit,* and she'd gaze at little Katie with all the love and adoration as if she'd carried her for nine months and suffered the labor pains herself. *Amanda can live in my shadow now. All she can ever be to Katie is an aunt,* Margie mused, as she cleaned up the cake plates and silverware after the party.

Two days later, Katie took her first steps. She was soon waddling around the living room on unsteady chubby legs, often falling but getting right up again. She usually laughed about it all, but it scared Margie to see her fall. Zoe brushed it off as normal and necessary for her maturity.

"If she gets hurt, you can kiss it and make it well, Margie." Zoe was matter-of-fact. "Just wait until she goes outside and wants to run. She'll be chasing the chickens in the pen."

Margie dreaded to even think about those days. She didn't chase the chickens, but as the years progressed, she did want to run. Elizabeth liked horses, and when the girls played together, Elizabeth pretended that Katie and she were horses. She'd run and whinny and bob her head up and down.

"Come on. Let's run and gallop," Elizabeth begged Katie.

"I can't run. I'm not allowed to." Katie was almost in tears. She marched to the back door of Elizabeth's house and knocked on the woodwork around the screen. Sara soon appeared, and she could tell something was wrong.

"What's the matter, dear? Isn't Elizabeth sharing?"

"She's sharing, but she wants to run, and I'm not s'pose to, so I have to go home now." Katie's brown eyes were sad, and she looked up into Sara's big brown eyes, which were orbs of sadness, too.

"Maybe you girls should come in the house and play with the dolls." Sara advised.

"No, I have to go home," Katie insisted, and away she went,

walking slowly across the street with her head down. Sara watched her from the kitchen window to make sure she got home all right.

"They're smothering her, Jess," she said to her husband. "They won't even let her run."

Jess was a man of few words, so he just nodded in agreement, as he could see it, too.

Amanda, too, thought Katie was over-protected and smothered, but she couldn't see that she herself contributed to the problem, just advising and watching from a distance. She tried not to over-indulge or spoil Katie with gifts, but it was a rare occasion when Amanda didn't return home from Spokane with the newest book on the market from John W. Graham's book department or a little outfit from the Crescent Department Store.

Margie objected. There was that shadow again. It wasn't as if she couldn't buy for Katie; she had some inheritance from her dad, but she just didn't see the sense in giving her more than she needed. She wasn't even in school yet, so all she really needed were some play clothes, one good dress for Sunday School and parties, and two pairs of shoes—the serviceable corrective brown shoes and the white high-tops for dress-up occasions.

Katie hated the brown shoes, even before she was old enough to realize they weren't fashionable. Mommy tried to explain to her that they were *special* shoes. They were good for her feet, just like the stewed prunes were good to keep her regular and the cod liver oil kept her healthy. Those were all bad things in Katie's eyes. "But Lizbeth doesn't have to wear ugly shoes."

"No, she doesn't, because her feet are not as special as yours, and you need really good shoes."

Margie didn't want to use the word *deformed* because Katie's feet weren't that bad. She just had very narrow feet, high arches, and her big toes were long and very crooked.

Except for being fitted for the ugly brown shoes, Katie enjoyed going to the shoe store in Spokane. The people were so nice there. Berg's Junior Shoes was just across the street from the Davenport Hotel, so Zoe, Margie, and Katie often made a vacation out of a shopping trip and spent the night in the grand old hotel. She'd leave with a balloon and a pencil and those ugly brown shoes. If she'd outgrown her white ones, she'd get a new pair of those too, but that was O.K. She loved those shoes, and now at four years old, she was observant enough to notice that the other little girls at Sunday School wore either white high-tops or black patent leather shoes with straps.

"I'll never get to wear those black shiny shoes," she thought, and she knew better than to ask. "My feet are too special!" But she didn't feel special; she felt very different from her friends.

Even though Katie was raised differently in the eyes of many, she was a typical little child in many ways. She had to learn not to repeat everything she heard. One day she told Hilda what she had heard at home about Laura, Hilda's oldest daughter.

"Mommy said that Laura had on the dirtiest pair of white shoes she'd ever seen!"

Hilda's nose was understandably out of joint at first, but when she told Margie and later learned that Katie had been reprimanded, she forgave both Margie for saying it, and Katie for repeating it. She rationalized it by thinking that at least Laura got to have fun and if she got a little speck of dirt on herself along the way, so what? Margie was just too fussy!

Katie wanted to ask Hilda why she called those little red vegetables in her garden r*edishes* instead of *radishes*, but after the scolding over the dirty white shoes, she decided to ask Mommy instead.

"I guess because they are red, but I am glad you know the right way to say it," praised Margie.

Speaking correctly and having impeccable manners were of great importance to Margie. Katie was taught to shake hands when she met a new acquaintance and to say, "How do you do?" When they'd stop by on rare occasions to visit someone, and especially at Mrs. O'Reilly's, the local banker's wife, Katie sat prim and proper on the flowered damask couch with her legs and feet together and her hands folded in her lap like a lady. Mrs. O'Reilly was always all gussied up and her house was immaculate with fine china and figurines sitting around. Zoe called them "dust collectors," but Katie thought they were beautiful.

Katie never said a word unless she was spoken to first. When she was offered a glass of milk or lemonade and a cookie, she always said, "Please" and "Thank you" without having to be prompted. She looked like Shirley Temple with her curls and dimpled cheeks, and she had that mischievous twinkle in her eyes, even though her demeanor was calm and polite.

Katie had limited contact with the world outside of the Wentworth home. Those that did come calling on rare occasions came to see Zoe and were in her age bracket, or there were funny little old men who came to do odd jobs in the yard or garden. But those were exciting times for Katie. She looked forward to the weekly grocery deliveries from Hudson's Grocery.

Blanche Hudson herself carried in the brown bags of food and paper products. She always looked tired and frazzled, but she'd take a few minutes to visit. She had six children at home, so she always had stories to tell. Katie sat on a kitchen chair, her big brown eyes roaming from Grandma Zoe to Mommy to Mrs. Hudson, trying to take it all in and understand their conversations. Unless they needed a plumber or a painter the only man other than family who they let in the kitchen was Peter Mathias. He farmed Zoe's quarter section of wheat south of town for her. He would arrive now and then with important-looking papers in an envelope. He'd talk about parity and yields and affidavits, and Katie sat and listened and wondered what all those big words could possibly mean. Zoe would sign the papers, and he'd be on his way. It seemed very official, and Katie felt like she'd been a part of an important transaction.

The other men who came to work never entered the back door. Zoe took care of instructing them on their duties outside, and when they were finished, she "settled up" with them, as she called it, and paid them on the back porch.

Katie watched from the window or, if Margie was outside to keep an eye on them, she could go out, too, and watch them more closely. They were interesting characters, all unique in their own way. When one of them had worked and gone home, Katie would think about that person for hours. Why did Ted Landers, who came to fix the fence and the chicken coop, always wear that red bandanna around his neck? He seemed ancient. Billy Jording used the old push mower to cut the grass. He drove an old green truck, wore coveralls, and had a big bushy white moustache. Katie wondered if he ever took a bath, as he didn't look or smell too clean. Grandma said he probably bathed in the lake once a month!

One day Billy brought a bobcat that he had shot down near Lake Roosevelt. He hauled it out of his truck and stretched it out on the lawn, so Katie could see how big it was. Margie took pictures of Katie and Billy and the bobcat. She wasn't scared of it; she just thought it was a big cat, and its name was Bob. Later she told Grandma that Bob the cat smelled as bad as Billy.

In late July, just after Katie turned five, a man came highly recommended to assess the state of the roof and the chimney on the Wentworth house. Katie never did know what his name was, but she called him Mr. Chimbley. He was short and fat and always wore nice clothes, but they were too tight for him. The buttons nearly popped off his white shirt, his tie was loose at the neck, and his belly hung over his gray dress slacks. He wore a straw hat on his head and beads of perspiration arose on his forehead and trickled down his rosy cheeks. He'd lean back on his wing-tip shoes and look up at the roof until Katie was sure he would fall over backwards.

"Now your chimbley is cracked," he said, after conferring with a younger man in work clothes who had scampered up and down a ladder to make inspections on the roof. "We really need to replace your chimbley as well as the roof." Zoe didn't know if she could trust anyone who didn't even know how to pronounce the word, but his firm had done other repairs around the town, so she finally hired him to replace the roof and the chimney. Katie was glad to hear he himself would return when the job was completed by his workmen; she just wanted to hear him say "chimbley" one more time, and see what would happen if he really did fall over backwards.

*   *   *

Katie's world changed dramatically when she entered kindergarten and finally was with people her own age. Twenty-three little balls of fire met mornings, five days a week, with their teacher, Mrs. Spencer, and a couple of volunteer mothers.

Katie loved kindergarten, once she got in the door. Quite often a big, friendly, collie dog who lived in the neighborhood was there, panting outside the heavy door of the old church building, where the kindergarten class was held. She was deathly afraid of dogs and all his kissing and tail-wagging panicked her, and unless someone was at the door to let her in, she ran all the way home—all of one block. She still wasn't allowed to run, but that was an emergency.

It was in kindergarten that she met her first boy friend, Rusty Harrison. He was the cutest boy in the class with long eyelashes and greenish-brown eyes that danced and sparkled when he looked at Katie. He had a crewcut and always wore blue jeans and a red and blue striped tee shirt. Oh, he was cute, and whenever he was in the neighborhood visiting his grandma, he would come over to play with Katie.

One day they decided to take a short walk together. They walked north up the road past the west side of Elizabeth's house and then darted through the weeds behind her garage. All of a sudden, Rusty came up real close to Katie and kissed her on the lips. It scared her, and she didn't tell anyone for years. From then on, though, she knew that she loved him, and the next year in first grade they made special Valentines at school for each other. They had learned to write "I love you," and they each printed it in their best penmanship. They didn't put their Valentines to each other in the Valentine shoe boxes that they'd decorated to hold all the cards, but they secretly handed them to each other after school on the playground.

Katie was sent to the principal's office several times when she was in the first grade. It was the most humiliating thing she'd ever experienced, followed secondly by being sent to the cloak room the same year. She felt that none of the infractions were really her fault. If she wouldn't have had to sit and eat either stewed prunes or sour rhubarb every morning for breakfast with her mother hovering over her, she wouldn't have dawdled over her food and would have been on time.

Facing Mr. Hale, the Principal, scared Katie even more than the ghosts she knew flew around her bedroom at night. Mr. Hale was short and stocky, looked like a bulldog, and hardly ever smiled. Katie was in tears every time he talked to her. She tried to explain that she didn't think she was such a bad little girl; she just didn't like her breakfast, and it made her late. Finally Mr. Hale and Margie worked it out; if she insisted that Katie eat that fruit every morning, then perhaps Katie should get up about twenty minutes earlier. Mr. Hale almost gagged when he thought of that poor little child choking down stewed prunes almost every day. The solution worked out fairly well, though, and Katie was not late again.

One morning Katie's teacher, Mrs. Pope, asked the students to put their crayons and pictures away, as she was going to read them a story. Katie didn't comply, although she always had before. She decided on the spur of the moment that she could continue coloring and listen to the story at the same time. That was a major infraction of disobedience, so off she went to the cloakroom to contemplate her naughtiness. She thought it was better punishment than going to see Mr. Hale until she saw a familiar face enter the classroom.

"Oh, no, there's Mary Jane," Katie thought to herself, as she peeked out the door. She was the older sister of Katie's classmate and friend, Jill, and if Mary Jane saw her sitting there in trouble, she would be so embarrassed. That was one of the big words she'd just learned and now she knew it applied to her. That was one of her worst days in first grade.

*   *   *

Katie's worst day in second grade was when Elizabeth and her parents moved to Spokane. Margie, too, was devastated, as she and Sara had become close friends. They got together on the last day and sat amid boxes in Sara's living room and cried and cried. Sara did not want to leave Wheatland, but a lucrative job offer called Jess to Spokane.

Elizabeth and Katie walked home hand in hand on Elizabeth's last school day. Who would help Katie watch for cars when they crossed Main Street, and who would chase off Phillip Minor when he tried to run over the little girls with his bicycle?

Zoe couldn't understand why anyone would move for any reason. She planned to stay in her home in Wheatland until her dying day. She hated to see them go, but not a tear was shed; she told Katie and Margie that they could always look them up when in Spokane.

Katie and her mommy cried together the next day when they sat on the front porch and watched the moving trucks pull out. Jess waved like he used to do every day when he'd drive by in his green pickup. Katie could barely see him that final time through all her tears.

Pride, envy, and avarice
Are the three sparks that have
Set these hearts on fire.
                    —Dante

Chapter XIX

Camille Rose, the oldest of the three Wentworth girls, left Wheatland in 1913 at the young age of nineteen, and no one in the town, except for the family, really knew why. Speculation ran rampant through the town that she'd gotten herself in "a family way," while others thought she'd gone off to New York to study art.

The train of thought of her body being marred and strained by a pregnancy was way off track. That would ruin not only her body, but her pride. She'd never had any desire to have some "snotty nosed kids," as she called them, hanging on to her coattails.

There was a grain of truth in the second idea. Actually she'd gone to Canada to study art with Pierre Le Deux, a great French artist.

Camille and Zoe had never gotten along. Even as a baby, Camille and her mother were at odds. Camille wouldn't nurse, and she screamed when Zoe changed her diapers or clothed her. Being a new mother, Zoe thought that maybe her techniques were all wrong. Perhaps the diapers were too rough on her baby's delicate skin, or maybe she pinned them too tightly. Maybe she was hurting her in some way. She tried every way of being a good mother that she could think of but, as time went on, Zoe decided that Camille had a mind of her own.

Although she never bonded with her mother, Camille was close to Papa Wentworth. His theory was that Camille and her mother's personalities clashed because they were basically very much alike. Papa, on the other hand, had a gentle spirit and a calming way about him that touched Camille's heart and drew her to him.

At ten months old she was walking, and she'd stagger into his outstretched arms. He'd grab her and embrace her, and then spin her around and away she'd go to do it all over again. They made a game out of it, which Zoe thought was ridiculous.

Papa helped her learn the alphabet, and by the time she started school at age six, she could read her little books. She loved the pictures in her books, even more than the stories "Look at the colors, Papa. Aren't they pretty? I like the pink and yellow flowers and the green grass and the blue river." The *Little Prudy* books that she loved didn't have pictures, so when Papa read those to her, she would picture the people and their homes, and try to draw what was in her mind's eye. Art became her passion, even as a child. She had an innate eye for color and design and could see a flower or a pastoral scene and transfer it to paper.

"Papa, may I please have some paints?" She'd implore, and he could not deny her. He'd do his best to produce what he could find to satisfy her desires. Supplies were scarce in Wheatland, and he seldom made it out of town to the bigger stores. Sometimes all he could find would be a stick of charcoal, but even that made her happy. She could draw in black and white.

Camille was a good student all through grade school, but when she got older, she had to be reminded daily to study her math and learn her Latin. Her mind would wander, and she'd sit and draw on her school papers that she had to turn in to her teachers. It was the first time that her algebra teacher had ever received an illustrated assignment!

Zoe had very little patience with her, and they grew further and further apart. Camille retreated to her "studio," as she called her bedroom at the top of the stairs. Zoe called it "the blue room," as the flowers in the cream-colored wallpaper picked up the blue in the carpet.

Camille wanted to redecorate her studio, but Zoe insisted that it was perfectly fine the way it was. Papa just shrugged his shoulders. He knew he couldn't change Zoe's mind, so he did what he could to make Camille's room into a retreat for her to pursue her art. He made a wooden easel and a drawing table, and he got her a stool to accompany the table. There were two windows, so there was natural light during the day, and Papa got her a light to clamp onto the drawing table, so she could work on rainy gloomy days or in the evenings. She spent her happiest moments in that room.

Zoe hated Camille's paintings She'd shake her head at Camille. "Get up there and study your Latin, or you'll never graduate or amount to anything."

Camille heard that last phrase, "You"ll never amount to anything," repeatedly over the years. Sometimes she thought she believed it herself, but instead of letting it defeat her or give her a complex, she grabbed onto it as a lifeline to prove herself and show her mother how wrong she was. She did graduate with perfect grades, which made her feel good about herself, but her greatest happiness came when it was announced at graduation, that "Miss Camille Rose Wentworth is the recipient of the art award of twenty-five dollars for her talent and achievements in all aspects of art and especially for her oil paintings and watercolors." Papa was proud of her and led the audience in a standing ovation for his daughter. Zoe sat and sniffed. The parents were sitting in the two front rows of the auditorium with the graduates up on the stage. It cut Camille like a butcher knife to see her mother still seated when everyone else was on their feet, clapping and cheering for her.

That's the last blow. I'm leaving home, Camille said to herself, as the audience took their seats again, and before that summer was over, she was gone. Her Papa tried to discourage her, but only because he hated for her to be so far away and on her own. Zoe urged him to let her go. "She can handle herself. Let her lead her narrow little life of a paintbrush and a piece of paper. She'll soon tire of it and want to come home." The money she won and the money she earned in July at the Wheatland Chataqua in sales of her artwork enabled her to travel to Canada. She arrived in Calgary almost broke, but in a week's time she had been hired as a clerk in a dress shop and was offered a little room over the shop.

After her second pay check, she enrolled in night classes at Pierre's art studio. Going to bed dog-tired every night, she was still the happiest she'd been in her entire life. She wrote long letters to Papa, and when he could sneak it without Zoe's knowledge, he would send her a little money now and then. She was a closed subject between Zoe and Papa. Zoe had slammed and padlocked the doors of her heart long ago as far as Camille was concerned.

Margie was thirteen when Camille left home, Amanda only eight, and they missed their older sister, but they knew better than to dwell on it. Sometimes they'd ask Papa questions about her, and he tried to give them honest answers, but omitted some of the difficulties and conflicts between Zoe and Camille. He just said she went away to study art. He couldn't answer their questions about if and when she would come back.

There was a span of several years when not even Papa heard from her. Finally she wrote and said she had married a Canadian named Jake Dallas, and they were living in Calgary. She had her own art studio and was teaching art classes as well as selling her own works.

Papa broached the subject with Zoe, and she did listen to the letter about her daughter's life, but she made no comment. Papa just had to prove to his wife that Camille's life was not wasted and that she was not a failure.

In the 1930's Papa heard from her again. She had divorced Jake and was now living in California with her second husband, Richard Stone. He was a Naval officer, and they had traveled overseas. She said she was very happy. She did art work just as a hobby now, as she was so involved in her husband's life and their travels and friends. Margie was in awe of her older sister as she read the letter that Papa had received. Amanda admired her and said she was ahead of her time. She knew enough to escape and do as she wanted, which Amanda wanted to do as well, and she envied her.

Amanda notified Camille when Papa died, but she was out of the country and didn't receive the news until the funeral was over and Papa was in his grave. She doubted that Camille would have come anyway, and Amanda wouldn't have held it against her. Zoe snorted and thought that it was a good thing Camille had an excuse, although she really didn't want her there anyway. The folks in Wheatland had all but forgotten that there was an older sister, and they'd given up speculating about her whereabouts. Camille was listed as a surviving daughter, living in California, in the local paper's obituary, so her name was bandied about town for a few days, but soon forgotten again.

In 1950, Richard Stone passed away suddenly of heart failure in Long Beach, California. Camille was devastated and, although he had family scattered around the country, she barely knew them, and she felt very much alone. He was buried with military honors, and she spent almost a year taking care of his affairs. He left everything to her, and she was very well provided for—a healthy life insurance policy, stocks and bonds, a government retirement plan, and valuable treasures and antiques that they had acquired during their travels. She sold their two bedroom house and moved into a high rise apartment building in Long Beach. Unfortunately, all the money in the world did not make up for her loneliness. With no children from either marriage, Camille wandered the shops and drove the beach alone. Her closest friends were still married, and although they included her in dinner parties and outings for awhile, she felt like a third shoe, and she began turning down their offers.

She scoured the want ads, looking at the employment opportunities, but really didn't need to work, and didn't want to take on another art studio. She set up her easel in the spare bedroom, painted a few pictures, and sat on the beach sketching people as they strolled by or surfed the ocean, but she soon tired of that as well. She seemed at loose ends, and nothing satisfied her.

Finally she went to the Humane Society and adopted a five-year old Boston bull dog named Sugar. At least he was someone to talk to and take for walks. He loved to ride in the car with the window down, so sometimes they'd take long afternoon drives, stop, walk, and drive some more.

He was great company and a good companion, but she needed human contact. She needed her family. Trying to shut them out of her mind hadn't been too difficult with her career and marriages, and their travels and friends, but that was all gone now. There was too much free time to sit and think.

She thought about her sisters and wondered where they were and what had happened in their lives.

Let's see. Margie is fifty-one now, and Amanda is forty-six. Wow! Time is passing us by. She shoved the thoughts of her mother back into the dark recesses of her mind for the time being. Oh, sure, she'd thought of her over the years, but the hurts of the past had always still been there, piercing her heart. She'd never heard one word from her in all these years. What kind of a mother is that? She wondered if Zoe's heart had softened any throughout the years, and finally one day she allowed herself to realize that her mother was eighty-two years old.

I wonder how they all are? Is it just my loneliness or do I really care? Do they care about me? What would happen if I called them? She pondered these questions for two weeks off and on and finally came to the conclusion that the only way to find out would be to act on her questions.

Finally, one lonely Sunday afternoon, Camille poured herself a cup of coffee, lit her tenth cigarette of the day, and dialed O for Operator. Yes, there was a Z. Wentworth listed in Wheatland, Washington. Her number was 4471. Her hands shook as she took a long drag on the cigarette and laid it in the ashtray. Sugar looked up at her with his head cocked, as if to say, "Are you all right? Are you sure you want to do this?" She'd run it by him over the course of the last two weeks, so he felt he should have some say in the matter!

In less than a minute, an eight year-old girl in Wheatland answered the Wentworth phone.

"Hello," a young melodious voice sang into the receiver.

Camille feared she had the wrong number. What would a child be doing there? "Is this the Zoe Wentworth home?"

"Yes, it is," Katie responded politely, and as she had been so carefully instructed, she inquired, "And who may I say is calling?"

These are the days when
Birds come back—
A very few, a bird or two
To take a backward look.

—Emily Dickinson

Chapter XX

Zoe's head jerked up from the Sunday paper she was reading, and her hand flew to her chest, when Katie turned from the phone and said, "It's Camille. She wants to talk to Margie."

"Good heavens! Why is *she* calling?"

Question marks were buzzing around in Katie's head, too, while Margie talked on the phone. She had heard the name mentioned over the years as some obscure relative who had been gone for a long time, but very little was said of her. Grandma Zoe certainly didn't want to discuss her oldest daughter, and when Katie had asked a few questions, Margie always changed the subject quickly, so Katie soon put her out of her mind.

When Margie hung up the receiver and sat down, she was quite stunned. She had little time to mull over the conversation or translate her emotions into thoughts.

Mother repeated her question of fifteen minutes ago and added a new one. "Why is she calling? What does she want?"

"Just a minute, Mother. I need to think about our conversation. Let me get us some tea while I try to gather my thoughts, and then I'll tell you."

Later, pouring two cups of scalding water and handing her mother a tea bag, she asked, "Do you want anything, Katie?"

Before she could answer, Zoe jumped in with her opinion. "I think she should leave the room."

"No, Mother, I think she should stay and hear this conversation about her Aunt Camille."

"Aunt Camille?" Zoe and Katie spoke in unison.

"Yes, she is your aunt, Katie. She is an older sister to Amanda and me." Margie thought it was time to tie the family shoe strings together and maybe even try to reattach the umbilical cord between Camille and her mother—a delicate surgery, for sure.

"You still haven't told us what she wanted," Zoe persisted, "and how did she know you were here?"

"She didn't know; she just took a chance. Now, Mother, get prepared. The bottom line is she wants to come home for a visit."

"Oh my! Good heavens to Betsy! You didn't give me any time to get prepared for *that* news!" Zoe shook her head in disbelief. "What brought this on after all these years?"

"From what I could gather from our short conversation, I would say she is lonely since her husband died, and she wants to reconnect with her family. Plus, she realizes we are all getting older."

Zoe sniffed. "Hmpf . . . She probably hopes I'll die soon, and she can get in my good graces and in my will, and get my money. But I can assure you, that will never happen. She'll never see a dime of my money!"

Katie's eyes were like the revolving beam in a lighthouse, searching from one face to the other. The talk of Grandma Zoe's impending death disturbed her, and she let out a cry of pain.

"Oh, honey. It's all right. Grandma's not dying; she's just talking through her hat." Margie tried to soothe her upset daughter. Katie had heard that saying many times over the short eight years of her life and had finally figured out that a person could say that without wearing a head covering.

Zoe still had unanswered questions. "What did you tell her? When does she want to come? How long does she want to stay? Can you imagine all the preparations we'll have to take care of?"

"So you're agreeing to it?" Margie thought her mother must have a streak of forgiveness hidden somewhere after all.

"Oh, no, not so fast. I will have to ponder on this awhile. It's too much to throw at an old lady and expect an answer back the same day." As a post script she added, "I wonder what Amanda will say."

Margie had forgotten about Amanda temporarily, but she lunged for the phone. Then she remembered that it was Sunday, and Amanda would be out at the farm. "I'll call her tomorrow."

"Yes, let her have a calm, relaxing weekend with Robert. We'll drop the bomb tomorrow."

Monday arrived as scheduled, and Margie stopped by Amanda's apartment on her way downtown. The news surprised her, but her reaction was more like a Fourth of July sparkler than a bomb. The two sisters had often talked about Camille when Zoe wasn't around, although they mostly wondered about her and asked each other unanswerable questions. They knew so very little about her. At least their interest in her was something they had in common, and now they both agreed it would be exciting if Mother acquiesced and allowed her to come home.

One day, later in the week while Katie was at school, Margie and Amanda hashed it out with their mother. Zoe was thinking only of her feelings, and they tried to open her eyes and her heart to what Camille might be going through.

"What caused the falling out anyway, Mother? I've never really understood it all." Amanda asked the definitive question at long last.

"From day one, we just never got along. She was an obstinate child, and your dad catered to her, and that pushed us farther and farther apart. He encouraged her in her art work, but that just gave her an escape from everyone and everything else. Mildred was her only friend, and she was a strange nut, too, all involved in drama and music, but at least she came out of her obsessions and settled down and married Gilbert Reynolds and became a farmer's wife. They just retired and moved into town, you know. In fact, they live across the street from Belle and Ed."

Amanda tried to get her mother back on track, but she'd had enough talk about Camille for one day. "Maybe she's changed,

Mother." Amanda ended the conversation with something for Mother to chew on. "Let me know what you decide," and Amanda was out the door.

On Sunday, exactly one week from the shocking phone call, Mother summoned Margie into the kitchen while Katie was at Sunday School. "O.K., Margie. Call Camille and tell her she can come. Find out when she wants to come and how long she wants to stay. I've been thinking that maybe she could stay out at the farm with Robert and Amanda, but we can work that out later. Just call and get it over with! Maybe she's changed her mind and decided to take off and fly back to Canada." Zoe was clinging to that hope.

*   *   *

One month later, early in May, a two-door yellow and white Chevy Bel Air pulled up in front of the Wentworth house. Camille drove with all the car windows down, and Sugar, sitting in the front passenger seat, loved the fresh air. Camille liked to feel the sun on her bare arms, plus the air helped dissipate the heavy fog of cigarette smoke from her two pack-a-day habit.

Katie was home from school for a quick lunch when Camille and Sugar rounded the house and stepped up on the back porch. One of Camille's spike heels got caught between the boards of the rickety old porch, and when Katie opened the door, there stood a lady like she had never seen before. The tanned leathery skin was stretched over her thin, bony body. Her hair was a bluish silver, short and curly. From her eyeglasses hung a gold chain, and from her ear lobes dangled the longest, gaudiest earrings Katie had ever seen. In one hand she held a purple shoe with a damaged spike heel, and in the other was a red cigarette holder with ashes falling from the cigarette onto the old porch. At her heels was the ugliest black and white dog Katie had ever seen.

"Someone's here," Katie turned and spoke to her mother, "and she has a dog." Katie was still fearful of them.

"I'm Camille," the strange-looking lady announced, and by then Margie was at the door to greet her and usher her in with a hug. Sugar was right behind her.

Zoe sat in her kitchen chair and didn't get up. She could use her old arthritic body for an excuse for remaining seated, if necessary. She was appalled at her daughter's appearance and her husky voice, apparently deepened from years of smoking.

Camille asked for an ashtray, but since they'd never had one on the premises, Margie produced a small sauce dish.

Camille was taken aback by her mother's appearance as well. She'd last seen her as a well-upholstered, proud and stylish lady with brown hair and rouged cheeks. Now, as she formally shook her mother's soft hand, she saw an old, thin, faded-out, wrinkled woman with hair the color of steel pulled back in a bun. She wore a drab gray house dress and no make-up. They stared across the table as if they'd never laid eyes on each other before. Neither one could say, "You're looking well," as they'd both changed and aged so drastically, so they just said, "Hello."

Katie broke the ice by pointing to the clock above the kitchen sink and saying, "Mommy, it's time to take me back to school." Margie hated leaving Camille and Zoe alone so soon after Camille's arrival, but it was just a short drive up to the south hill, and she'd be home in fifteen minutes.

Katie was bubbling over like a pot of hot pudding boiling on the stove. "So that's my Aunt Camille. Wow! She is nothing like you and Aunt Mandy. I've never seen anyone who looks like her or talks like she does. I wish I didn't have to go back to school; I just want to sit and stare at her all afternoon." Katie babbled on and on.

"You'll be home soon, but no staring. It's not polite and you know that. Now, run along, honey, and I love you." Whenever they parted, they always kissed and said "I love you" to each other. Margie thought those were the three most important big little words in the English language, and she had no one else who expressed love to her.

"I love you, too, Mommy. Don't forget to pick me up today. I have to bring home all my books for Aunt Amanda to see."

Margie had forgotten that Amanda wanted to write down the names of all of Katie's text books, so the next time Amanda went to Spokane, she could purchase copies of the text books at John W. Graham for Katie to have at home. Katie was doing perfectly well in school, but Amanda insisted on having the books at home for further study.

Katie tried hard to concentrate all afternoon, but once her teacher, Miss Robbins, had to speak to her about her lack of concentration. That was unusual, but all Katie could think about was that strange lady at home. I wonder if she's an actress. No, Mommy said she was an artist. I'm sure glad that Aunt Mandy isn't like her. Aunt Mandy is sort of nosy and bossy, but at least she looks like a normal person. Aunt Camille is so different. I wonder if she's adopted. That was a new word that was swirling around the lunchroom and playground. Several of her classmates said they were adopted, and Rusty Harrison whispered in her ear, "and so are you." Katie had no idea what it meant. She thought it had something to do with whether or not a person looked like his or her parents, but was vague on the whole concept, and when she had asked her mommy, her answer was that it meant that a person was chosen. She still didn't understand and thought that the resemblance theory fit Camille, because she didn't look like anyone else in the family that Katie had ever seen.

The sign under the clock in the third grade classroom said, "Time will pass. Will you?" Time was barely moving for Katie that day, but finally the bell rang, and she loaded up her chubby arms with all her books and headed for the car. Margie was waiting and had Camille with her. Several of Katie's classmates wondered who that was in the car, and Katie shyly said, "Camille. She's from California." She was too embarrassed to claim her as an aunt. She needed to find out if Camille was adopted before she acknowledged that she was a relative.

They drove by Mildred Reynold's house, just two blocks from the school. Camille wanted to visit her old friend while in town, and needed to know where she lived, so she could call Mildred to make arrangements to get together.

When they arrived back at the Wentworth house, Camille thought it was time to ask where she would be sleeping. She was prepared to stay at a motel or hotel, if that was her only option.

Before Camille could even get the question out, Zoe said, "You'll have the blue room." What else could she do? Her hands were tied! The neighbors, in fact, the whole town, would be whispering about Zoe farming out her prodigal daughter.

"Oh, my old room. That will be nice. Does it look the same?"

"Go and see for yourself." Zoe had never entered the room since Camille left. She'd left it all up to Margie—the cleaning years ago and even now. It was too hard for her to manage the stairs, so that was her excuse. Sometimes the infirmities of old age came in handy!

"Would you like to help me, little Missy? I have some things you could carry in from the car." Camille motioned for Katie to follow her to her car.

"Why don't you use the front door? It's a lot closer," volunteered Margie. Zoe glared at Margie as if she had just spoken a string of swear words, but let it go. It did make sense.

In just a few minutes, Zoe covered her ears. "What is that horrible racket?"

"That's Camille, dragging her trunk up the stairs," Katie yelled over the noise. She had brought a box of dog food into the kitchen. Katie was intrigued with the trunk. Aunt Amanda carried what she called a *grip,* and when Katie went to Spokane with Grandma and Mommy, they used suitcases, so a trunk was something new to Katie. She was glad she was home from school to see all of this.

"What's that clicking sound?" Zoe was still disturbed.

Katie explained that the sound she heard in-between the trunk scraping the stairs was Camille's high heels as she climbed each step.

Zoe threw up her hands. "The stairs will be ruined. I knew I shouldn't have let her stay here. She's causing trouble already."

Margie tried to calm the raging seas of Zoe's blood pressure. "Now, Mother. It's all right. She must be at the top. I don't hear the noise any more. It's all over. We won't hear it again until she leaves for home."

But it wasn't over. Every day they heard the clicking of heels on the stairs. Even Sugar's toenails made a sound that upset Zoe, whose hearing, all of a sudden, was sensitive again to every little noise.

Sugar slept in the bed with Camille, and every morning at 5:30, while the rest of the family was still buried deep in sleep, Camille, in her pink slippers, carried Sugar down the stairs and took him outside. She retrieved the Spokane newspaper from the yellow box by the alley gate, spread the stock market report out on the kitchen table, brewed a pot of coffee, lit her first cigarette of the day, and studied her portfolio of stocks. Her blood pressure went up as her stocks went down, but if Texaco and American Tell and Tell were doing better, she smiled at Sugar and relaxed.

Margie and Katie came quietly down the stairs at 7:00 sharp every morning. If it was a school day, Katie had to get busy immediately with her breakfast. She was still on the prunes, but now she'd added Puffed Rice or oatmeal to the menu.

Zoe stayed in bed as long as possible while Camille was visiting. Although they were civil to each other, it was a challenge for them both, so Zoe holed up in her room as much as she could and got up for breakfast around 8:30 or 9:00.

All Camille ever wanted was toast and interminable cups of coffee. Complaining about never being able to find her favorite foods at the market, as she called Hudson's Grocery Store, she had to settle for plain old bacon and toast rather than bagels and Canadian bacon for breakfast, and lettuce and cucumbers instead of watercress and avocados for a salad at 11:30. She finally secured some liverwurst from the meat market. Katie tried it, but couldn't swallow it. Spitting it outside over the fence, Katie declared that it had a good name. It was definitely "worse than liver." Zoe liked brown eggs from her own chickens and bacon and toast, which Margie fixed for the two of them every morning.

Camille's two-week visit went slowly for Zoe, but rapidly for the other family members. Camille had lunch with Mildred twice at the Reynold's home and rode out to the farm with Amanda during the week on two afternoons. Being a free spirit herself, she thought the marriage arrangement between Amanda and Robert was ideal.

Margie and Katie enjoyed Camille's eccentricities, but Margie was fearful that Camille and her mother would come to blows. It didn't happen, and when the two weeks were up, and Camille dragged her trunk down the stairs to her Chevy, Margie felt a great sense of relief that nothing had arisen to cause a battle.

The only thing that really stuck in Camille's craw as she waved "good-bye" was the absence of any of her paintings on the walls. Little did she know that for two weeks, she had been sleeping on a bed that covered her two favorite works done years ago. They'd been there ever since she left home, all those many years ago. If only canvas and oil paint could speak.

If you forgive people enough
You belong to them, and they to you,
Whether either person
Likes it or not—
Squatter's rights of the heart.

       —James Hilton

Chapter XXI

When Camille drove down the hill and left the city limits of Wheatland to begin her long journey to California, she was taking more baggage home with her than what she brought. They weren't tangible souvenirs or gifts from the family, but thoughts and feelings coupled with wishes and regrets.

There were no gestures of love from Mother, and that was a letdown, but maybe she had expected too much. Her sisters and Katie seemed happy that she came, so she was torn between feeling the continuing loss of maternal love, and joy in finding two sisters and a niece, "Little Missy," as she liked to call her. Margie and Amanda promised to write, and they invited her to come back for a visit.

There were no apologies or outward signs of forgiveness, yet Mother did allow her to come and stay, and she was fairly civil to her. They tolerated each other and their different lifestyles for two weeks and didn't touch on any of the heartaches of the past. So Camille took with her a feeling of satisfaction—not that all was forgiven, but that they could tolerate each other.

Finally, there were regrets—not that she had left home all those years ago—but that she had stayed away so long. She should have tried to reach her mother's heart before it got so hardened. She should have come home sooner before her mother got so old. In some ways, the homecoming turned out to be a guilt trip, and her baggage was heavy with regrets.

"And, Sugar, where were my damn paintings?" She growled at her dog, whose buggy eyes said, "Under the bed, but don't blame me. It's not my fault!"

Life was never the same again at the Wentworth house after Camille went home. There was a pall, almost as pervading and encompassing as after a death in the family.

Margie felt a big letdown. Even though she was on edge the whole time of Camille's visit and worried she would have to referee a battle, she loved having company. It meant more work for her—cooking, washing, cleaning—but this was her long-lost sister, her flesh and blood, so she didn't mind at all. Camille *was* different than the women in Wheatland, but, after all, this was a farm town. Some of these ladies had never gotten further than Spokane, whereas Camille had traveled the world, been married twice, owned a business, and was an artist. She had every right to be different, and if she wanted to say "Eh?" like they do in Canada, that was all right, too. It just added to her individuality!

Margie felt pride in Camille's accomplishments, but then the dam burst when she thought of how lonely Camille must be now, and Margie often cried softly in her room at night. She'd never done half the things Camille had done, and she was one of those women who'd never gotten any further than Spokane, except for a medical trip to the Mayo Clinic, but she had Katie now, and Camille had no one. Margie made a promise to herself to be a good sister and cried so much that her migraines began to flare up again.

Zoe was a changed woman. She'd always been a complainer and a stern taskmaster, but now that old wounds had been reopened, she grumbled and demanded even more. The remnants of Camille's visit, such as the pervasive and lingering smell of cigarette smoke, made her irritable.

"Our curtains are ruined," and she threw up her hands in despair.

"No, Mother. I'll take them down, one by one, wash them, and hang them outside on the line. They'll smell like the breath of spring in no time." Margie rescued her mother from defeat.

"All right, but just don't do it on a Sunday. What would the neighbor's think?"

"I'll do it on Monday, Mother."

"What about the stairs? Are they all scratched?"

"They look fine, Mother. I rubbed and polished them with Old English oil just yesterday. Remember, you asked me what that smell was?"

"Oh yes, but what about the dog droppings? The lawn will be turning brown, if it isn't already."

"It's green, Mother. Camille picked them up and buried them every day."

"What's that awful odor in the fridge? I can smell it every time you open the door."

"It's the liverwurst. I'll throw it out," Margie said with resignation in her voice.

When she wasn't complaining, Zoe was as quiet as the deafening silence after a clap of thunder. She went downhill, not so much physically, but mentally and emotionally. She even quit the bridge club, and Margie took her place. Margie and Amanda thought it was old age, inching its way in and grabbing a toe-hold. Zoe wasn't sharing her heartaches, but ever since Camille had visited, she'd felt unsettled and disturbed, torn apart in many directions.

I should have been a better mother, but she was so obstinate. I should have encouraged her more, but she ran to her Papa for that. I should have known she'd leave home, but I didn't acknowledge the warning signs. I should have written to her, as any good mother would have done, but I didn't know how to reach her heart. I should have apologized for all of this and more, but I couldn't. I should do it now, but I can't. Not just yet. Zoe's bags were packed with guilt, too, but her trip was confined to the four walls of her home.

Katie's life was changed by Camille's visit, too. School was out for the summer, so she had time to sit in her swing hanging from the old apple tree or ride her blue and silver Schwinn bike around the block and think about her Aunt Camille. It disturbed her to think that she had an aunt who was so unlike the people she knew, yet she liked her. Her clothes, her voice, her food, her dog, and even the things she talked about and the phrases she used were all so foreign and intriguing to Katie, who still wondered if Camille was really a part of their family. Maybe she'd gotten mixed up and belonged somewhere else with some other family. That brought to mind again that strange word, *adoption.* She'd asked Mommy again what it meant, but Margie put her off and told her she was busy, and they'd talk about it some other time.

Katie had a children's dictionary Aunt Amanda had purchased for her in Spokane, but the word was not in there, so she'd searched the big dictionary that was in the bottom drawer of the hall wardrobe, but she couldn't understand the meaning.

"And so are you," Rusty had said.

"I'm adopted, and I don't even know what it means. Maybe I should ask Rusty. He seems to know what it means."

Another thing that bothered Katie was Grandma Zoe's attitude toward her. All of a sudden, Grandma seemed mad at her most of the time. She told Katie that she was obstinate and incorrigible, so out came the big dictionary again, but since Katie didn't know how to spell the words, she couldn't even find them.

Katie liked to tease, and whenever Grandma Zoe said she had something under her plate, Katie would pick up her dinner plate and look all around on the table cloth. The more Katie laughed, the more annoyed Grandma would become, and Margie had to step in and put a stop to all of Katie's amusement.

"You'll be sorry when I am gone, young lady." Zoe barked at her granddaughter.

"Oh, are you going on a trip?" Katie teased, knowing full well she meant she would be going up on the hill to her grave. Grandma had announced her impending death quite often lately.

Sometimes Zoe would hug Katie, but other times she'd tell her to get away, so Katie was unsure of where she stood and if her grandma loved her. The little girl had a lot of unanswered questions, and although Margie didn't think it was right to ignore her, she didn't want to face the issues just yet.

"Rusty and his big mouth!" Margie thought to herself. From then on, she dreaded seeing him walk up the sidewalk to play with Katie. But if she'd have only known, she had a greater worry than Rusty Harrison.

Katie, curious Katie, who would never leave anything alone or unanswered, decided to try another avenue for her questions— Aunt Amanda, who seemed to know everything about everything.

So one day just out of the clear blue sky, Katie stopped by on her way home from the soda fountain and knocked on Aunt Amanda's apartment door. That was the first time she'd ever gone alone there without her mommy. The rapping startled Amanda who was dozing over her library book.

"My goodness! What a nice surprise, honey! Are you here by yourself?" Amanda looked up and down the hallway for Margie.

"Yes, I've been to the drugstore. Patricia makes the best chocolate sundaes." Patricia and her husband, Daniel, the druggist, insisted that everyone call them by their first names, and although that rubbed Margie wrong, she allowed Katie to dispense with the more formal Mr. and Mrs. Benson.

Aunt Amanda could see just a hint of chocolate around Katie's mouth, and she got her a wet washcloth.

"Now, what brings you here? Did your mother send you?"

"Oh, no, she doesn't know I'm here. I just wanted to stop and see you to ask you a question." At this point, Katie started to get scared and wished she'd gone on home. She seemed visibly upset, and Amanda moved over to the couch, sat beside her, and took her hand.

"What is it, honey? Is something wrong? Is Grandma sick or is Mommy having one of her headaches?"

"No, it's just that no one will answer any of my questions. Rusty Harrison told me that I'm adopted, but I don't know what that means, and Mommy won't tell me." There, she had blurted it out.

Amanda was understandably taken aback. Of all people for Katie to turn to with a question like that! It was just like Margie to avoid the issue and leave the poor, little girl with questions.

"She didn't tell you anything?" Amanda was astonished.

"Well, once she said it meant that I was chosen, but what does that mean?"

Amanda was on the spot. She could tell her she should go home and ask her mother again and run the chance of Katie still not being told much of anything, or she could tell her the basic meaning of the word without revealing too much.

"Please tell me what it means," Katie begged and looked at her aunt with sad eyes. "Does it mean there is something wrong with me or that I'm different?"

Having to tell her something that would satisfy her questions, Amanda said, "Yes, your mother was right. It does mean that you were chosen. Your mother told me that someone wasn't able to keep you when you were a baby, so she chose to take you and raise you as if you were her very own child."

That was a good start, but it opened the door to more questions. "Why wouldn't someone want a baby?" Katie couldn't imagine that.

"Well, sometimes there are different reasons. I don't know what happened, but perhaps your real mommy didn't have any money or maybe she didn't have a house." Evading the true issues was a necessary tool in this case.

"But where did I come from?"

"You mean what city?" Amanda didn't want to get into a discussion of reproduction with Katie, and yes, that was what she meant. "I think you were from Spokane. Now that should clear things up for you." Amanda was anxious to close the subject.

"Yes, that helps me know where I came from, but what about Aunt Camille? Is she adopted, too?"

"Oh, my goodness, no. Where did you get that idea?"

"Because she is so different looking. She doesn't look like anyone else in the family or even like anyone else I know. Maybe Grandma Zoe adopted her and then didn't like her and tried to give her away."

"No, that's not true at all. She was not adopted. She was home for awhile, but you know she was an artist, so she went away to art school after high school. Now, that's all I know, Katie. You'd better get on home before Mommy gets worried about you."

"Okay. If I have any more questions, I'll come and ask you, Aunt Mandy, because you give good answers. Thank you," and with that, she hugged Amanda and hurried out the door.

"Isn't that just like Margie?" Amanda belly-ached to Robert that night over dinner at the farm, as she told him of her afternoon visitor.

"What do you mean? Maybe Margie thought she was too young to know." He stuck up for Margie, and didn't care if Amanda noticed. "I think she is a good mother."

"You always stick up for her. Well, I intend to tell her to answer her child's questions herself," and she had every intention of jabbing Margie with just those instructions. "She even asked if Camille was adopted. She thought it had something to do with whom a person resembled. Can you imagine?"

"She's not so far off base; people usually do look like someone in the family."

Oh Lord, Amanda thought to herself. I hope Robert doesn't see any similarities between Katie and her real mother.

"Katie sure is a cute little girl, wherever she came from. Her mother must have been a real beauty."

"Tha . . ." Amanda almost said thank you. "That's for sure," she agreed.

*   *   *

At her first opportunity Amanda called Margie and told her they needed to talk. "Your daughter is asking questions, and I don't think I should be the one to give her the answers. Get down here now!" Amanda commanded in the tone of Robert's former Marine Corps drill instructor.

"Do I have to come today?" Margie whined. "I have a migraine."

"You don't even know what a migraine is, but you will when I get through with you. Is Katie home?"

"No, she went to Brownie Scouts with Jill."

"Good, then, stay home. I'm coming up there," and Amanda slammed down the phone in anger.

"Oh, my head." Margie moaned, as she headed for the couch. She wished Mother could get her a cold compress, but she was in bed. She was taking her afternoon nap, which was a new development, too, that started after Camille had gone home.

Amanda soon arrived and lambasted Margie up one side and down the other. "Just answer her questions," Amanda implored, after half an hour of filling Margie in on what had transpired during Katie's visit, and Margie promised she would do a better job of being a mother.

"Just leave; I am so sick." She pleaded with Amanda, and as soon as Amanda went out the door, she was in the bathroom, literally making full use of the term "a sick headache."

The next day when she was feeling better, she asked Katie if she had any questions.

"Just one. Aunt Mandy answered all the rest."

Margie was apprehensive, but knew she'd have to supply the answers from now on.

"What do you need to know, honey?"

"Well, I was just wondering if I could have any brothers or sisters?" She asked several times over the next couple of weeks. Each time Margie told her that it wouldn't be possible. She was getting too old to choose another baby. Finally, Katie seemed to give up or at least accept the explanation. She resigned herself to the fact that she was going to be an only child, and she felt lonely. No brothers, no sisters, no daddy. Oh, that was another question.

Crabbed age and youth
Cannot live together.
Youth is full of pleasance,
Age is full of care.

—Anon.

Chapter XXII

Zoe stared at the fragile petals of the pink peonies that lined both sides of the sidewalk where the grass ended and the flower and vegetable gardens began. Just a little over a month ago Margie had driven her mother up the hill to the cemetery to place an arrangement of flowers on Frederick's grave. Now she felt as tired and withered and shattered as the fallen petals on the ground. Peonies had always been her favorite flower, and as she leaned on her cane and stumped back up the sidewalk toward the back porch, she felt like it wouldn't be long before her grave would be decorated with the pink flowers she loved so well.

She often sat in front of the dining room window where the summer sun heated her chilled body. She was never warm enough any more, even with a shawl around her shoulders or a sweater over her house-dress.

Amanda complained to Margie that "Mother is just not getting out enough, and she's not getting enough exercise. Her blood is barely moving."

Margie knew it was true, but told Amanda that it was rather difficult to budge an immoveable object. From then on, Amanda made the supreme sacrifice of her precious time to get Mother out at least once a month and drive her around town. Amanda wanted to drive her in the evenings, but Mother didn't like going out at night. "She wants to go after dark, so she can look in everyone's windows and see what people are doing," That was Margie's theory, and Mother agreed with her. Amanda said that was the only time it was convenient for her.

Margie and Amanda were mature enough to know that age and the infirmities and burdens that often accompany it weigh on a person's mind and heart and can change one dramatically. However, Katie was only ten years old and too young to understand why Grandma was changing right before her eyes. She'd always been in awe and just a little fearful of Grandma's sternness, but now everything that Katie did seemed to bother her, and Katie began to resent her.

"Grandma hates my puppy," Katie cried to her mother, after she'd had her Springer Spaniel for two weeks. In lieu of siblings, which were impossible for Margie to produce for Katie, she'd finally given in to her need for companionship and gotten her a puppy.

"No, honey, she doesn't hate her. She's afraid of tripping and falling over her, and we have to train Daisy to not jump up on her. We'll work together, and it will be okay."

Katie shrugged and hoped her mother was right. The resentment was building, so Katie tried to keep busy and stay out of Grandma's way.

Jill and Karen, Katie's two best friends, invited her to their houses to play many times during the summer, but whenever Katie asked if they could come to her house for a few hours in the afternoon, Margie quickly came up with an excuse.

"It's because of Grandma, isn't it?" Katie figured it out immediately.

"She's just not feeling too well right now; it's her stomach. Maybe they can come next week."

Oh sure. Next week it will be something else wrong with her, Katie thought to herself.

Finally Margie gave in and opened up the parlor, which previously had been used only for the Bridge Club and at Christmas for the tree. She dusted the furniture and opened the curtains, and Dottie across the street wondered what was going on.

Margie let the girls in through the front door, so Mother wouldn't hear them, and she supervised them as they played and ate popcorn behind the closed French doors that led to the living/ dining room where Mother sat by the window. They were good little girls, but their giggles soon reached the ears of Grandma, and on their way out the back door to play on the swing, they wondered why Katie's grandma had her hands over her ears. Katie knew she would never be able to invite them again.

"She always complains about being so deaf, so how could she hear us? We weren't very noisy," Katie tried to figure it all out after her friends left.

"Her ears are just real sensitive to noise. She can't help it. I hope you can understand." Katie tried to meld the ways of old age and youth together.

The problems worsened that fall when Katie joined the elementary band. Margie wanted her to have every opportunity to broaden her education, so she allowed her to join on a trial basis. They borrowed a very well-worn trumpet from Hilda Johnson. It was silver, and the other students all had gold horns, but Katie endured the dents and sticky valves, and when she was sure that was the instrument she wanted to pursue, Margie purchased a used one from a music store in Spokane.

"The teacher said I have to practice every day," and she'd lug that case home every afternoon, often to be told that Grandma was sleeping or her ears were bothering her. Her teacher knew the situation and understood, but without the extra practice, Katie struggled to perfect the songs. If the weather was decent, she'd sit outside and go through the scales and the songs.

Karen's mother was a piano teacher and several of Katie's classmates took lessons from her, so Katie, wanting to be like them, asked to learn that instrument as well.

Margie's direct response squelched that idea immediately. "No, I don't want you sitting around, tinkling on some piano keys. Anybody can learn to play the piano."

She'd already lined up something different for Katie. She was going to take elocution lessons under the tutelage of Patricia Benson, the druggist's wife, and a graduate of the Cornish School of the Arts in New York City.

So every Wednesday afternoon Katie walked to Patricia's house for her weekly lesson. It was near the school, and about the time that Katie was knocking on Patricia's back door, Margie was pulling up in front of the house. Margie wanted to take it all in and make sure that Katie had perfected the exercise for breathing correctly from the diaphragm or had the right inflection of the Italian language from last week's lesson, and then key in on what was assigned for the next week, so she could coach her at home. Sometimes it would be a short poem to memorize and recite or a pantomime to act out.

Katie loved Patricia and the flashy gold in her teeth when she smiled, and she began to dream about being just like her and of becoming an actress. Soon Katie was asked to give readings for events around the town. Her first performance was at Christmas at the Presbyterian Church. Aunt Amanda hadn't darkened a church door since her wedding, but when Katie personally invited her, she said, "Oh, yes, Robert and I wouldn't miss it for the world!" So, at the Sunday night service one week before Christmas, the Shaws and the Wentworths were all in attendance—even Zoe, who was, after all, a charter member of the church.

Robert and Amanda picked up Zoe, Margie, and Katie; Belle and Ed gave up their Sunday night service at the Assembly of God Church to hear Katie give her recitation. They all sat proudly in the second pew. Margie wanted to be close to the front, so if Katie should forget a word, she would be near enough to inconspicuously prompt her. It wasn't necessary, and they smiled and hugged her when it was over. Margie and Amanda bathed in the warm accolades of the applause.

As Katie joined them in the pew, Margie whispered in her ear, "You were perfect, dear. Every syllable was just right." Katie loved hearing it, and she knew that her mother would settle for nothing less than perfection.

Even Zoe patted her on the back and managed a smile. She highly approved of her taking lessons because Patricia taught her to have lady-like poise and to stand properly when speaking with the heel of her left foot meeting the inside arch of the right foot and pointing outward at an angle. Patricia also taught her how to have a smooth, balanced voice and not to yell like some of those other "ill-mannered rambunctious brats," according to Zoe.

That same night at church, somewhere in the dimly lit pews in the back, sat Patricia. She was of the Catholic faith, but she just had to sneak in long enough to hear her prize pupil. Katie didn't know she was there until Patricia told her at the next week's lesson, "You were great on Sunday night! Now let's take two weeks off for the holidays, and I'll see you next year."

Katie was so happy and gave Patricia a hug. The sun rose and set in her heart with Patricia.

All was not well at home. There was jealousy brewing. Certainly Amanda was proud of Katie that night at the church, but she was tired of hearing about how wonderful Patricia was and all she was doing for Katie.

"What are you trying to do, Margie—make a child actress out of her? She was so dramatic that she made her Christmas recitation sound like a heroine in an MGM film. She's not Shirley Temple!"

"You're always so critical, Amanda. I'm trying to do the best I can, and everyone said she was wonderful."

"That's what's important to you—what everyone thinks of you and your perfect little specimen, isn't it?" She wanted to add, "You should hear the things they say behind your back," but she didn't.

Margie was mad and on the defensive. "Isn't that what everyone wants—approval?" Margie was sure she was right in that area of thinking.

Amanda wasn't finished. "And by the way, while we're talking, why did Katie take Dan Benson to the Girl Scout Father/Daughter Banquet instead of Robert? I'm sure it was your idea; you think they're both so wonderful."

"Oh, no. It was totally Katie's idea," Margie lied. She was not normally the liar in the family, but she was tired of being the bad mother. "Katie said she barely knows Robert, when I suggested she invite him. You hardly ever invite us out to the farm, and when he's in town, he never stops by."

"Well, I wonder why that is!" Amanda's comment puzzled Margie.

"Did he say he was jealous and would have liked to have gone?" Margie would never want to hurt Robert.

"No, he knows nothing about it."

"So, you're the only one bothered by it."

"Well, after all, he *is* family." Amanda concluded the argument and had the last word, as always.

Actually, Amanda wasn't the only one bothered by the whole situation. The question of, "Who's my daddy?" had never been answered to Katie's satisfaction. Nobody seemed to know. The other adopted kids in her class all had daddies. No matter what substitute father would have escorted her to the dinner, it wouldn't have been the real one pulling out her chair and cutting her steak, and that made her feel very different once again.

Grandma Zoe chose not to get involved in the jealousy and conflicts on child-rearing between her daughters; she had her own problems.

"I have enough of my own internal fires to put out, which reminds me, Margie. Where are those paintings that Camille did so long ago and liked so well—the forest fire and the pink peonies? Have you seen them? They must be upstairs in a closet somewhere."

"How odd that you would remember them! You always hated them, Mother."

"Yes, but you know, the one of the peonies were actually rather pretty, and I've been thinking that if you could find them, maybe we should hang them in the dining room. We could hang the forest fire on that big, bare, east wall, and I could sit with my back to it. We could put the pink peonies on the wall over the dining room table. I could see it when I sit at the desk by the window. I miss the flowers outside terribly when the snow covers them."

Margie was surprised at Mother's well-laid-out thoughts and plans. Obviously, she'd given it a lot of consideration.

"I did see them when I cleaned the blue room. They're all framed and ready to hang. They're under the bed, covered with plastic. Oh, Mother, I'm sure Camille will be so pleased to see them hanging on the walls when she comes again."

"Oh, is she coming again?" Mother was surprised.

"She mentioned in her last letter that she might come again next summer."

Zoe wondered if she would live to see it.

Memory put a red star in the corner
Like pictures in a gallery
That get sold.

—James Hilton

Chapter XXIII

The picture-hanging took place late in February—much later than Zoe had anticipated, but once again it was Amanda who was too busy to help. Granted, she had been called to substitute many times during January and February's flu epidemic, which laid both the teachers and students low. Somehow they all escaped the flu, but then the chicken pox hit town, and Katie was an unlucky and miserable victim. She was covered from head to toe with scabs and itched like she was bombarded with red ants. Margie wished she could buy Calomine Lotion by the gallon. "Don't scratch," was admonished many times over.

Finally, when Zoe determined that all the germs had subsided and that Amanda was free of what she had picked up "in that germ-infested incubator of a school," Margie was allowed to call Amanda and schedule a time to help hang Camille's paintings of long ago. On February 28, about as late as one can get in February unless it is a leap year, Amanda arrived with her hammer and nails.

"Oh, you didn't need to bring your tools; I have what we need."

"But are the nails strong enough to hold the pictures?" Amanda was sure they wouldn't be quite right if Margie had selected them from the storehouse of their dad's old supplies.

It was quite a session of getting it all just right. Margie's nails would have held a thirty-pound framed canvas, so they were very adequate for Camille's three-foot long paintings.

"It's crooked. A little to the left, Margie. No, that's too much. Move it back." It went on until Amanda's perfect eye had the forest fire at just the right elevation. Then they went to the other wall for the pink peony presentation. It was more square in dimension, but took just as long to hang properly.

"Well, Mother, what do you think?" Amanda inquired of Zoe, when the art gallery was ready for inspection. Somehow Zoe had slept in her chair the whole time through all the hassle. She awakened with a start and rubbed her eyes.

She surveyed the forest fire first. "You hung it nicely, but it's just as wild and ugly as I remembered it. But maybe Camille will be pleased that it is on the wall." Then she turned and gazed at the other wall. There was a long silence before she answered. With unheard-of tears in her eyes, she slowly stammered, "Now, that one I like. Yes, I like it a lot. It reminds me of spring and the flowers in the yard and the cemetery." She turned and looked out the dining room window, so no one would see the hankie she pulled from her dress pocket. Just then she caught a glimpse of something moving across the yard near the window and heading in the direction of the porch. "Who's that?' She asked.

Margie had seen the person too. "It's Katie, Mother. She's home from school."

"Oh, my goodness! For a moment I thought it was Camille, who'd come home to see her paintings already. You know, Katie is getting so tall and thin. I think she resembles Camille."

Margie and Amanda looked at each other with raised eyebrows and shrugged their shoulders.

"Don't worry; I haven't lost all my marbles. I know who her mother is."

The two sisters were trying to hush their mother up, as Katie by now had entered the dining room. Apparently she didn't hear her grandma's comments, as she focused on the decorated walls. She looked from one painting to the other.

"Hi Mom, Hi Aunt Amanda, Hello Grandma. Wow! You've all been busy today." She went closer to look at the forest fire. "Aunt Camille did this? I love it, but then, of course you know I like bright colors and especially red."

"Yes, it is bright, but look over here," and Margie pointed to the pink peonies. "Do you like them too, dear?"

Katie wrinkled up her nose. "Oh, they're okay. They look all faded out and boring." *Boring* was one of her favorite words of the moment, and she used it to describe anything she didn't like. She even thought Grandma was boring, but she didn't tell anyone.

"Which one do you like the best?" She looked first at Aunt Amanda. "I bet you like the same one I do." She knew her aunt liked bright, vivid colors.

"You're right, Kiddo. It's the one of the forest fire for me, too." Amanda agreed.

"How about you, Mom? I bet you like the flowers."

Diplomacy was Margie's forte. "Oh, I like them equally as well, just because Camille painted them."

Zoe had no opinion, unless her snoring was her answer.

*   *   *

Camille chose not to come that summer. Her letters just said she had other plans—a trip with friends; she did send a postcard from Boston in August. The two sisters and Katie were disappointed, and Zoe said, "Well, maybe it's for the best." She clung tenaciously to life like a little boy hanging onto a frayed rope, swinging out over a cold, deep lake. Maybe Camille would come back to Wheatland once more before Zoe died, and maybe they could settle their differences. If not, Zoe would just let go.

Margie tried to entertain her mother and keep her mind sharp. She'd read the highlights of the morning paper to her, which started off with the obituaries and ended up with the society page. Mother couldn't be bothered with the sports or the comics, so some mornings their time of reading went quickly. Mother would do some mending if the light was just right coming in through the window, and she hoped her eyes held out until after the big shopping trip of the year in Spokane. This was the first year that Mother was not accompanying Margie and Katie; but Mother's work would start when they returned from Spokane. Katie was not allowed to wear her new clothes until Zoe had reworked the button holes, reinforced all the seams and tightened the buttons with heavy-duty thread. It was a lot of work for her tired, old eyes, but it was routine.

Around the middle of August, Margie engaged Amanda to check on Mother during the day, while Katie and she went to Spokane. They usually spent the night at the Davenport Hotel, but Amanda didn't want to stay over with Mother, and Mother didn't want to go out to the farm, especially during harvest, so Margie and Katie crammed everything into one day.

Their first stop was the Town Topper Hallmark and Gift Store on Sprague Avenue where Sara Fosberg worked. They went in strictly to visit with her, but they always picked up something. If she had time to talk, they got all caught up on Jess and Elizabeth Anne. If not, they'd have to wait until Sara wrote her Christmas letter. This day they arranged to meet for lunch.

Next they went to Berg's for shoes for school. Katie was so thrilled to be out of the brown special shoes and into black suede oxfords and alligator shoes with straps for special occasions. Mr. Berg and family still wanted the best for her feet and would roll the heel and adjust the toe, so they fit her properly.

Sara met them under the clock at the Crescent Department Store on the main floor, as planned. That was the one of the most popular meeting places downtown, especially for shoppers and those having a luncheon engagement.

It was their lucky day in the Tea Room upstairs, as it was the day of the weekly fashion show. Models would mingle through the luncheon tables and model the latest outfits, as the ladies enjoyed their lunch. Katie was so in awe of the slim, attractive models, that she could hardly swallow her clam chowder and crackers. Sara and Margie enjoyed it as much as possible, but they were too busy talking.

"I tell you true. This has been so much fun, girls," Sara gushed when it was all over.

"Can we do it again soon?"

Katie was really hoping next time they could take the Manito bus up to the Fosberg's house, so she could see Elizabeth, but it was always left at, "We'll see."

A trip to Spokane would not be complete without a stop at the Davenport Hotel. Because of Grandma, they could not spend the night this time, so they dashed in for some strawberry ice cream with fresh berries and then sat for a few minutes in the lobby and listened to the birds sing and watched the big gold fish swimming around the base of the fountain.

After some shopping for school clothes at the Palace, it was time to retrieve the car, pay the parking attendant, and head west toward home.

"It's been fun, Mom." Katie yawned and laid her head back on the seat of the car.

"You mean you weren't bored?"

"No, I still look forward to our special times together, and it was really better without Grandma dragging along behind."

"Now let's not ruin a good day with talk like that. She can't help it if she's slow."

"I know, and I'm sorry, but she just fouls everything up. Like tomorrow when it's my turn to have 4-H club at my house; because of her, we have to have it at the Community Hall."

"Just stop and think about it, Katie. It's really for the best."

Katie didn't agree, but there was no use arguing. She really didn't want her mom to get a migraine after they'd had such a nice day together. They had to get home safely with the new clothes, so Grandma could start the next day, if the light was right, making the reinforcements.

*   *   *

Zoe made it through the winter of 1956, but Ed Shaw did not. He'd just never regained his strength after that last year on the farm during the war years, and although Belle cooked as much as she ever did on the farm for the two of them and pampered him with vitamins and afternoon naps, he continued on a downward spiral.

The flu bug ran rampant through the town that winter, and it attacked Ed and never let him go. His last days were spent in Spokane at Deaconess Hospital, battling pneumonia in an oxygen tent. The pneumonia won. Robert consoled his mother by telling her that, "Dad lost the battle, but won the war; and he's in a much better place than we are." She was devastated, but she knew Robert was right.

Ed was laid to rest four days later in the family plot north of Wheatland on the way to the farm. Several hundred townsfolk and farmers turned out to pay their last respects to a good man and good friend, and the biggest shock of all was that Michael came from Seattle. At first he told Robert, who called him with the news, that "The pass will probably be snowy and icy, and I won't be able to make it."

"You'll be here if you have to take a dog sled. Mother needs you; we all need you. Is that clear?" He sounded like he was talking to a little kid, but it must have worked. Michael arrived the next day and stayed an extra day after the funeral. Robert insisted that his mother, Amanda, and Michael stay out at the farm. Michael and Amanda did escape in the afternoon after the services. The house was full of mourners paying their respects, and nobody noticed their departure until it was too late to call them back. They would have just said that they needed more groceries for breakfast the next morning. Both were professionals at shading the truth.

On the way into town, Amanda told Michael the whole story of her pseudo-professorship in Iowa, her pregnancy, and of her beautiful baby girl, whom she had put up for adoption. The only thing she didn't tell him was that Katie was her very own. She didn't have to. As they sat on the couch at Amanda's apartment, Michael held her face in his hands and looked into her eyes. They told the whole story.

All that Amanda was required to do when Michael asked, "She's ours, isn't she?" was a nod of her head. The eyes truly are the windows to the soul.

The print may be a standard
Black and white, but God intends
For life to be colorful.
——Brian Bruya

Chapter XXIV

The players in the game of hearts were changing places. The art teacher from Amanda's evening class and the man that was in Amanda's dream gave up his seat to the photographer, and the cards were shuffled and dealt again and the game went on.

Michael Shaw received the hand of fatherhood, but he could never reveal his cards. Katie must never know the answer to the question that was eating at her heart.

Anxious to leave town, Michael told Amanda as they drove back to the farm that he should never come back to Wheatland for any reason.

"Never say 'never,'" she wisely said. "We don't know what the future holds. Your mom may need you—who knows?"

Michael was nervous. "But the resemblance, Amanda. What if someone can see it—even today?"

She shrugged. "Guess it's just a chance we have to take. I suppose the old busy-bodies around here are still trying to fit the pieces of the puzzle together, especially on occasions like we had today when everybody gathers with the family, and our business is brought to the fore-front. But then in a few days it all blows over. I live here, you know, and I think about it every day, but if I felt too guilty and let it show, then the game would be over. By the way, how did you figure it out?"

Michael rubbed his forehead, as if in deep thought, but really the answer was very easy.

"I just put two and two together, but mostly it's her eyes. I feel like I'm looking in a mirror." They had turned into the lane and were nearing the farmhouse. "Oh good, most of the cars are gone." Michael was relieved.

"Zoe and Margie and your daughter are still here." Amanda observed their car. "Can you handle it?"

"Yes, but don't call her *my daughter*. I'm not ashamed of her, but I just never wanted to be a father and especially not like this. This is bizarre! You have to admit it, Amanda."

"Oh, I do. It's a very strange situation, but it's workable. Well, let's go in. It's getting late in the afternoon, and I"m sure the three Wentworths will be leaving soon. Zoe won't allow Margie to drive after dark."

They carried one little brown grocery bag into the kitchen to prove the necessity of their trip to town. Robert wondered what took them so long.

Amanda spoke up quickly. "We were just driving around the town. Michael wanted to take some pictures of the trees and the park. It's so unusual to see them uncovered this time of year." The snow had melted shortly after Christmas and, except for a skiff or two, it had been an exceptionally dry winter. "Now he wants to take some family pictures, don't you, Michael?" This hadn't been mentioned between the two of them, but Amanda had her reasons.

"Yes, you're right. I do. Just let me get my camera ready," Michael agreed, and after everyone else was gone, they all gathered in the living room, and Michael arranged the family in a professional manner. Zoe protested, but he cajoled her into sitting in the middle, with Katie front and center on the floor with the family behind her. They all noticed again the absence of Ed, which forced Michael to use the tricks of his trade to bring forth unforced, genuine smiles. He snapped three shots, "Just to make sure," and then the group dispersed. Robert dashed outside to check on the chickens before they went to roost. Margie, Amanda, and Belle wanted to make sure the kitchen wasn't in a mess. Zoe, anxious to get home, hobbled into the bathroom and then into the spare bedroom to retrieve their coats.

"Hey, Katie," Michael said quietly. "May I take a couple snapshots of you? You know—close up."

"Okay. If you want to." Katie had always been photogenic and loved to pose. She thought it was good practice for when she became an actress.

Michael motioned with his head. "Here, just sit on the arm of the couch," and he gently touched her chin and turned her head just so. "The light's not real great, but maybe it will be all right," he worried aloud. A few clicks, and he was done. "Those should be good." He wanted to tell her she was beautiful, but Zoe, returning with the coats, saved him just in time from saying too much.

"Let's go," she barked and ushered Katie into the kitchen.

The day was nearly over—the day that Michael buried his father and the day he found his daughter, whom he didn't even know existed.

The next day Michael left the family to return to his life on the other side of the state. Belle cried, Robert solemnly shook his hand and said, "It was great having you here. Now don't be such a stranger," and Amanda gave him a quick hug. She walked him out to his car, and he handed her the film.

"Send me some shots, if they turn out."

"When haven't your pictures turned out?" Amanda couldn't believe he'd have a failure.

"I am still experimenting with a lot of the new color films."

"Well, good. Keep practicing. Next time you can use color to get some shots of Katie."

"Next time?"

*   *   *

The school year proceeded with several upsets for Katie. In March, Patricia and Daniel Benson sold their drugstore to Andy and Julia Monroe and moved to Spokane. When school was out in early June, Rusty Harrison and his family moved to Yakima, Washington.

Katie was devastated with both losses, but before the summer was over, Margie had found another dramatics teacher, much to Amanda's dismay. Her name was Emily Stafford, and she herself had at one time been a pupil of Patricia's. It wasn't long before Katie loved Emily and her lessons. Emily lived on a farm west of Wheatland, and Margie and Katie both enjoyed the drive through the wheat fields and by the herds of cattle.

Katie wrote a couple of letters to Rusty, but he didn't write back. Margie said that was typical of boys; they weren't much for letter-writing, so not to take it personally.

In August, Camille announced by mail that she would be visiting in September, and would call with a specific date. Zoe expressed surprise—both that Camille was coming again and that she was still around to see it. She perked up a bit and commandeered the house-cleaning on the main floor from several vantage points. Katie helped Margie clean the blue room and polish the stairs. Zoe wished they could put a protective coating on the steps to protect them from all the torture of Camille's wear and tear.

She soon arrived much the same, and the trunk, the high heels, and the dog banged and clicked their assault on the stairs once again.

Camille thought her sisters had aged and that her mother looked terrible—and then there was Katie.

"Little Missy, how you've grown! Look, I think we are the same size now. I bet we could wear each other's clothes."

Katie looked at her mother with a pained expression. The blue corduroy jumper and plaid wool skirts hanging in Katie's closet just wouldn't look right on Camille's skinny bones; Katie, who felt different enough already, would be booted out of school if she showed up in Camille's skin tight silk dresses with a split up the back seam and the long dangling earrings and high spike heels.

"She was just making a comparison, honey; she really didn't mean it." Margie assured her daughter later in the evening.

Camille had been there one whole week before she verbally acknowledged her paintings on the wall. Just to see them hanging there had opened up a flood of emotions, and eventually the sandbags weren't strong enough to hold back her feelings.

One evening after dinner, as they were sitting in the living room, Camille broached the subject, and the raging waters of forty-plus years of anger and rejection poured out and over-flowed. "So, Mother, I've been admiring my paintings on the wall. I wondered where they were and remembered how you hated them. What made you hang them now?"

Mother tried to be diplomatic, but with Camille's attitude, she was in no mood to offer the long-awaited apology. "Oh, you know me. I just like flowers and frills and more subdued colors, and I thought you'd like to see them displayed."

Camille's face was turning as red as the fire in the painting. "No, I don't know you, Mother. I never have. You wouldn't let me get close to you, and now I've come back to try again, but it's just the same. In fact, it's even worse. You never cared about me, so why would you care about my feelings now? You sit there with your back to me and look out the window or face the wall and hardly ever say so much as one word and if you do, it's negative." She was on a tirade, and her voice got louder and louder.

Margie was about to explain quietly as an aside to Camille that Mother was aging, and noise and commotion upset her and not to take it personally, when Camille jumped up and dashed into the pantry. When she returned in just a few moments, Margie saw her right hand drawn close to her side, but she didn't see the butcher knife until Camille approached the forest fire and raised her arm. Margie jumped from the couch and grabbed Camille's arm just as the shiny instrument gouged a long rip right in the center of the painting.

"Let go," Margie screamed.

Katie put her hand over her mouth and ran to the bathroom and slammed the door. Mother cowered in her corner and knew that her apology was now useless.

Camille dropped the knife, and as she turned to grab her quivering dog from the couch, she yelled at her mother. "There, how do you like the forest fire now? I never want to see it or you again!"

And she never did.

Katie slept on a cot in Grandma's room that night. There was no way she would ascend those stairs and walk past the blue room with Camille still in it.

A shaken Zoe had been put to bed immediately with a cool compress on her forehead. Margie hovered over her like a nurse and finally sat in a rocker until both Katie and Mother were asleep. Mother had a little cowbell by her bed that she could ring if she needed anything, and Margie listened for it with one ear all night. Like a mother checking on a very quiet newborn baby, Margie crept quietly down the stairs around 2:00 a.m., worried that Mother had died in her sleep, but she was snoring loudly with her mouth wide open. Katie was tossing and turning and having weird dreams. She jumped when Margie tucked her in again and kissed her on the cheek.

Camille banged down the stairs one final time early in the morning and roared out of Wheatland in a cloud of dust, like a teenage boy spinning his wheels. She left behind a battered and bewildered household and a surprised and saddened sister down the hill in her apartment. Amanda's disappointment lay in the fact that she had hoped Camille would use the black and white photos of Katie and do some charcoal sketches or maybe even paint a colorful oil, but after Margie called with the news of Camille's quick exit, Amanda shoved the pictures in a drawer.

"Maybe I'll send a copy to her one day and commission her. Surely she's not mad at me!"

I am ready to meet my Maker.
Whether my Maker is ready
For the ordeal of meeting me
Is another matter.
—Winston Churchill

Chapter XXV

Zoe's health began a downward spiral almost as soon as Camille's dust had settled. She struggled through each day, buffeted by problems from every direction. The senna laxative, for example, cleared up her constipation temporarily, but then she became dependent on it more and more, and sometimes she took too much. It became a vicious cycle and created more work and anxiety for Margie when it worked too well.

Katie often heard her mother say, "Grandma didn't quite make it again. Oh, how I wish she had her own bathroom."

"As if I couldn't tell!" Katie held her defiant little nose. For the first time she wanted to be away from home as much as possible. Margie didn't like her attitude, but she thought, in a way, who could blame her?

Zoe's blood pressure skyrocketed, but she refused to take the little white pill. "What does Dr. Petersen know? He's not from the Mayo Clinic, is he?" Those were the only doctors she trusted, although she'd never been examined or diagnosed by one.

In addition, she was sure she was having serious heart palpitations.

"It could very well be, Doctor. She's been under a lot of stress lately." Margie was trying to help with the diagnosis, but the EKG showed nothing terribly wrong.

Whether her problems were real or imagined, Mother was miserable, and Margie was at her wits' end. Also, she was trying very hard not to overdo and get sick herself; but as long as she stayed on her non-fat diet, she was better able to cope. Katie thought the diet was so boring, but Margie explained that it was better for all of them to eat healthy.

"Mother's heartsick over Camille, but she won't admit it." Margie tried to confide in Amanda when she visited.

"So what if she did admit it? It wouldn't make the problems go away. They should have aired their differences years ago, but it's too late now." Amanda had her own problems, and they wouldn't go away either.

"But I just thought maybe you could talk to Mother and get her to open up. Sometimes it helps to confide in someone, and then she'd feel better."

"Margie, you're just grasping at straws. She won't talk to me. Besides, don't you think that a lot of her problems are just old age? The body does wear out, you know."

As usual, Amanda was no help. Margie knew better than to bring up her worries about Katie, because Amanda would just switch it all around and blame Margie for being a bad mother.

Amanda mentioned Katie herself. "By the way, before I leave, why doesn't Katie ever walk by my apartment any more? When I'm home, I watch for her every afternoon."

Margie could have told her that was the very reason Katie took another route; she didn't like being watched and used to hate it when she'd walk by and Amanda would call her in to see how well she could read. She was a top student in reading and always had been, reading most of the *Reader's Digest* when she was in the third grade.

"Oh, I think she's been getting a ride with the Grahams. She has so much to carry—trumpet case, books, gym bag—you know, so when Henry picks up his girls, she goes home with them—I mean he drops her off." Actually, she did go to their house quite often. Henry ran the ambulance service and was the local mortician, so he wasn't always available; then Katie would walk, by-passing

Amanda's, and drop by to see Hilda Johnson, but Amanda didn't need to know that; she was jealous enough already.

"Well. I could bring her home," she said defiantly. "If I'm teaching, she could wait for me after school, or if not, I could run up and get her." Amanda was quick to volunteer.

"I think it's really better for her this way, Amanda. At least when she's with the Graham girls, she's with people her own age. If you really want to help out, then please help me with Mother." She sounded almost desperate.

"Oh, I will. Call any time."

And you'll be busy, Margie thought, as Amanda hurriedly grabbed her jacket and was out the door. She didn't even take the time to tell her mother good bye.

*　　*　　*

Zoe suffered her first stroke the day that Katie's dog, Daisy, died in October. Daisy was sleeping on the kitchen floor when she shuddered, gave a horrendous, bone-chilling moan, and went limp. Katie witnessed it and shrieked for her mother, who was in Zoe's bedroom changing the sheets.

When Margie saw her, she had a good idea what had happened. "Oh no. He got her again, and this time he killed her." Margie had gotten Daisy to the vet in time to save her the previous time that she'd had the poisoned hamburger, but it was too late now.

"I hate him! I hate him!" Katie cried, as her mother held her in her arms.

"I know. I don't like him either."

The person in question was a creepy, middle-aged man named Elmore Carter, who lived alone about three blocks from them in a shack that Margie had named "The Kotex Cottage." It was thrown together from all sorts of scraps of material, and Margie was sure it was padded for warmth on the inside with a woman's necessities. He enjoyed walking through their alley, smiling and sneering and whistling at Daisy. She was a gentle dog and wagged her tail at everyone, except Elmore Carter. She snarled and growled, and instead of him just taking another route, he threw poisoned meat over the fence. They couldn't absolutely prove he was the culprit, but the fact that he liked to go to Hudson's Grocery and eat raw hamburger in the back room made him just that much more suspicious.

Margie called Amanda, and she in turn called Robert, who drove quickly in from the farm to dispose of the dog. He carried her outside, but it was dark, and he thought he should wait until morning to bury her.

Meanwhile, Margie had told Zoe what happened, and even though she didn't care that much about the dog, it upset her so she had a bad spell. She got rigid, then went limp and slumped over the desk by the dining room window. Robert came in and picked her up in his strong arms. Margie tucked a blanket around her. They left Katie all alone and drove Zoe to the nearest hospital twenty-two miles away in Coulee Dam, Washington, where she remained for five days. Much to the dismay of the town folk, the local Wheatland Hospital had been turned into a nursing home.

It was the worst night of Katie's life. Her friend and companion, who'd run up and down the sledding hill with her in the winter, who knew twelve tricks and displayed them at a talent show at the county fair, and who waited for her at 4:00 p.m. every day at the corner of their yard, was dead. To top it off, Grandma had a bad spell, so they all left her. She trudged up the stairs to bed and cried and cried. She wanted to call Hilda to come over to stay with her, but it was dark and raining, plus Katie had a cold and knew she shouldn't share her germs with her.

It was 2:00 a.m. when Robert and Amanda finally dropped Margie off. He told her he'd be back in town later when the sun was up to bury Daisy. Margie threw the blanket that they'd wrapped Mother in over the dog, and then she crept quietly up the stairs to check on Katie. She was still awake. Margie sat on her bed and took her in her arms, and Katie sobbed her heart out.

"Grandma will be okay," she assured her.

"Yeah, but Daisy won't. I loved her so much."

"I know; she was a good friend."

Margie stayed until Katie was asleep, and then went to her room across the hall. She was exhausted, but she lay awake thinking. What a horrible day! The only good thing is that Robert's coming in the morning.

He arrived alone about 8:00 a.m. Katie was awake, but wanted to stay in bed and let Robert take care of Daisy's burial. Later Katie would go outside when she felt better and see where Daisy was sleeping among the parsley and the sage. Katie knew she'd get over her cold, but Daisy's death would haunt her forever.

Margie had been up for hours. She was still worn out from the night's ordeal, but she'd bathed and dressed and cleaned up the house a bit for Robert's arrival.

Robert looked very somber as Margie let him in the back door. They hugged, and she asked if he wanted coffee or tea before they began the chore.

"Maybe after?" he questioned.

"Yeah, we'll probably need it to warm up." She was agreeable to anything, at any time—even a pet's burial—just to be with Robert. She saw him so rarely, but thought of him daily.

He grabbed the shovel from the shed and worked quietly, digging the hole and then gently lowering Daisy, still wrapped in the blanket, into the grave. Margie stood on the grass and watched him work. She looked up once toward Katie's dormer window. She thought she saw a shadow move away just as she looked, but couldn't be sure.

Robert was finished, and walked toward Margie. He held the shovel in one hand, and with the other wiped away a single tear that was thundering down her cheek.

"I'm sorry, but Katie and I loved that dog."

"I know; she was a good companion for her. I was thinking. I know a breeder in Spokane. Maybe *we* can get her another Springer."

Margie heard all his words, but *we* was underlined with a row of exclamations marks in her mind.

"Margie, did you hear me?"

"Oh yes." Margie snapped to attention. "It's a little soon, but we can ask Katie what she thinks about it after some of the pain goes away." Margie really didn't want to train another puppy, but *we* together, she and Robert, were all that mattered.

"I'll put the shovel away, then how about that cup of coffee?"

The tears were dammed up in her throat, so she just nodded her head. She wanted to slip her arm through his, but the neighbors were no doubt peeking through their curtains. Once inside, he hung up their coats while she made the coffee.

"I need to wash my hands." He pointed to the bathroom, and Margie nodded.

"Oh sure. Go right ahead. I'll put some banana bread on a plate to go with our coffee."

But they never got around to their little party. When he walked back into the kitchen, he couldn't control himself any longer. He took the plate of bread from her hands and set it on the table. Then he turned and embraced her with all the years of wanting and waiting pouring out. She melted into his arms and nestled against his chest. He wanted to kiss her, but he knew if he ever touched those lips with his, they'd be locked together forever. They both pulled away, but stood holding hands and facing each other.

"Katie could come down at any minute, so we have to be careful," Margie warned.

But it was Amanda, not Katie, who caught them. All of a sudden, the kitchen door opened, and there she was.

"Where have you been? What are you doing?" Amanda's voice was loud in desperation. "The hospital's been trying to reach you. Mother has taken a turn for the worse."

*   *   *

Zoe's condition did worsen before she got better, but the pride and determination that had sustained her all her life once again gave her some strength to carry on a while longer.

"Get me my hair pins. Where are my teeth?" She barked on the fifth day. "I'm going home. Call Margie," she commanded the nurse, and with the doctor's reluctant permission, she was set free. "That place was like a jail. All I got was some bread and water," she grumbled on the ride home. "I want some meatloaf and mashed potatoes."

Margie cooked and cleaned and babied her mother even more than usual, so by Christmas, Zoe felt that she was strong enough to celebrate the family get-together at the Shaw farm once again. "This will be my last Christmas; then I'll be up on the hill," she predicted.

The day went smoothly, and everyone enjoyed their gifts and dinner. Ed's absence left a big gap, and they missed Michael, too—some more than others.

"Oh, I ate too much," Zoe complained shortly after the big meal. She and Katie were sitting in the living room, while the other women worked in the kitchen. "Oh, my stomach," and then she was sick. Her hands clapped over her mouth couldn't hold it back.

"Help! Amanda! Mom! Somebody! Grandma's sick!" They came running from the kitchen.

"Go get Robert, honey." Belle gently shoved Katie toward the back door. "I think he's in the barn." Katie was glad to get out of the house and stayed out on the porch after Robert went in the house. In a few minutes, Margie called her inside.

"Sit down here in the kitchen while we wait for the ambulance."

"The ambulance? Did she die?" She wasn't sure about her feelings toward her grandma, but she'd had enough of death for one year.

"No, Katie, but she's really sick. She's had another spell—much worse, I think, than the first one."

"Do I have to be home alone again?" Katie was nearly in tears.

"No, you and I will go on home. Robert will stay here with Belle, and Amanda will ride to Spokane in the ambulance with Grandma."

Katie was so relieved and hugged her mom.

Just then Henry pulled into the lane, and he and his helper for the evening jumped out of the front seat of the ambulance, opened the back doors, and yanked out a stretcher.

"She's in there on the couch." Margie said, as she ushered them in. "Sorry to call you out on Christmas."

"Oh well. It's our job." Henry answered, as if he wasn't too bothered.

Robert helped them load her up, then kissed his wife. The ambulance made a u-turn and roared away for the Deaconess Hospital in Spokane.

When Zoe Wentworth passed away six days later, the whole town of Wheatland was shocked. Of course, those few friends who had come to visit her at home over the fall and early winter months could see her aged and frail body failing. Somehow, though, they foolishly thought that maybe she'd be the first person in history to live forever. However, the eighty-seven-year-old matriarch of the Wentworth family barked out her final orders on December 29, just before she slipped into a coma, silencing once and for all the commanding presence she held over the family. Two days later, Zoe heaved her final sigh.

Amanda notified Camille by phone that evening.

"Don't expect me." Her cold heart was frozen like the pink peonies covered with snow.

The rest of the family, the people of the town of Wheatland, and the residents of the surrounding farmlands buried Zoe.

Her reign of terror was over.

One was never married
And that's his hell;
Another is, and that's his plague.
                            —Robert Burton

Chapter XXVI

Hilda Johnson was so saddened by Zoe's death that she'd hardly been able to write the obituary, but she finally pulled all the pieces of the family together and summed up Zoe's life in four paragraphs. When it was published, she brought two extra copies over to Margie.

"Just in case you want to send one to Camille or to your relatives back East," she offered, as she handed them to Margie.

"Thank you. Come on in and sit a spell. It's so good to see you. Amanda and I were just going through some of Mother's papers, and we do need a break." She and Hilda embraced. "Hilda's here," she called to Amanda, who was in Zoe's bedroom.

Hilda sat at the kitchen table in Zoe's chair, and when she realized it was Zoe's empty spot, she burst into tears. "I've lost my best friend," she cried. "Do you know that in her Christmas letter to me, she truly believed she wouldn't be here much longer? She said it was the last letter she'd ever write to me."

Margie took Hilda's emotions hard and began to cry, while Amanda, who had inherited or acquired her mother's stoicism, only frowned and said, "You mean she sent you a Christmas card when you live just down the alley?" Amanda thought it highly unnecessary. "Couldn't you just pick up the phone and say, 'Merry Christmas?'"

Hilda was drying her tears. "Oh, but that wouldn't be the same. I've loved her letters, and I've saved them year after year."

"What a lot of clutter! Where would you keep them in that little house?" Amanda just had to keep beating a dead horse.

Hilda was tired of the questions. "I just keep them in my heart." With that, she and Margie burst into tears again.

Amanda shook her head in bewilderment, got up, and stepped into the dining room. In just a minute she returned with a cellophane bag in her hand. She was anxious for Hilda to go home. "When you leave, Hilda, why don't you take this little sack of horehound candy with you. I found it in Mother's desk drawer, and none of us can stand it. Now, don't save it as an inheritance gift; be sure to eat it." Amanda laughed, but no one else could see her humor.

"Thank you, Amanda. It's one of my favorites." She stood up and tucked it into her apron pocket. "Well, I must go. We have a paper to put to bed in a few days again." Sometimes she sounded as if she owned, edited, and published the paper all on her own.

"I suppose you're going to write about how you came clear down the alley for tea with the Wentworth girls. You know, I could never understand how a visit from a neighbor could be very newsworthy."

Margie rose to Hilda's defense. "Sometimes that's all the excitement there is in a small town, Amanda, and sometimes there are other things going on that are secrets. Why don't you just give it up and quit badgering her? Did you get up on the wrong side of the bed this morning?"

With a smirk, Amanda said, "No, I'm just taking over where Mother left off."

*　　*　　*

For Katie's twelfth birthday, Margie took Katie and three of her friends—Jill, Karen, and Annette—down to Park Lake, about sixty miles from of Wheatland, for an afternoon of swimming, games, and a picnic supper. Margie very rarely took Katie anywhere just for fun, so this was a real treat. If it was an elocution lesson, a dramatic performance, or a Bi-County spelling competition, Margie was right there, but entertaining her daughter was not high on Margie's list of priorities.

When they returned home that evening around 7:00 p.m., Robert's pickup was parked out in front of the Wentworth house. He and Amanda were sitting on the front porch, and Katie could see he was holding something in his lap—and it was moving.

"Oh, my gosh! It's a puppy. Let me out here, Mom, while you put the car in the garage." Katie jumped out, almost before the car had stopped.

"Happy birthday, Katie," Amanda and Robert said in unison, and they held out the squirming spaniel to her.

"For me? Oh, my gosh," she said again. "She looks just like Daisy." She didn't know whether to laugh or cry. "Thank you. Thank you," and she hugged them both.

Just then, Margie rounded the corner of the house. "Oh, you shouldn't have," was all she could think to say when she saw the little brown and white bundle in Katie's arms.

"Well, we talked about it, Margie," Robert responded. There was that word *we* again. Did he mean he and Margie, or he and Amanda, or both?

Before she could even try to figure it out, Robert had another idea. "I know you're probably worried about training a puppy, but you can bring her out to the house, and I can help, and I could even teach her to hunt. You know, Springers make great hunting dogs."

Katie yelled and scared the little puppy, who snuggled even closer to her breast. "Oh no. She might get shot!" She'd seen enough of death lately to last her a long time—first Ed Shaw, then her beloved Daisy, and then Grandma.

Amanda hadn't bargained for all this generosity from Robert, but she supposed he felt sorry for Katie and was trying to be helpful. "You're scaring her, Robert, after all she's been through; but maybe I can drive her and the dog out, and you can at least help Katie with the obedience training." She turned to Katie. "What do you think you'll name her?"

While Katie and Aunt Amanda were giving that some thought, Margie and Robert's eyes met. Amanda was fouling up their hopes and dreams.

I can drive her out myself! Margie hoped Robert could read those words in her eyes, and when he smiled and nodded, she was sure the message that she was the one who wanted to come out to the farm for the dog training got through to him.

"Well, we'd better go, Mandy, now that we've made Katie happy. Enjoy your puppy and come out any time."

"We will. Thank you both so much." Katie hugged them both again, and they were off.

"Oh, Mom. Isn't Robert the greatest? I wish he was my father." She gasped. She'd never thought of that before. "He isn't, is he?"

*   *   *

The puppy training out at Robert's didn't turn out as well as some had anticipated. When school started in September, Katie was a busy seventh grader, so Margie decided she'd take little Dixie out to the farm while Katie was in school. She'd surprise Katie with what a smart dog Robert had selected, and what a good trainer he was.

Margie was no longer on a party line, so she didn't have to worry about people with big ears and even bigger mouths; but the three times she called him to see if it was convenient, it did not work out at all. She wanted to make sure Amanda was teaching at school all day for one thing, but the first time she called, Amanda answered the phone herself, so Margie hung up quickly. When her bravery returned later in the week, Margie phoned again, but there was no answer.

Well, I suppose it's for the best. He *is* a married man—married to my sister, of all people.

Just when she'd resigned herself to putting her feelings back in her dresser drawer and turning the little lock, Margie answered a knock on the door to find Robert standing there.

"Well, for heaven's sake! It's you!" Margie patted her hair and ran her fingers through the top to rearrange and style it. "What a nice surprise! I've been trying to call you. Come right on in."

"Are you busy?" Robert queried.

"I try to keep busy, but no, not really. I was just ironing Katie's new dress. She's going to her first seventh and eighth grade party on Friday." Margie was babbling nervously. "I tried to call you about the dog training, but could never reach you. Should you be here today? Where's Amanda?"

Robert tried to reassure her. "Calm down, Margie. It's okay. Amanda's in Spokane, and if any nosy neighbors need to know, I am just delivering the eggs you ordered."

"But I didn't order . . . Oh, I get it." She laughed and took the carton from him.

"I only brought one dozen, even though you might have wanted two, but see, that way I can come back next week with another dozen." Robert had it all planned.

"We don't use as many as we did when Mother was alive, but we can have scrambled eggs for breakfast and egg sandwiches for lunch." Margie was sure she would need more next week. "You are so clever, Robert." That was the very least Margie could say.

"I can't stay long, but how is the puppy doing?" Robert hoped he'd selected a good one.

"It's a slow process, but she's learning. Katie doesn't spend the time with her, though, that she did with Daisy."

"There's nothing like a first love," and with that comment, Robert grabbed Margie and sealed his statement with a long, passionate kiss. He finally pulled away. "Oh, man. This can't be happening. I can't be doing this." He wiped his mouth with the back of his hand, as if that would erase his sin.

"We'd better sit down and talk, Robert." Margie was so shaken. She felt dizzy and sank into the chair across from Robert. "We'll have to hurry. Katie will be home soon."

"I just don't know what to do, Margie. I try to deny my feelings for you, and I pray, and I feel so guilty. Sometimes when I talk to God, I say, 'But God, you just don't understand.' But that's so stupid! Of course He understands; He knows more about me than I know about myself. I know that He forgives me, but I am such a hypocrite!" Robert leaned back in the chair, rubbed his hand over his crewcut, and looked at Margie. He'd maintained his Marine Corps spit and polish, if not his Christianity. He knew the latter was eternally more important than the first.

"Maybe you'd feel better if you went to church," Margie was desperate to help.

"I think I'd feel worse, and besides, I can't get Amanda to go on Sundays when we're supposed to be doing things together. Sometimes I take Mom and go to Bible study on Wednesday nights. We both enjoy that. We need the fellowship and the lessons. Boy, do I need the lessons!"

"Are you happy, Robert?"

"Yes. I mean no. I try to be, but it's no kind of a marriage, really. Just weekend get-togethers. I feel like we're dating, and when I try to talk her into giving up her apartment and coming to the farm exclusively, she says she has her reasons for staying in town. I often wonder if *she's* having an affair; and the worst part is, I often think it would be easier if she were."

"Oh, Robert. I don't think she is, but I suppose she could be hiding something from us."

Margie knew the real reason was to watch over Katie, but that was another secret in the game of hearts.

"I guess I just don't understand her; she's always so busy." Margie knew that from years of experience with her little sister. "She's always been like that. Whenever she's needed, she's busy. I sure could have used her help with Mother, but it was only toward the very end that she even showed much concern, and then there wasn't all that much to do as far as housework, because Mother was in the hospital."

Robert let his pity show. "Yeah, I tried to get her to help you more. I know it wasn't easy." He wanted to take her in his arms and hold her forever, but he crossed them over his chest instead. "You do love me, too, don't you, Margie? I just want to make sure. You know, we've never really talked about us and our feelings."

"We've never had to talk. Oh, Robert, if you only knew how much, but you'd better go now. Katie is due at any moment."

As he got up reluctantly to go, he looked around and sniffed. "What's that smell? Is something burning?"

"Oh, no, the iron. I forgot to turn it off," she cried! She dashed into the living room and, jerking the iron away from the scorched nylon material, she cried again, "Katie's dress is ruined!"

We are not like blades of grass
Swept away by a lawn mower.
We have roots like trees.

—Maya Angelou

Chapter XXVII

A scorched dress and a burned-out marriage—the dress was easily repairable by cutting two inches off the bottom and hemming it again; but it would take more than a pair of scissors and a needle and thread to salvage Robert's marriage.

Katie was late getting home that day, and by the time she slammed the screen door, the scorched material had been removed, but the odor lingered.

"What smells so funny?" Katie wondered.

"I was about to ask you the same thing," Margie sniffed at Katie's hair, "but I can tell you've been to Hilda's house."

Margie showed her the dress. "I'm sorry, honey. The iron was set too hot for this sheer material, and it scorched it a little, but I fixed it. Does it look okay? It's not too short, is it?"

"Yeah, it's okay," she said nonchalantly, barely looking at her new dress. "I'm not sure if I even want to go, though."

Margie was shocked. "Why not? It's only for two hours."

"But I don't know how to dance. Rusty and I used to dance to *Round and Round* in the gym when Annette brought her Perry Como record to school. He'd twirl me around so fast that everyone else sat down and watched, but that's the only dancing I know how to do."

Margie encouraged her to go. "Probably no one else will be

any better than you. You'll have fun." She sincerely hoped no one would be any better than her daughter. She wanted her to be the best in all things.

Katie reluctantly went, but returned home tired and disillusioned. "The girls sat on one side of the gym, the boys on the other. The teachers tried to shove us together and make us dance, but it didn't work too well."

"Didn't you dance at all?"

"Yeah, twice—once with Frank, but he smelled bad, and once with Dave, but his hands were all sweaty. I kept wishing Rusty would walk in."

Margie could relate to that; she knew what it meant to hope that someone special would enter the door. "It will get better. Everyone will feel more at ease next time."

It seemed to get better for everyone else, but not for Katie. Although she went to every dance through the seventh and eighth grade, and most of the high school dances she could attend without a date, she hardly ever danced. She wasn't popular, and she tried desperately to figure out why. She was smart—maybe too smart. All the adults in her life told her she was pretty, but she wasn't allowed to wear make-up, and her hair was not the same style as the other girls in her class. She had a ponytail clear into high school, but then she got it cut really short. Her mother loved the natural waves, but nobody else had them. She was quiet and shy, especially around the boys, and on those rare occasions when one of them asked her to dance, she didn't know what to say. Her mother usually answered for her at home or out in public, so she had little practice in the art of socializing.

One day Hilda asked Katie a question. Before Katie could answer, Margie had butted in with the answer.

"No, I asked Katie the question, and I want her to answer it." Hilda could see what was going on.

The band teacher often told Katie that she was non-committal. Margie wasn't there to speak for her, so Katie's silence proved the teacher's observation correct. Trying to figure out her unpopularity took hours, and there was no explanation or resolution.

The other bothersome problem was the lack of understanding of the whole adoption thing. The other students in Katie's class who were adopted were not as obsessed with the subject as was Katie. They seemed to have happy normal lives with a dad in the house and brothers and sisters, but for Katie it was a different home life. Often quizzing Hilda to see if she knew anything, Katie got nowhere. Surely someone would confide in Hilda. She'd been Zoe's best friend, and now she and Margie seemed very close.

Hilda had no information to offer and told Katie that if she did know anything, she probably shouldn't breach the confidence that anyone had entrusted to her. Hilda remembered hearing that phone call that someone had placed to Iowa, but it happened so long ago that Hilda wasn't sure any more if she had heard correctly or whose voice it really was. It sounded like Amanda's at the time, and then she did go to Iowa, but that was to teach, so Hilda had stopped trying to make a case out of that; but she, too, wondered how it had all come about, and with the investigative mind of a reporter, it was intriguing. She felt sorry for Katie, and she couldn't imagine not knowing all about one's heritage. Hilda was from strong Swedish stock, and the genealogy way back into the old country was interesting to her. "I'd help you if I could," Hilda had sincerely told Katie several times. Katie believed her, but still had no answers. Maybe this was the cause of being unpopular—nobody else knew who she was either. That answer would have to suffice for awhile, but someday when the declension of nouns in Latin had all been learned and that "idiotic" periodic table in chemistry had been deciphered, there would be more time to study and figure out her heritage. With Margie demanding perfection, even to the point of having Katie reading all the library books out loud, so Margie could write the book reports to get an A, she had little time to dwell on her problems.

When Katie was a senior in high school, her life changed dramatically. It was one of the most bittersweet times in her life. There was more freedom to study on her own, even reading a book to herself and going to the bedroom upstairs to write her own book report. The bedroom was off-limits for everything, except sleeping, so Margie made quite a concession in allowing that to happen. It paid off, though, when Katie came home with an A on the report card.

Margie took all the credit. "Well, you got a good grade because you learned from me how to do it."

Much to Margie's dismay later on, she allowed Katie to get a job after school, stocking shelves at Hudson's Grocery. The Hudsons were very accommodating, letting her work around other activities—4-H club and playing in the band at football games or parades. She worked for two hours most nights after school and every other Saturday.

The most accommodating of all the Hudsons was their oldest son, Teddy. He had graduated from Wheatland High the previous year and was employed at the Chevron station, trying to earn money for college. When he had time to pop into his family's store, he'd stop to help Katie lift a heavy box or place some cans up high on a shelf. If Katie would have known how to flirt, she'd have tried to catch Teddy's eye and lead him on, but capturing the attention of the opposite sex was not high on her list of accomplishments. But no expertise was needed. Teddy asked Katie out late in November, and by Christmas they were going steady. He loved everything about her—the brown, wavy hair; sad, hazel eyes; and her pretty, dimpled smile. She was a perfect compliment to his curly, blond hair and dancing, blue eyes.

Margie protested with all the ammunition possible, and not just to Katie, but to Amanda, as well. "But he has a car. His family just runs a grocery store. They're all uneducated." But she reluctantly let Katie date him, mostly because Amanda was demanding that Katie be allowed to live a little. "Yes, she can do better, but it's just puppy love; it won't last. Let her have some fun."

Katie had to defend him every time he asked her out, although they'd never done anything wrong. "But, Mom, we're just going to the Marquee Lights. Elvis is playing in *Kid Galahad*, and then we're going to Burgers and Fries. Then we'll be home," or "The prom will be over at midnight; we'll skip the party at Karen's, and I'll be home by 12:30."

They were always on time, but there was Margie, stationed at the front door, peeking through the vertical windows to make sure that Teddy kept the car running, and Katie got out immediately.

"There's Mother," Katie would say to Teddy, as they kissed good-bye. "Now, she'll chastise me for falling in love with you."

Katie politely listened at first with respect, remembering Margie's teachings not to answer back, but it was becoming harder and harder to keep quiet.

The night that Margie jumped all over her for being five minutes late was the night that Katie became defiant.

"I rue the day I ever let you go to work at that grocery store! I don't sanction any of this!"

Finally Katie exploded. "Just because you've never had a boy friend! You don't know what it is like!" She'd never yelled at her mother before.

Margie's face turned red, the tears crashing down her cheeks. "You know nothing about my life. You don't know what's gone on."

Katie yelled again, "Well, at least you know who you are; I don't even know that!"

They both felt bad for yelling, but neither apologized. Margie decided perhaps Katie needed someone to love her for the time being, so she let her date Teddy occasionally during the rest of the school year and into the summer, but she demanded when Katie went to college at WSU that she turn off her feelings, just like turning off the faucet.

Margie should have known it wasn't so easy; as her feelings for Robert were just as strong as ever. They had decided the weekly egg deliveries were not a good idea, so they had to arrange other ways of meeting. The only possible arrangement was for Margie to go to the farm, which had to be carefully worked around Amanda's schedule, although they didn't often know where she was at any given moment unless she was teaching or off to Spokane.

They had to play the game of hearts carefully and keep the cards close to their breasts. Robert continued to feel guilty, but his loneliness and his love for Margie won out every time. While Margie certainly didn't want to get caught, she felt she deserved a little happiness in her life, too, and the game went on.

Amanda went blithely on her way with her life of freedom and monitoring Katie. She tried to talk Katie into pledging her sorority at WSU, but Katie knew she'd never be accepted.

Amanda blamed Margie. "I thought you wanted the best for her. What is wrong with my sorority? I suppose you talked her out of it."

"Nothing is wrong with it. She just doesn't think she'll fit in. Let her live in a dorm for awhile. She can always pledge later, can't she? This is her first time away from home, and she's scared."

"Sure, because you never let her go anywhere or do anything."

Margie came back with the ultimate retort, and she thought she was going to see Amanda cry for the first time. "Could you have done better?"

*   *   *

Margie packed Katie's new Samsonite suitcases that had been a graduation gift from Aunt Amanda and Robert, and hired Dottie to drive them to Pullman. Amanda was furious once again, because she hadn't asked for her assistance.

Amanda was a full-time chemistry teacher at Wheatland High now, so, of course, Margie wouldn't think of asking her. It was the third week in September. Amanda would surely be busy, and she didn't really feel right about asking Robert.

"Well, I could have easily taken the day off." Amanda's nose was so far out of joint that it actually looked crooked.

"Maybe another time. We got her all settled in. Who should we run into, but Sara and Jess? Elizabeth is in the same dorm. Isn't that nice to live close by someone she knows?"

Amanda had acquired her mother's old habit of sniffing. "Oh, I suppose." Amanda had really never thought too highly of any of them. "Sara and Jess have just never done anything with their lives," so to Amanda they were a waste of time.

Margie was quick to defend them. "No, they don't have a string of college degrees, but they're good, upstanding people. They've worked hard to send Elizabeth to college. I'm glad Katie and Elizabeth can renew their friendship."

Although her suitcases were so full she had to sit on them to get them closed, Katie felt like she'd left her whole lifetime at home. She was not allowed to communicate with Teddy by mail or phone or see him when she came home, and her heart was broken.

"You need to expand your horizons," her mother told her, "and meet new people. Don't sit around and think about Teddy. He'll probably forget about you the minute you leave town."

In spite of their disagreements over Teddy, Katie and Margie missed each other terribly. This was their first separation ever, and Margie felt terribly alone. All she had left to care for was Katie's dog.

For Katie, college was an eye-opening experience. For the first time in her life, she had to make her own bed. Margie had always done it, so it would be done right with never a wrinkle to mar its perfection. Katie, who had always gotten straight A's in English, was struggling to write college essays. She had to think on her own, and that was foreign territory for her. Her mother told everyone that she graduated from high school with a 3.80 g.p.a., when in actuality, it was a 3.08. Funny how those numbers got turned around! But she wouldn't be bragging about Katie's grades in her first college semester. Margie was notified through the mail about Katie's low grade point. She couldn't believe it and didn't know who to blame. Maybe it was poor advice from her college advisor, perhaps the professors were too demanding, maybe her roommate was too noisy; whatever it was, it couldn't be Katie's fault. She told no one, and she wrote encouraging letters to Katie at least once a week.

The problems did stem from all of those reasons that Margie imagined, but it went far deeper. Katie was a troubled girl.

When Cassie, a gal across the hall, asked, "So what did your father do for a living?" the questions of Katie's adoption loomed bigger than ever.

"He was a farmer," was Katie's answer to Cassie, but to those coeds with whom she began to form a bond of friendship, she told the truth. Then, of course, the girls had all sorts of questions. The one that opened up a whole new avenue of thought like a mind-expanding drug was, "How was it possible for a single woman to adopt a baby? It just wasn't done then."

Katie had never thought about that before, but she spent valuable hours when she should have been studying the circulatory system of the frog for zoology, or trying to understand the poetry of the English writers, trying to figure out who her mother could have been. If she couldn't have adopted her, as the girls said, then Margie must have given birth to her herself! Then Camille entered her mind. She went away, maybe to have a baby, and to keep it in the family, maybe somehow Margie was able to take her, sort of like a gift. That's probably why she came back to visit—to see how the baby turned out.

Camille seemed to like me a lot, she called me 'Little Missy,' and said we were the same size. She must be the one. But later Katie discounted those thoughts; Camille was just too old. Katie had no clue who her father could be, but finally decided that Margie must be her mother. The oddest part was that she never once considered Aunt Amanda.

When I want your opinion
I'll give it to you!
—Nick Anderson

Chapter XXVIII

Belle Shaw passed away suddenly in the fall of 1966. Amanda answered the phone out at the farm when Belle called for help. It was a Tuesday, but Belle was so sick that it didn't seem odd that Amanda would be there on a week day. She'd been trying to spend more time with Robert, but Margie thought it was just for show. She selfishly hoped it wasn't working.

Belle could hardly talk. "Help, Robert. Help!" was all she could get out.

"We'll be right there. Just hang on." Robert was way out in the field on a tractor, and Amanda knew she wouldn't be able to get his attention, so she grabbed the phone again and called Margie. Damn! Her line was busy. Wouldn't you just know it? When she needed someone, nobody was available. After all she'd done for everybody else!

The gravel was flying as Amanda peeled out of the driveway and headed down the lane. Between her dust and Robert's out in the field, the air looked like the dust storm that often arrived before a thunder storm. Amanda was in town in eleven minutes and found Belle lying on the kitchen floor with the phone at her side. Her eyes were rolled back, and she was unresponsive. Belle's house was close to the local hospital, but Amanda couldn't pick her up and carry her there, so she had to call the ambulance. She called Margie again while she waited, and the line was finally free. "Who in the world have you been talking to all this time?" She never missed an opportunity to berate her sister. "Oh, it doesn't matter. I'm at Belle's. We're waiting for the ambulance. I think she's had a stroke or heart attack."

"Is she still alive?" Margie hoped so. She loved Belle, not just because she was Belle, but also because she was Robert's mother.

"Yes, but just barely. There'll be no time to get her to Spokane. So, can you do something? Can you come and help me?"

Margie thought about Robert. "Where's Robert? Is he there? Why don't I run out to the farm and see if I can get him off the tractor?" Margie volunteered, when she heard he wasn't with her.

"Okay, you do that." Amanda sounded sarcastic, but Margie told her he really should be there.

But Robert never made it in time to see his mother alive. He had stopped for lunch and was headed into the house when Margie arrived; but even so, by the time he washed his hands and face, quickly changed his clothes, and revved up the pickup to follow Margie back to town, it was too late. He found Amanda talking to Dr. Baker in the hallway; her eyes were as dry as the dusty field at the farm. When the doctor stepped forward to shake Robert's hand, he shook his head, and Robert knew it was over.

"I'm sorry, Robert. She had a massive stroke, and there was just nothing that we could do for her." Dr. Baker patted Robert on the back. "Would you like to spend a moment with her?"

"Yes, alone." Robert answered, and tried to swallow down the tears, as he plodded down the hospital corridor with the doctor.

Margie and Amanda sat down in the waiting room. Margie was in tears, but Amanda just sat and looked around the room finally asking, "Do you want some coffee? Oh, and here are some fresh-baked cinnamon rolls."

Margie thought they looked like Belle's and cried even harder. In between sobs, she blurted out, "Is that all you can think about at a time like this—eating? Don't you feel anything, Amanda?"

"Oh, well, she was just an old woman. Something was bound to happen sooner or later." What she was feeling was the delight in the thought that someone would have to call Michael. She might as well take the burden off of Robert and do it herself.

"I thought you liked Belle. She was always good to you, even though you live your own life, mostly apart from Robert," Margie persisted in trying to get some emotion from Amanda. She got it, all right, but not the sympathy or grief one would expect.

Amanda lit into her so loudly that a nurse popped her head out of a door to remind her with a touch of a finger to her lips that hospitals are quiet zones. "Look, Margie. You have no idea what you're talking about. Our arrangement works out just fine. Robert has his life on the farm, that I never wanted, and I have my life in town, that I love, although I wish Wheatland had more to offer. As for Belle, she kept trying to shove me out there to live all the time and kept nagging me to go to church. She should have known that I'm too independent for that, and I'm going to do what I want to do! No church for me!"

"Yeah, everybody else knows it, but really, Amanda, all she wanted for you and Robert was happiness. I can't imagine her shoving and nagging." But Margie knew that any little, delicate touch with a tip of a finger would feel like a shove to Amanda.

"I just wish that everyone would keep their opinions to themselves. Oh, here comes Robert now."

He looked at both Amanda and Margie. He wished one of them would hug him, preferably Margie; but she couldn't right now, and Amanda wouldn't. "Henry is on his way to take her to the funeral home." He sat down for a minute.

"Do we have to wait for him?" Amanda was anxious to get out of there.

"No, Mandy, I just need to rest for a minute. He'll call us when we need to come into town and make the arrangements—probably tomorrow. Margie, I was thinking. Why don't you go home, get some things and come out to the farm to stay. I know this has been a shock for you, too, and you're all alone." He needed her like never before.

Margie was so astounded. "Oh, Robert, I don't think that would be a good idea right now. You have so much to do, and you and Amanda should be alone. There will be a big gathering later on, and I'll be a part of that, and, oh, I need to call Katie. I doubt if she can come, but she loved Belle and needs to know what happened. Thanks anyway." How she hated to turn him down!

He turned to Amanda. "You're coming, aren't you, Mandy?"

"Well, of course. I was already there."

The funeral was scheduled for Saturday. Michael arrived on Thursday. Katie had an important Saturday lab, so she wasn't able to be there. As much as Michael wanted to see her, Amanda and he knew it was for the best. He stayed out at the farm, which was somewhat awkward, but when Robert went outside to do the chores every morning and evening, Amanda and he had a little time together.

He had questions about Katie. "How is she doing at school? Is she happy? How often does she come home? Does she still resemble me?"

Amanda answered as best she could. "As for her happiness, I think she is still very curious and unsettled about the whole adoption issue and not knowing who her parents are. I wouldn't be surprised if she searched for them—for us—someday."

"Doesn't that worry you? It scares me to death, Amanda."

"Yes, but I've been thinking about a plan to steer her in another direction. I have a friend who is a private investigator. If I pay her enough, she will handle my plan, and Katie will be led astray and think someone else is her mother. I've already talked to my friend about it, and she's agreeable when the time comes, and Katie makes a big issue of it. I think it will keep you totally out of it too, but she probably won't bother to search for quite awhile with school and all. Plus, I hear that she has a new boy friend—someone named Paul Chapman."

"Oh, Amanda, you are up to your old tricks. How do you come up with these ideas?"

"I have a lot of time on my hands to think. Robert thinks I am so busy, so don't tell on me."

"Don't tell what, Amanda? What are you up to now?" Robert heard the last part, as he came in from feeding the cows.

She came up with an idea rapidly, "Well, I was thinking that when your mother's affairs are all cleared up, perhaps I could move into her house."

"Just hold your horses, Amanda. We haven't even buried her yet. We'll talk about that much later."

Once again the Shaws and Margie made the pilgrimage, first to the church, and then to the cemetery. The little family was dwindling in rank, and Margie thought, "We are all getting older, too." She missed Katie more than ever and wished she were there. She needed someone to hug, and the special someone wasn't available.

Belle had many friends from church and the community and, as they had done after Ed's service, Robert and Amanda greeted most of them at the farm. Margie had cooked a big ham at home, and the ladies from the church brought casseroles, salads, and desserts. Ham was not on Margie's non-fat diet, so she'd never cooked one before, but it turned out fine, and everyone raved over it. Amanda had done very little cooking, but that was nothing unusual. She'd never really bothered to learn, and the cookbook Belle made for her of Robert's favorite recipes was as new as the Christmas Day she'd received it. In fact, it was shoved so deep in a drawer that Amanda had forgotten it ever existed.

Not long after Belle's death, when Robert was looking for a utensil in the kitchen at the farm so he could fix another dinner without his wife, he found the cookbook. It was buried under some dish towels, like it didn't mean a thing to Amanda. He sat down at the kitchen table and thumbed through it, tears clouding his eyes, thinking of how his mother used to love to cook his favorite dishes, and how Amanda on weekends would throw together some spaghetti out of a package or put a chicken in a pot. She thought she was really cooking, but she didn't know how to season or make a dish appealing to the palate or the eye. He came to a decision as he sat there all alone, and it wasn't just the cooking that made him say aloud to the empty room, "I've had enough!"

One week later he filed for divorce. It wasn't what he believed in as a Christian, but then he hadn't been living the Christian life up to God's or his own expectations for a long time. His marriage was just a sham, but he'd held it together as long as his mother was alive.

When Amanda received the divorce papers, she had the shock of her life. At first she thought there had been a mistake. They must have been delivered to the wrong person; but no, they had her name on them—Amanda Wentworth Shaw. Then she tried to put the blame on someone—anyone—but herself. She'd been a good wife. She'd let Robert have his life on the farm that he'd always wanted. She'd been good to his mother and never criticized her in front of Robert. She'd really liked Belle at first, but then her running around doing good for people finally got to Amanda. She called her "Miss Goody-Two-Shoes"—not to her face or to anyone else, but she was just too sweet for Amanda's taste, and she'd never really done anything with her life to be an independent woman.

Maybe Robert was having an affair, but who could it be? Sometimes she thought he seemed rather smitten with Margie, but she was family, after all. Surely he wouldn't be interested in his wife's own sister. How disrespectful! And not her, of all people. She was the epitome of a non-entity. With Amanda's help, she'd raised Katie fairly well, and she'd been a caretaker for Zoe, but other than that, her slate was blank in Amanda's eyes.

The divorce proceedings were long and messy. Amanda wanted more than Robert and the courts were willing to give her. She still thought she should have Belle's house, but she was doomed to spend the rest of her days in an apartment or buy her own home.

"At least there are no children to fight over," she told Robert.

"Yeah, that's another sore point," he retorted. "You know how much I wanted a child."

"Oh, but by the time you got back from the war, we were just too old!"

When the One Great Scorer
Comes to write against your name—
He marks, not that you won or lost,
But how you played the game.

—Grantland Rice

Chapter XXIX

Paul Chapman and Katie wasted no time falling in love. They met at a dance at the student union building in October of her senior year and, by February, they were engaged. Paul had gone to Wheatland for Christmas dinner with Margie and Katie and, because he wasn't a college graduate, but working in construction, Margie took an instant dislike to him.

"He's not for you, Katie. He has no diploma, and what future is there in pounding some nails into a board?" Amanda agreed and thought Katie could do better, but didn't voice that opinion to Katie, just to Margie.

Margie was sure Katie would never graduate, but all she had left to accomplish was her student teaching in high school English. Margie threw up her hands in despair, yelled and screamed, and threatened to disown her. Even though Katie loved Paul, her mother's tirades only drove her into marriage faster and with more determination to get away from her. Katie couldn't believe this was happening; the only time they'd had any real disputes were over boys—Teddy and now Paul.

Hilda probably knew the real answer to Margie's dislike of the men Katie chose, and when she told Katie, it came as a big surprise. "You know, Katie, I've decided that your mother wouldn't like any man you chose. It's not really Paul, nor was it Teddy; she wants to keep you just for herself. You've been her pride and joy, and she's carried you around on a silver platter, so to speak, for all the world to see and admire. I suppose she wants the best for you, but you didn't happen to fall in love with a professor or a doctor, did you? There's nothing wrong with construction workers. My husband worked building Grand Coulee Dam, and there wasn't a finer man around, God rest his soul. Now, be happy, and I'm sure Margie will relent and give you a beautiful wedding." Hilda kissed her on the cheek, and Katie went back to summer school hoping Hilda was right.

But Hilda didn't know Margie as well as she thought. Margie not only did not give Katie the wonderful wedding she dreamed of, she didn't even attend. Paul and Katie were married in September in a Presbyterian Church on the college campus with Elizabeth as her attendant and two other college girls at the guest book and gift table. It was a long walk down that aisle alone to meet her groom and the pastor, but she knew of no one to give her away. Robert declined, thinking that Amanda would be in attendance. Jess wanted to do the honors, but Katie thought it best that she leave a substitute dad out of the affair.

Paul's family was all there—even cousins and aunts and uncles from out of town, and they helped fill up the cavernous sanctuary, pour the punch, and cut the cake. Paul and Katie were thankful for their help. At least someone's family came through and acted like they cared!

Aunt Amanda didn't even show up, and even though Katie knew she wasn't all that crazy about Paul, she thought she might come, so some family would be there. Katie looked all over for her before and after the ceremony, but was disappointed once again. She didn't see the black car hiding in the shadows after the evening wedding. Amanda felt it wouldn't be right to make an appearance and cause questions to be asked when Margie wasn't there, but at least she saw her daughter in her wedding dress as she and Paul ran out of the church and into the waiting car to take them on their honeymoon. She followed from a distance—just close enough to see the taillights, as they left Pullman and headed south to Lewiston, Idaho.

"Good-bye, daughter. Have a happy life! I'll tell Michael all about it," Amanda said to herself, as she waved at everyone and no one.

*   *   *

After Katie graduated and taught school for two years in Spokane, she and Paul were blessed with a son, Andrew Paul, and three years later, little Angela Joy arrived to round out the family. The babies helped heal the broken bonds between Katie and her mom, but there would always be tension if Paul was present. Katie often thought of Hilda's wisdom and decided she was right.

Katie remembered all the good times they had when she was growing up. At the time, she knew her life was different than most, but she could see that her mother tried to raise her in the only way she knew how, and that she certainly did love Katie. She remembered how patient and caring her mother was for Grandma Zoe and how she put up with her ill health and crankiness. Katie came to understand and forgive her grandma for her elderly ways that she probably couldn't help. She forgave her mother, too, and wrote Margie a long letter, apologizing for the times she yelled and stormed out in anger. Margie wrote a beautiful letter in reply and said there was nothing to forgive.

The one person she couldn't understand or forgive was Amanda. She could never fathom how two married people who should be in love would live apart. She'd heard all of the reasons from Amanda over the years, but now that she was a married woman herself, she could grasp it even less. She hated it when Paul was out of town two or three days on a construction job. She'd felt sorry for Robert, but now that he was free of Amanda, she hoped he'd find someone to make him happy.

*   *   *

Margie and Robert had kept their distance all through the time of the break-up and divorce proceedings and even for a few more months just so the wagging tongues in town wouldn't think she was the cause of the disaster. They'd all seen the situation over the years and wondered why Amanda couldn't be the wife Robert needed, but sometimes gossip gets twisted and turned and the truth becomes a lie or a story is made up out of nothing, so they thought it best to wait in this particular game of hearts.

Many nights when Robert was out on the farm alone, Margie would go outside and stand by the fence and look up into the sky. On a clear night, she tried to count the stars, and when she found the north star, she would whisper, "Oh, Robert, 'you are the true north in the compass of my soul.'" She'd read that in a book one day and, although she couldn't remember the author, she decided that would be her touchstone to Robert. Some couples had their own special song; they could have this saying. She'd tell him next time they talked.

They started meeting in secret again. Sometimes she'd drive out to the farm, leave her car, and they'd go for long rides. Robert didn't like to call them trips; that sounded too risque, and he was trying to mend his relationship with God, although like between Katie and her mother, there was unconditional love, and all was forgiven.

Once they drove clear to Kamloops, British Columbia, and spent the night in a motel—same room, but separate beds. They both thought this was the only right way until they were married. They went to church in Kamloops together, and Margie promised him that they would never miss a Sunday in church when they were man and wife. That brought tears to his eyes.

Their love was born of a passion that had grown and matured over the years. Why he'd ever married Amanda, he had no idea, but now that chapter in his life was over. He was eager to turn the page and start on a new life with Margie so they could grow old together.

God had other plans. Margie had ignored an aching in her abdomen for many months.

Probably my gall bladder is acting up. I should never have eaten that bowl of ice cream, she'd tell herself. Maybe it's just stress, she hoped, but one day as she was standing over her sink, washing the one plate and knife and fork from supper, the pain was no longer an ache, but a stabbing of a steak knife. She bent further over the sink until her head almost rested in the dishwater. The pain subsided somewhat after she took some Pepto Bismol, but the aching grew worse, and she knew she must see a doctor. She kept it from Robert, who would just worry. It was probably nothing.

Dr. Petersen examined her, but thought she needed some tests, so he sent her to Spokane—once again unbeknownst to Robert or anyone. She spent two nights at a hotel in the city, and Robert wondered where in the world she had gone. This was so unlike her. Amanda had done it all through their married life, but he thought Margie told him everything. Not this time. When the tests came back that she was full of cancer, there was nothing they could do, and she had just a few weeks to live, she became even more secretive. He noticed the dramatic weight loss and the tired, drawn look that enveloped her face, and he couldn't stand it when she didn't answer her phone.

"Oh, I was just napping," she'd tell him. "I stayed up too late last night watching television." She was napping, but it was from the pain pills and the tumors that zapped her strength a little more every day.

Finally, she knew she could keep it from him no longer and invited him for lunch. She didn't care if the neighbors saw his pickup there or if someone told Amanda. She would soon be in the hospital to rest up for her final nap. The lunch she fixed was out of a can, and even using the electric opener was a chore, but she got it on the table, and they pretended to smile and eat. Margie choked frequently and could only swallow water.

"Honey, you're sick, aren't you? Please tell me the truth."

She finally told him everything. "I won't be able to marry you, Robert," and that was the final crushing blow. "We just wouldn't

have very long to be man and wife, so it's better this way. I don't
even think I have the strength to go through with it."

Robert had never felt so sad. "Does Katie know? What about
Amanda?"

"Yes, Katie will be here tomorrow, and as for Amanda, she was
dashing out the door when I called her and wanted her to come up
and talk. She said she'd have to get back to me later, as she had a
plane to catch out of Spokane for a trip to Seattle. Why would she
be going to Seattle?"

"Who knows and who cares?" Robert shared her sentiment.

Margie lived for two more weeks, and Robert and Katie were
constantly by her side. They took her to the hospital in town the
day before she died. She was in so much pain and so miserable—
incoherent at times and other times more rational than they were.
Her eyes opened wide just before she closed them for the final
time, and she said, "Love you," to them both at the same time.
They were holding her as she slipped away.

They were inconsolable as they planned her funeral, and they
had no help from Amanda. They still didn't know where she was
or how to reach her. They considered calling the police to track her
down, but thought surely she would show up in time. They never
once thought of calling Michael Shaw.

*   *   *

Henry slowly closed the snow-covered doors of the black hearse
with finality, brushing the winter whiteness away with his gloved
hand as he securely adjusted the handle.

Oh, Henry, you've been here so many times when I've needed
someone, Katie thought. His blue eyes were sparkling as always,
not in laughter, but in just a gentle, caring way. You took me
to school when I was young; you fixed my poor, old, broken-
down sled; you gently reassured me when Grandma died; you've
helped me so much in so many ways. Why couldn't you be my
daddy? Who is my daddy? She wondered for the millionth time,

at least. How comforting that Henry should be there now when she needed him most. Yes, she had Paul and the kids and Robert, but Henry was not only the one who had taken care of all the arrangements in such a professional manner; he was also her friend.

Winter is not a good time to die. Why, a body could freeze to death if it's not careful. Now why would Katie's dry wit want to add a spark of humor to a dying ember on the day of her mother's funeral? She felt guilty and hung her head.

Margie surely didn't plan this death nor choose a snowy December exit with the numbing cold of an Eastern Washington winter. She often told Katie that she hoped her burial would call for a late May afternoon service when the birds were singing and the smell of flowers were in the air. Her own pink peonies that Mother liked so well should be delicately laid on the fresh soil. Margie could even cut the flowers ahead of time, if she knew when they were needed and refrigerate them to last, as she'd done for years and years in preparation for Memorial Day. Every May she'd carefully cut each peony stalk with the yellow kitchen shears. Then she'd rearrange the sparsely stocked Crossley refrigerator, moving the one percent milk and the corn oil to accommodate the vases and pitchers of flowers.

The day before Memorial Day, so she wouldn't see too many people, she'd carry the flowers, shears, grass clippers, buckets of water, and boxes out to the car and drive the back road under the north bluff and on out to the cemetery. There, with the wind blowing through closely cropped gray hair and whistling up the legs of worn peddle-pushers, she'd begin cleaning grave sites and arranging flowers. The main area of concentrated clipping, raking, stone-washing, and flower arranging were her mother and father's graves; but her long legs, like Ichabod Crane's and large feet, clad in holey tennis shoes, could be seen springing across the grassy turf to visit the graves of old and true friends.

With tears coursing down her cheeks during the few times that Katie had recently accompanied her, Margie had asked, "Will anyone do this for me when I am gone?"

Katie turned once more, just as Henry was driving down the last lane and heading for the cemetery exit. As she looked back to the burial plot, she could see the caretakers shaking the snow from the large bouquet of roses and carnations to place on the mound.

'There are no pink peonies today, Mom, but just wait until May," she whispered into her handkerchief.

Yes, Margie was different. Everyone in the little town of Wheatland knew her and her ways. They liked her for her kindness, and yet they talked behind her back They wondered at her lifestyle. Although they didn't envy her, they admired her garden and flowers, her way with words. In their social cliques or over a game of cards, they ridiculed the strange hours she kept, the clothes she wore that looked like hand-me-downs from Amanda, and her odd diet. Mostly, they wondered about her daughter.

But on the day of her burial, they wondered about Amanda's absence. At least they had been there to do their duty; the tribute was paid.

The Angel that presided
O'er my birth said,
"Little creature,
Formed of joy and mirth,
Go, love without the help
Of anything on earth.

—William Blake

Chapter XXX

Katie was in the process of closing up the Wentworth house for the rest of the winter when Amanda returned home from Seattle two days after Margie's funeral. Katie had so much to do and so many people to notify to make changes—the post office, the bank, the furnace oil company, city hall, the telephone and power company and on and on. She could have used her aunt's help, but still no one knew where she was.

Just as she was pulling the shades in the living room, she saw Aunt Amanda come into view, and she heard her heavy step on the back porch. Katie hoped she wouldn't have to be the one to tell her what had happened to her sister while she was running loose on the other side of the mountains. The school secretary had told Katie that Amanda had taken a short leave of absence, but she and Robert wondered what her story would be.

She burst in the back door before Katie could get there to let her in. She was red in the face, and Katie actually thought she saw her eyes full of moisture.

"It's so windy out, my eyes are watering," Amanda said, as she fumbled for a tissue in her coat pocket. "I heard what happened and couldn't believe it. Mildred Reynolds was at the post office when I stopped to get my mail, and when she offered her condolences, I had no idea what she was talking about. Then my post office box was overflowing with sympathy cards. I pretended I knew what was going on when Mildred mentioned Margie's death, but I was totally in shock! Why didn't someone try to get in touch with me? I should have been here!"

Katie couldn't agree with that more. "Yes, you should have, but how could we get in touch with you when we had no idea where you were?"

"The school should have told you; I was at a conference for science teachers," she lied.

Katie rolled her eyes. "I don't think so. The secretary said you had taken a leave of absence, but she didn't know how to contact you."

Amanda lied again, "Oh yes, after the conference, I did spend some extra days seeing the sights. I desperately needed some rest and relaxation." Sleeping on Michael's couch wasn't all that restful, but who's to know? It was a little crowded trying to share his single bed.

Amanda sat in the rocking chair, as Katie finished pulling the shades on the north side of the living room and then in the big bedroom that had been Zoe's. Margie had slept there during her last few weeks of illness, as she couldn't navigate the steps any longer.

"Didn't you know that anything was wrong before you left, Aunt Amanda? Didn't she tell you she was sick, that she was in the advanced stage of cancer?"

"Good heavens, no. Do you think I'm so cruel that I'd go off and leave a dying woman? You know how private she was, and when I noticed her weight loss and tired, drawn face, and asked her about it, she put me off. I had no idea she was so sick, and I feel terrible."

She really did feel a great loss all of a sudden, sitting there in the darkened room, in the home where they'd shared their differences, their personal losses, and even their lies. But it was home, and Amanda knew that soon someone would inherit it and maybe it would be sold. She quickly came out of her doldrums when she thought, maybe she left it to me. I've always thought that if it had a couple more bathrooms, it would make a great bed and breakfast.

Katie was finished with her chores for the time being. She turned the furnace down to fifty-five degrees and hoped that wouldn't be too low if there was a hard freeze. She'd come and check on things from time to time. She had read her mother's will a long time ago, and even though Margie had threatened to disown her over her marriage to Paul, she had left her everything. Amanda would find out in due time.

"Maybe you should go to the cemetery, Aunt Amanda," Katie thought it was the least she could do, since she'd missed everything else. "Would you like me to go with you?"

"No, I think I'd rather go alone," and she left the Wentworth home for the last time. She had a key, but she never used it again.

Katie had some business to do downtown at the bank, so she was very glad to turn Aunt Amanda loose. She had often felt suffocated around her anyway, and with the depression Katie felt over her mother's death, she could hardly breathe as she entered the bank. The gals were so kind and helpful as they made the arrangements to send Margie's latest statement to Katie's address in Spokane. "Your mother was a jewel," the bank manager told Katie.

"When things are settled, I'll be back to close up her accounts," Katie told the teller, with tears in her eyes, "but right now, I need to get into Mom's safety deposit box. Can someone help me with that?" She'd signed the papers six months ago and had the key for access, but she'd never felt the need to see what her mother had put safely away. Maybe it was a little soon after her mother's death to snoop, but on the other hand, perhaps there were some important papers there that she would need. Maybe, just maybe, there would be some information she'd longed to know for years. A swarm of butterflies took flight in her stomach with that thought.

"I'll let you in," offered Betsy, a teller who wasn't busy at the moment, and after Katie had signed in, she led Katie though the swinging doors, past the bank manager's desk, and down the corridor to the vault. The short hallway seemed to stretch on forever for Katie. It was like the reoccurring dream of trying to get somewhere, but slipping back one step at a time, gaining nothing. Her legs ached, and her feet hurt, although she'd only gone a few yards. I wish I could stop and rest. It's useless; I'm getting nowhere.

"Here it is, Katie." Betsy sounded far away. "You can use the little room just across the hall. Take all the time you want. Just let me know when you are finished."

"Thanks," Katie mumbled, trying to climb out of her reverie. She shook her dazed head and pulled the drawer out of the metal cavity that Betsy and she had opened together. She stumbled across the hallway and sat at the desk. The safety deposit box didn't look very big, and there wasn't much in it. There were a few papers on top—deeds to the farmland, an insurance policy, and some papers about the house. In the back was a brown, leather bag with a drawstring knotted at the top. Katie found extra coins from her Mom's Indian Head penny collection, which Margie had given Katie just before she went to the hospital. The collection was hidden away safely in Katie's trunk until she could get home with them to Spokane.

A manila envelope underneath the papers caught Katie's eye. It was sealed, and the clasp was securely fastened. In bold writing in the middle of the front was the single word, *Katie*. At the bottom the same determined writing, only smaller, read, *Personal and Confidential*. Katie dropped the envelope twice before she was able to pull out the sheets of typing paper. Her hands shook, and the writing blurred before her eyes, but soon she began to read:

"My Dearest Daughter, Katie,

      I am writing this on a cold and lonely winter night. My beans are a frozen mess on the alley fence. It was too hard for me to dig my potatoes this fall, and all my various kinds of squash froze before I could lug them from the storehouse to the cellar stairway. The leaves are covered with snow, but I was just too tired to rake them this fall. This is the first time that this "poor farm" has ever been in such a mess.

All I have left are memories of you, my dear. You were such a tiny baby when you came to live here. Someone said you were precocious, but I already knew that.

I remember your first Christmas, when you lay sweetly sleeping by the tree and how you enjoyed so many others out at the Shaw farm. Then there was the night you gave your first reading at church and how proud we all were of you, your first fancy dress, your first job, the tears you shed over JFK, and the day you went to college.

Then those bitter memories—the boy you dated, the wedding I didn't attend, the words we hurled at each other, the conversations we faked, and our stilted letters until we forgave each other. Your two darling children helped take the pain away and heal our hurts, but they grew up too fast like you did.

It's so late, and my eyes are tired. In fact, I'm so tired all over. I haven't even told you the real reason I am writing, but I'll have to finish this another time."

That was the end of the first page. Nothing new had been revealed about Katie's background and her identity still seemed like a jumbled mess. She couldn't wait to read on:

Back again, Katie. I'll try to finish this tonight. It snowed again last night. Oh, how I hate the cold!

Katie, you asked me many times about your background. I'll tell you again just as I always have. I wanted a baby very badly, but thought I was too old and was single and, therefore, not eligible. But then you came along, and I was able to get you. You mother just didn't feel that she could keep you. I know absolutely nothing about your father, so I can't help you out there, either. I understand your curiosity, and I want you to know that no other mother could have ever loved you more than I have. Yes, there were some disappointments and lots of regrets. I could see the handwriting on the wall many times, but you wouldn't listen, like most kids, so you had to learn for yourself. I did the best I could, being alone and all. I hope you have some pleasant memories of your childhood and of me.

I won't be here to boss you around much longer; the doctors say I only have a few weeks to live, but maybe I can fool them and stay around awhile longer. I was so sure I'd never get cancer. I ate my bran every day and broccoli and cauliflower—no bacon or other fats or preservatives—but it snuck in there somehow.

So, this will be good-bye, my darling daughter. I will be leaving this world 'ere long. I will leave you with two thoughts. Remember what our favorite poet, Emily Dickinson, wrote: "The world is not conclusion, a sequel stands beyond. Invincible as music, but positive as sound." We used to love to read her writings together—don't forget. The other thought is that if you are still so terribly bothered about your background and finding out who you really are, may I suggest that you turn to your Aunt Amanda for help.

With all my love, Mom.

The sheets of paper were covered with wet splotches from Katie's tears when she finished reading. It was a beautiful letter—so full of love and understanding—but it didn't answer any questions. Square one looked just the same as it always did—maybe a little more square. Why do I always have to go back and start all over? She didn't say anything new that I haven't heard over and over again. She stuck to her story, and it wasn't of any help. Aunt Amanda, how could she possibly help me? Katie tried to think it all through, as she put the letter back in the envelope. She shoved it under her arm to take home and reread. Maybe she'd missed something.

Betsy came when she called for her and helped her finish up her business. It was nearly closing time and starting to get dark outside when Katie bid farewell to the girls at the bank. She decided to drop by Aunt Amanda's, although she didn't know why. She certainly didn't want to show her the letter, and the last time she quizzed her, she got nowhere, but that was years ago. It didn't matter; Aunt Amanda's car wasn't there anyway. Next time I'm in town, I'll ask her some questions. By then, I'll be ready to pursue this until I have the answers.

I leave this rule
For others when I'm dead—
Be always sure you're right,
Then go ahead.

—David Crockett

Chapter XXXI

A large vase of pink peonies on a small table in the hallway just inside the front door greeted each guest as they arrived to spend a night at Katie's Bed and Breakfast. It was in late May of 1986, just one weekend before Memorial Day when Paul and Katie opened their new venture in the old, but newly remodeled, Wentworth home that Katie had inherited from her mother two years ago.

She had remembered the day many years ago when Amanda had said that the old house would make a lovely bed and breakfast, but at the time Katie thought that both her Grandma Zoe and her mother, who were both very private people, would perish the thought of strangers climbing the stairs and sleeping in their beds or eating at their dining room table. After Margie passed away and Katie had to make a decision about what to do with the house, it seemed like the perfect thing to do. The timing was right, as both Andrew and Angela were out of high school and on their own. Angela was a bank teller and shared an apartment with a girl friend in the Spokane Valley, and Andrew was in his first year of college at WSU, so Katie and Paul were free to sell their house in Spokane and make the move to Wheatland. Paul was a good compliment to Katie. She took a long time to make up her mind to do things, while he jumped right in, sometimes before thinking of all the angles and twists and turns. But this time when he said, "Let's just do it, Katie," she was sure he was right, and so they went ahead with their remodeling plans. Because of Katie's generous inheritance, Paul was able to retire from big construction jobs, and he hoped that when they moved to Wheatland, and he had the time, he'd be able to bid on a local building project from time to time.

The first remodeling project on the old house was to build on a large bedroom for Paul and Katie. Right off the existing bathroom on the west side of the house seemed like the logical place. It was handy to the kitchen and pantry, too, so in the early mornings Katie could get up and get to work on breakfast while the guests were still sleeping or getting ready for the day in the other part of the house.

The next room Paul updated was the kitchen. Because of his former work in Spokane, he knew how and where to buy wholesale so was able to outfit the kitchen with all new appliances, sinks, counter-tops and flooring, at greatly reduced prices. It was modern and efficient when he was finished. Katie thought it was beautiful, too.

Paul then worked his way through the rest of the house. He laid new carpeting in all the downstairs rooms and installed a bath in the huge closet in the downstairs bedroom that had formerly been Zoe's. Upstairs he added a bathroom at the end of the hallway, for the guests to share. It was huge with two sinks and a shower, decorated with mauve and gray with lots of towel racks and shelving. Katie loved shopping for all the extra little amenities to make it homey.

Two of the bedrooms upstairs were remodeled with carpeting and new curtains, but the only room that didn't require much work was the blue room. It had barely been used except when Camille was home, so only a good cleaning and new curtains were required. Katie found the painting of the pink peonies stashed under the bed, so once again she brought it down and hung it in the dining room.

When spring arrived, Katie was busy in the yard, planting and grooming the flower beds, painting the front porch and, with Paul's help, installing a porch swing. She also painted some old Adirondack chairs she found at a garage sale and placed these in the back yard under the shade of her favorite old apple tree where her swing had once hung.

It was a big, old place to remodel and redo, but they enjoyed working together, and by May when it was time to open their doors to their first guests, they were tired but happy.

Katie had mailed a personal invitation to Camille, wanting her to be their first guest in the blue room. She didn't hear anything for several weeks, but finally received a note from a friend of Camille's in California, who was apparently working with Camille's lawyer and who had inherited some of Camille's belongings. The note started as a pleasant thank-you type variety, but soon turned into a diatribe about how Camille had died and nobody in her family knew it or cared about her. She had never answered any of the letters that Margie or Amanda had written after she left home after the painting stabbing, so they finally gave up. She had apparently turned the story around. Who knows what all she had told that lady about her family? Probably even "Little Missy" wasn't exempt from her anger. Katie thought it was sad that she had died as a bitter, old lady, but as Grandma Zoe had always said, "She made her bed; let her lie in it."

Katie asked Aunt Amanda if she'd like to stay in the blue room during their first weekend, but she was going to Spokane. She had retired well past the usual age. They had kept her on at Wheatland High. She said, "Well, I still have all my marbles, and I have nothing else to do, so I might as well be teaching. They have to learn their chemistry from someone."

When Amanda declined the invitation, Paul said, "You sure are anxious to fill that room. Are you afraid no one will come and stay?"

"No, it's just a special room. It was always sort of off-limits, like it was holy or reserved for only certain people, so I just thought it should be used."

But neither Paul nor Katie needed to worry about the lack of guests that weekend or any other weekend during the summer. They were busy, too, during the week until school started and vacation times were waning. They tried during the summer to find fun things for the younger kids to do. During the day they encouraged them to visit the park and the free swimming pool downtown, and in the evenings they had croquet, lawn darts, and badminton equipment on the back porch for their use in the spacious yard. Inside two card tables were set up for board games or cards in the parlor. Sometimes Katie would make popcorn in the evening and set a huge bowl on the dining room table. The coffee pot was always on, and Paul had found an old soda pop machine which he kept full of pop on the back porch. Katie thought it looked tacky, but the kids loved it.

Paul and Katie were thrilled when their guests raved over the good food, comfortable surroundings, and homey atmosphere. Katie thought maybe even Grandma Zoe and Margie would be pleased with all they'd accomplished.

While Katie enjoyed being back and living in Wheatland again, some of the changes in the town made her sad. Hudson's Grocery was no longer there. Teddy had joined the Air Force and had been killed in Vietnam many years ago, and all the other Hudson children were grown and had either moved away or hadn't wanted to take over the store when their folks retired.

A new post office had been built over near the Marquee Lights Theater. It was modern and nice, but Katie liked the old one better. She remembered the musty smell that mingled with the cleaning powder that they used on the floor to sweep up at night. She could almost smell it when she thought about it long enough. Those old post office boxes were so worn and used, and she had had to stand on her tip-toes to reach her Mother's box, but she missed all that. The new post office just seemed too sterile and business-like.

There were other changes too—new homes and new people. When Katie read the Wheatland newspaper, there were many names she'd never heard of, but she learned who they were when she had time later in the winter to become an active part of the community. Both she and Paul joined the Chamber of Commerce, and he became a Lions Club member. She was a great reader like her mother before her, so she joined The Friends of the Library group and enjoyed their monthly meetings.

All these things kept her busy, and she really didn't have much time to sit around and think, but when she did she often had nostalgic thoughts. That's what going back to one's roots does, she assumed. Roots, background, genealogy—words she'd thought about so many times. Some of the ladies at the library talked about doing their genealogies and what all they'd found.

"Why, did you know that my mother was related to Betsy Ross?" Mildred Reynold's daughter announced one day over the refreshments after the library meeting. No, nobody knew, but they all oohed and aahed, and they threw in what they knew about their heritage. All except Katie.

Once again, she had nothing to offer, so she sat and nibbled on her cookie. Amanda just happened to be sitting across the table from her, and Katie thought once again of her mother's letter and suggestion that she ask Aunt Amanda for help. Hilda, too, God rest her soul, had thought that Amanda "might know something," but that's all she could tell her. Aunt Amanda, the holder of secrets and lies, glanced at Katie quickly, then looked out the window. Katie decided then and there that soon she would be knocking on Aunt Amanda's apartment door for some help.

*   *   *

As Katie was contemplating her decision, her thoughts traveled to the innermost recesses of her soul. There is an emptiness in the human heart that runs deeper than the lowest depths of the ocean, an absence so hollow that friendships and relationships cannot fill the void. Time does nothing to soothe the emotions or heal the loneliness bred by uncertainty. Suspected lies supposedly told for protection and shelter are only band-aids over open wounds; secrets revealed as gossip and rumors, only make an uncertain and aching heart hurt more.

Katie was feeling all of these emotions and knew that there is one thing in life and only one thing that can fulfill a human heart when the mind has heard only secrets and lies, and that is the truth. The absolute truth can only come from God, and that is the most comforting in which to trust and in which to believe. The truth from human beings always carries with it an essence of doubt. Can a person be trusted?

The search for truth is not an easy journey. Katie Wentworth Chapman knew that as well as anybody, but when she made the decision to find her true identity at all costs and no matter what the outcome, after forty-two years of emptiness, she felt the truth would set her free.

Katie made an appointment with Aunt Amanda, just to make sure she would be home. She didn't run around as much as she used to, but she often took a nap in the afternoon, so the visit was scheduled for 3:30 p.m. when Amanda would be rested and fresh.

Aunt Amanda had a feeling she knew what the meeting was all about and was prepared, but then she'd been ready for years—way back to when she was seeing Michael quite often. Her plan was ready to be executed. She held the cards to the outcome of the game.

As she had long ago, Katie broached the subject with trepidation, but Aunt Amanda was much more open to helping her this time. She had no concrete answers herself to Katie's questions, but she knew someone who could help her find them.

"I just happen to have a friend in Spokane who is a private investigator. Her name is Julia, and I've known her for a long time. Actually, we met in college, so, you see, it has been centuries ago." They both laughed. "She is excellent—very honest, has a good reputation, and a high success rate of finding misplaced people. The only problem is she is quite expensive. I don't know just how much she charges, but I could find out for you before you make a final decision."

"I've made my decision, no matter what the cost. Aunt Amanda, you have no idea how important this is to me. I have to know who I am! Now, please, give me her phone number so I can call her. I want to get started on this today."

"I'll have to find it, dear. My address book is like a Bible to me, and I just don't know where I've put it. I've been looking for several days. It has all my many friends and connection's addresses and phone numbers. What I am going to do without it!"

Katie could see that she was becoming distraught and tried to be helpful. "If you just give me her name, I can look her up in the Spokane phone directory when I get home and place the call."

"Oh, I'm so upset. I can't even think of her last name. It's Mitchell or Michaels or something like that. It will come to me in due time. You know how it is if you completely clear your mind of what you are trying to think of—it usually just pops into your head. Why don't you run on home? I'll think of it, and call you. Okay?" She was still good at dismissing people when she'd spoken her piece—even her own daughter.

Amanda listened for Katie's footsteps as she went down the hall and stairs, but she couldn't hear them like she used to. Her hearing was fading, even though her mind was still as sharp as the knives she stabbed in people's backs. She ran to the window, and as soon as she could see Katie on the sidewalk down below, hurried to the phone and dialed Julia Jamison's number, which she knew by heart.

"Yes, of course, I'll help. It will be fun to be devious once again. I haven't done anything underhanded for a long time. I hope I haven't lost my touch." Julia sounded excited to hear Amanda's plan, especially when she told Julia how much she would be paying her over and above the regular fee from Katie.

"Okay, then, Julia. I'll have Katie call you. Now, be your old, professional self, and do what you have to do. Katie must never know the real truth."

Julia assured her that she knew how to handle it all, and they hung up. In two minutes, Katie had the name and phone number from Aunt Amanda, who'd just happened to find her address book moments after Katie had left. She was straightening up the cushions on the couch, and there it was where it had slipped down in-between.

"Good luck, Katie, darling. I know how important this is to you. Keep me posted, and I hope you find out something soon. Sometimes it takes a little while, though, so try to be patient, dear," Amanda gushed. She was ripe for an Academy Award for Best Actress that afternoon.

The house of cards
Came tumbling down.
                                      —Anon

Chapter XXXII

Katie called Julia at nine the next morning and made arrangements for her to begin the search. She sounded like a pleasant older lady, very professional. She had one other case, but it wasn't too time-consuming, and being semi-retired, probably wouldn't have any more jobs coming up very soon, if at all, so she would make it a priority.

"Sometimes it takes weeks or months, and then just about when you've given up—bingo! Oh, and by the way, I expect payment up front, and the charge will be $350.00."

Katie didn't think that was too high a fee; she'd really expected it to be more, and if she found her parents—or even one—it was worth every penny and then some. She got Julia's address and sent the money that afternoon, even though she was working without a signed contract. Katie assumed that since she was Aunt Amanda's friend, she must be trustworthy.

Julia called Katie every month for the first three months, but she had nothing yet. Aunt Amanda said she hadn't heard anything from her, but then, she wouldn't since the only thing she had done was to put them in touch with one another in the first place.

Actually Amanda had sent her two payments of $500.00 each, and she knew exactly what was going on and when Julia was going to call Katie with the news that she'd been dying to hear.

*   *   *

When the phone call finally came on a late April evening, Katie was knee-deep in cans and jars in the pantry. She'd worked hard that day, cleaning and organizing for what they hoped would be another busy and profitable summer. She had little energy left to even find the phone on the cluttered table, let alone talk. Paul was downtown at a city council meeting, trying to obtain a permit for building a new house on the south hill for a family that was moving into town, so he was no help in answering the phone, which rang again, punctuating the stillness, as only a telephone can do. The sense of urgency as it rang a third time and then a fourth demanded Katie's attention.

"Hello," Katie barked sharply, as if to shut up the incessant noise.

"Where have you been? I've been trying to reach you for two days."

It was a pleasant woman's voice, and Katie knew she'd heard it before, but she couldn't quite place who it might be. "Who is this?" She demanded with fatigue draining the life out of her voice. "If you are one of those telemarketers, no, I do not have a cracked windshield, and I don't want to change my long-distance carrier!"

Julia laughed. "No, I'm not trying do sell you anything. I have some news about my search. Are you sitting down?" Before Amanda could answer, she continued, "I found your birth mother!"

"Ohmygosh," Katie ran the words altogether into one. She slumped to her knees and ended up on the floor somewhere between the boxes of scone mix and the cans of raspberry filling. "Oh my gosh!" Katie repeated again, this time as three separate and distinct words. She went from complete fatigue after collapsing on the floor to an erect standing position, as a shot of adrenalin surged through her body like an electrical shock.

This was the call, the news she'd been yearning to hear forever, it seemed. Katie had a myriad of questions, and they all seemed to tumble out at once.

"Who is she? Where does she live? Does she want to see me?"

Julia's voice broke through the emotions Katie was struggling to control. "Calm down, dear, and I'll tell you as much as I can right now. I just talked to your mother, and, of course, she was very surprised and wondered how I'd found her. She sounded very nice, and did admit to having a baby daughter whom she had given up forty-two years ago. But because it was such a shock to her, Katie, she said she'd have to think about whether or not she wants to have a relationship."

Katie gasped. It was so much to absorb.

Julia continued, "You have to realize, Katie, as we discussed before, there are other lives involved here—not just your adoptive family and your husband and children, but your mother had other children after you were born, and they know nothing about you. If she decides to establish a bond with you, she will have to swallow her pride and tell them. So, Katie, she has a lot to consider."

Katie continued to gasp. "You mean I have brothers and sisters?"

"Well, they're half-siblings. You have two half-sisters and one half-brother. Oh, and by the way, your mother works in a bookstore.

"Where does she live?" Katie wondered aloud.

"Oh, I can't tell you that just yet. But I am sending her the letter you mailed me a couple months ago that tells a little bit about you, and she said she'd write to you through me while she's deciding what to do. Do you have any more questions that I might be able to answer right now?"

Katie pondered for a moment. "I wonder if she ever thought about me or had tried to find me."

"I asked her that, Katie, and she said she'd thought about you often, but just assumed you'd had a normal family and had been adopted by a couple, and she didn't want to interfere. She was shocked when I told her a little of your upbringing. I have a gut feeling that because of that alone she will make an effort before too long to make some things up to you. Can you wait just a little longer, Katie? We'll keep in touch, okay?"

There was deadly silence.

"Are you all right, Katie?"

"Yes, I guess so, just in shock and happy and scared."

"I'll talk to you soon," and Julia and Katie said their good-byes.

Katie didn't know it then, but the ghosts of the past who once flitted mysteriously up and down the staircases and in and out of dark closets of all the family homes involved were about to slide down the banisters and collide in human form. Would the dirty linen, yellowed with age and moth-eaten with deception, be hung on the clothesline for all the world to see? Secrets, padlocked with missing keys, would suddenly open and reveal silent wounds. Truths would be told as the human heart was stripped to bare-nakedness. Then and only then could the questions be answered. Would the loud, clarion call of truth and honesty sound at last for Katie Wentworth Chapman?

*   *   *

Two long weeks later, Julia called again with more good news. Katie was more calm this time until she heard what Julia had to say, and then she thought she was having heart palpitations, like Grandma Zoe used to say she was experiencing.

"Here I am again, Katie. Had you given up on me?" Julia inquired.

"I could hardly stand the wait, but I knew you'd call one way or the other. So, what's the verdict?"

"It's very good news. She wants to meet you as soon as possible. She's close by. In fact, she lives in Spokane."

Katie put her hand on her chest to try to silence her pounding heart, but it didn't work.

Katie couldn't believe it. "Wow! Maybe I've even seen her before. I go in all the nice bookstores."

Julia didn't know in which one she was employed. "She can tell you all about that, but let me tell you her name. It's Gracie Ensler."

Julia gave Katie her phone number, too, and Gracie's permission to call her at any time.

Katie couldn't thank Julia enough.

"Just be sure to let me know how it all works out. It usually does turn out okay, but not always. Oh, and one more thing. I'll slip your birth certificate in the mail to you. I had to get a court order to get the real one. I will send it along as soon as possible."

That evening Katie was alone again, as Paul had another meeting. She fixed herself a cup of hot chocolate, turned the television off, and locked the front and back door. She wanted no interruptions when she dialed her mother's phone number for the very first time. A lady answered on the second ring, and Katie listened to a voice she'd never heard before.

"Hello."

"Hello. This is Katie."

"Oh, my goodness. I knew you'd call, but I didn't know it would be this soon."

"Are you busy?"

"No, I was just relaxing. I just got home from work."

They talked on and on. Gracie asked a lot of questions about Katie's family. She asked where she lived and was surprised they lived within sixty-five miles of each other. They made arrangements to meet on Gracie's first day off from work, which would be on Sunday—just three days away. Gracie thought they should meet on neutral territory, so they agreed to meet in Spokane at Denny's Restaurant on Maple Street at 1:00 p.m. Gracie had a picture of Katie, mailed to Julia with the letter, so she thought she could recognize her. It was all set.

Katie finished off the week in a daze. Paul had to rub her back to relax her at night, and during the days she kept busy scrubbing the house from top to bottom. Not that it really needed it, but that's what she did when she was nervous.

Sunday finally arrived. Paul wanted to drive her into Spokane, but, no, Katie wanted to go alone. She arrived at the restaurant forty-five minutes early, sat in the car in the parking lot, and analyzed every woman who entered the restaurant. Some looked like they had been to church and others looked like they'd had a hard night and had just arisen for the day, if they'd slept at all. She hoped her mother was decent looking. She didn't have to be beautiful—just clean and presentable, and maybe they'd even resemble each other.

At five minutes to one, Katie entered the restaurant and sat on a bench just inside the door. She waited, and she waited. She fidgeted and shredded a tissue that was in the pocket of her jacket. One-thirty came, but no one had entered whom Katie thought could be the woman in question—her mother. She was shredding another tissue in the other pocket at one forty-five when a plain-looking lady came in and looked around. She was alone and glanced at Katie—then looked away and hurried into the women's restroom. Katie wasn't sure, of course, never having seen a picture of her mother, but she had a hunch that it was Gracie. She was probably a nervous wreck, too, so she'd just sit and wait until she came out into the restaurant again. Another eternity passed, and finally the lady came out. She looked like she wanted to bolt and run, so Katie made the first overture.

"Are you Gracie?" she gently asked.

"Oh, oh, um . . . yes, I am," she answered very hesitantly.

Katie, full of exuberance, nearly knocked her mother down, as she hugged her and said, "Well, I'm Katie."

Before either one of them could recover, the hostess was seating them and shoving large menus under their noses. They both wanted only water for starters. When the waitress came to take their order, Katie, who was too nervous to eat, just ordered a bowl of vegetable soup. Gracie ordered a full meal—a T-bone steak dinner. She could afford it; she was being paid well, and not the least bit nervous now. She was ready to play the game.

They sat for two hours over lunch. Katie's soup filled her up, then she had a cup of coffee, but Gracie never did seem to get full.

After she consumed her huge steak dinner, she ordered a piece of apple pie. Katie wondered how she could have any appetite on a day like this, and where was she putting it all? She was a petite woman—short in stature—and probably weighed about one hundred and ten pounds, Katie figured. Her hair was gray, shoulder length, and straight. She had a large, bulbous nose that didn't seem to fit on her otherwise thin and wrinkled face. Katie tried not to stare, but she was looking for some resemblance. After two hours she couldn't see one similarity.

She was disappointed to not find out details about Gracie's other children. After all, they were her half-siblings. Gracie tried to produce pictures and finally came up with one of each. Katie wondered if there were problems among them all or just why Gracie didn't seem to want to offer much information.

Gracie kept looking at her watch, as if she had another appointment, and when 4:00 p.m. rolled around, Gracie announced that she was sorry, but she really must be going. Katie had planned to pay for her own meager lunch, but Gracie grabbed the slip and insisted. "It's the least I can do after all these years." It was the closest she came to showing any feeling or regrets.

As they walked out of the restaurant together, Katie wondered, now what do I say? Do I hug her and try to arrange another meeting or is the ball in her court?

"Oh, there's my ride now," and Gracie pointed to a car parked just a few feet away and with the motor running. An older woman waved at Gracie. She gave Katie a quick hug and said, "I'll call you," and was gone. She didn't want to keep Julia Jamison waiting. Julia just had to see Gracie's "daughter" for herself.

Katie stood bewildered in the parking lot. Margie had always told her when you don't know what else to do or where to go, you can always go home, and that was certainly the only place she wanted to be right then. On the long drive home, she thought about that woman named Gracie. Any preconceived mental pictures and hopes for a wonderful reunion had been dashed. Something was wrong. Somehow she just didn't fit, and how is she going to call me? She didn't even ask for my phone number.

By the time Katie had returned to Wheatland, Amanda had received the call from Julia that she'd been waiting for all afternoon.

"Well, how did it go?" Amanda was eager to hear when Julia called. "Was she believable? Do you think we pulled it off?"

"Oh, yes, Gracie said they got along famously, and she promised to call Katie soon."

"So do you think I got my money's worth? One thousand dollars is a lot of cash for only two hours work."

"Well, Amanda, it takes a lot of acting and role playing to be a professional impostor."

Amanda hung up the phone, satisfied that Katie had just experienced a wonderful reunion with her so-called mother, and she would never have to worry about being found out. Katie would wonder in due time why she never heard from Gracie again. Oh, I suppose if I have to, I could dish out another thousand dollars for another meeting between Katie and Gracie in the future. I'd do anything to keep my daughter happy.

Katie wasn't the least bit happy. The next day when she went to see Aunt Amanda, she didn't know how to tell her that her mother had been a big disappointment.

Amanda listened intently at the surprising story that Katie related to her of the previous day's meeting at the restaurant. It wasn't the same tune that Julia had sung. She was so positive that it was a wonderful reunion, or at least that was what she had led Amanda to believe.

"It was probably hard for her, Katie," Amanda tried to soothe her daughter. "It's been so many years, and it was no doubt quite a shock to her to hear that you wanted to meet her. Also, we just don't know what's gone on in her life all this time. Our personalities are all colored by our life's experiences."

"My, you sound philosophical, Aunt Amanda, but I suppose you're right. I should give her another chance."

She hated to see her daughter so distraught and unhappy, and so she offered to help her once again. "Are your rooms all booked up for the weekend, Katie? I thought, if not, maybe I'd accept that offer to stay in the blue room. Of course, I'd pay for my lodging."

"Paul said we have one male guest registered for the downstairs bedroom, but that wouldn't bother you, would it? You can always eat in the kitchen with us if you don't like the looks of him." They both laughed.

It was the last time they would laugh together.

"Don't worry about that. I'll be fine. So, I'll see you Friday in the late afternoon then."

"It will be fun having you, Aunt Amanda. Oh, and thanks for all you did to put me in touch with Gracie."

"It was nothing, Katie. I hope the next time you see her, you can call her "Mother," Amanda lied.

*   *   *

Friday had been busy for Katie. The rooms were ready for the two guests, but Katie liked to go over things one more time with a dustrag and check the bathrooms to make sure they were spotless. The pantry was full of staples, but Katie wanted to have the freshest eggs and milk, so she'd shopped that morning, too. Everything was in order when Amanda arrived at 5:00 p.m.

"I hope you've had an early dinner," Katie said, as she took her overnight bag and handed it to Paul to carry upstairs. "We can have popcorn this evening. I made an angel food cake, too, and I never do this, but since there are only going to be two of you, I thought maybe I'd set some of that out later."

"My, this is going to be quite a party. Will you join us? Who is the other guest?"

Katie repeated Amanda's question for Paul, who was halfway up the stairs with the bag.

"Oh, I don't remember his name. Some fellow from Seattle."

The fellow from Seattle arrived around 7:00 p.m. Paul signed him in at the small desk in the front hallway. The last name sounded familiar, but Paul didn't think he'd ever met him.

"Shaw . . . Shaw . . . That's a local name. Do you have relatives here in Wheatland?"

Michael was hesitant, but what could he say? "Well, yes, I'm sure you must know Robert Shaw, the farmer. He's my brother."

Paul, who often wasn't taken aback by anything and who always maintained his composure, was very much surprised. "I'm amazed that we haven't met. You must not come to town very often."

"No, I very rarely get over this way, but I'm a professional photographer, and I like to come around once in awhile to capture some shots of the old homestead and the trees or the snow, if it's in the winter, and, of course, I like to see the family, too."

"They're pretty much all gone, aren't they, except for Robert?" Paul wanted to ask why Michael wasn't staying out at the farm with his brother, but he thought better of getting too personal. Just then Katie came into the hallway from the downstairs bedroom.

"Your room's all ready, Mr . . . ?"

Michael held out his hand to her. "Michael. Michael Shaw. You probably don't remember me. It's been a long time."

Katie was shocked. Yes, she remembered him. How could she forget those eyes?

One hour later when Amanda came down from her room for popcorn after a short nap, she saw the back of a man's head, as Michael was sitting, reading the morning paper. She'd know it anywhere. She had had no idea that he was the other guest.

At that same moment, Katie was sitting at the kitchen table, finally having some time to read the daily mail that Paul had picked up hours earlier, and there was the birth certificate from Julia; but she'd sent the wrong one—the original—the one that Katie should never ever have seen.

Mother: Amanda Wentworth Shaw
Father: Michael David Shaw

In the basic game, each hand of hearts
Is a game in itself;
Hence the player with the least hearts
At the finish wins the game.
                    —*The Key to Hoyle's Games*

Epilogue

The game is over. Was there a winner in the Game of Hearts? Going around the card table where the game began and ended, examining the hands that were dealt and how the players played their cards, may lend a winner, and then again, it may not. The various family participants in the game were unique in their personalities and in how they held their cards and tried to play them carefully, whether or not they actually had any knowledge of what was going on or what cards the other players held or played.

According to the rules of the card game of hearts, the player with the least hearts at the end of the game is the winner. That would be Robert. But how could that be? He ended up broken-hearted, having lost his wife and his lover. He took his losses and went home; but ultimately and eternally, he was the absolute winner. He turned back to serving God, to seek the prize of glorifying his Lord and Savior and that sustained and fulfilled his life. While never being able to experience the joy of fatherhood, he turned to helping with the youth at church. In spite of his years, or because of them, the kids respected him and his devotion to the Lord, and after all, isn't that the greatest prize in the game—to please the heart of God?

Then, there was Margie. How does one tally up the hand of a player whose cards were snatched away, first by Amanda who grabbed hold of Robert, and then by the Angel of Death? She never had the opportunity to play all her cards or finish the game; but she owned all the attributes of a great player. She was honest, loyal, and fair. She was able to "breast her cards," not show their face value, to keep the secrets of the family, and to raise her sister's daughter with all her love, as if she were her very own. Margie gained the heart of Robert early in the game, which she took with her into death. She left a legacy of devotion and love—often rare attributes in the warlike game of hearts.

The next player, who was in absentia most of the time, was Michael. He gained the heart of Amanda early on in the game, but often had to temporarily discard her, in a manner of speaking, to Robert, only to draw her heart again. He ended up with one heart. Amanda still loved him at their accidental meeting at Katie and Paul's bed and breakfast where they were soon not welcome to sit around Katie's card table or enjoy breakfast together, so they took their love to Amanda's apartment. Eventually Amanda moved to Seattle, and they continued their game of hearts now as an elderly couple without the love of other family members. Their game had been a sham all along. The only saving grace was the beautiful daughter they had produced together.

Amanda, oh, yes, Amanda, the dirtiest card player at the table. She cheated at the game from the onset. Robert—she won and lost; Michael—she drew and kept. Ending the game with one heart, the heart of Michael, actually made her a loser, as she never saw her daughter again.

Finally, there's Katie. How does one even figure out her role in the game? When the cards were first dealt, she wasn't even born yet, but because she *was* born, the whole hand had to be shuffled and dealt again. The game took other turns when she entered the scene, and she unknowingly changed the whole complexion and outcome of the game. One could only hope that somehow Katie was the winner or that at least she shared that honor with Robert.

She and Paul became strong Christian believers because of Robert's influence, and they shared many bittersweet times together as they all grew older. Katie's love was complete with Paul and their adult children and grandchildren. Katie worshiped the memory of Margie and her motherly love.

But is the Game of Hearts really over? As long as there is life and love, the game will go on. The true winner is yet to be declared.

CPSIA information can be obtained
at www.ICGtesting.com
Printed in the USA
FFHW02n1412171018
48832513-53020FF